CHANGING THE
PHOENIX
RICHARD AND MALLORY

Simone Quynn

NEWMAN SPRINGS PUBLISHING
320 Broad Street
Red Bank, NJ 07701

First originally published by Newman Springs Publishing 2022

ISBN 978-1-68498-478-7 (Paperback)
ISBN 978-1-68498-479-4 (Digital)

Printed in the United States of America

For my best friend, my love, my family.

Donnette
Myrle
John
Sylvester

Richard was tired from his long flight. He'd been out of the country for several weeks and wasn't ready for any parties, yet here he was, sitting alone at a party he did not want to be at. He was here alone by choice. The women he used for entertainment now bored him. He needed another change. Maybe he was just tired of the games, and it was time for something more long term.

"I see you made it."

Richard stood to greet the man who had invited him. They were old friends, which was the only reason he was here tonight. "I thought you'd be too tired to make it. I'm glad you're here though. There's someone I want you to meet."

He wasn't in the mood to meet any more stuffed-shirt assholes tonight. He would have to get the hell out of here before people started noticing him. He was incognito—no flashy tux, no flashy jewelry, no flashy woman, just plain old Richard. He followed his friend who was deep in a conversation that wasn't registering for him. "So be careful with some of these women. They are looking for their next ex-husband—or you know, child support."

Richard only caught the last part of the conversation. "I think I'll be all right. This is not my first rodeo." He was no fool. He'd been in these situations before. Though tonight he wasn't feeling very social, he was sure he'd be okay.

"These are some of the models we just hired. There's a very beautiful one that joined us about two weeks ago. I insisted she show up here tonight, or she would be waiting tables at the next party." Richard didn't know why that made him want to punch his friend in the back of his head, but he had the sudden urge to hit the man. They entered a room where not many were gathered. The room was filled with an abundance of beautiful women mingling with several figures he immediately recognized—"the Private Room"—the room of secrets as the wives had referred to it.

"I don't think I'm in the mood to mingle right now." He knew exactly what was going on from the looks of things. He didn't feel like playing bid wars with anyone. None of the people in the room could outbid him anyway, so what was the point? He was about to leave when a beautiful redhead sitting alone in the corner caught his eye. "Who is that one over there?" She didn't seem at all interested in being there.

"Oh, that one? I don't think…"

He watched as his friend tried to get the attention of the woman. She finally looked their way and was waved over to them. "I don't remember inviting any redheads tonight." He sounded disappointed, but Richard was intrigued. The woman was beautiful.

"Good night, Mr. Trembill."

Richard could tell that the smile the woman wore was as fake as they came; however, it made her even more beautiful.

"I'm here as you requested."

Trembill's eyes grew as he realized who he was talking to.

"Honey, weren't you blonde this morning?" He glanced at Richard with an awkward smile. Trembill had always had a thing for blondes, but this one wasn't interested in him or what he was selling.

"Oh, I was, but the girls and I were having such a great time doing makeovers that I thought I should spice it up a bit." She was lying. Richard had only just met her, but he could tell she was lying.

"I think it looks amazing."

He reached for the woman's hand and placed a gentle kiss on her wrist. The touch of his lips made her shiver just a bit. She tried to hide her reaction, but he was already aware of what his touch was doing to her. He, however, would not reveal what she was doing to him. He was a pro at this; she would need some lessons.

"Richard—Richard Embers—and you are?"

She glanced at the man Richard had subtly pushed aside.

"I'm Mal—Mallory Sweet." She flashed him a genuine smile that warmed him immediately.

"That you are."

She pulled her hand from his and took a step back. She knew who he was now. He was the one all the other girls were hoping to meet. They'd all made a pact that no one would get upset or try to sabotage the others if he chose them. He was known to travel with beautiful women on his arm. Never did he offer them more than a month or so, and yet they all flocked to him like flies on shit. Not that she couldn't understand why; he was quite handsome. He wasn't dressed to impress, as he usually was, but still, the man was drop-dead gorgeous.

"I was leaving. I have an engagement in the morning. Maybe you'd like to accompany me." Mallory glanced over her shoulder to see a few of the girls staring fervently at him. She wished they would rescue her from her current situation, but they would not speak to him unless spoken to. That was a rule they were to follow.

"I would love to, but I'm afraid I wouldn't be very good company. I haven't been feeling my best this evening—slight headache. I think I'm getting a migraine." Again she was lying, but this time she was lying to him.

Richard smiled and stepped closer to her. She tried to retreat, but he held her in place.

"I do not like being lied to. Make that the last time you lie to me. Now, if you do not want my company, just say so." He was smiling, but that scared her. He made her nervous, and she was not a nervous person. When he touched her, he gave her chills, goose-bumps, and other things came to life like never before. This man was too dangerous to play with.

"So." She hadn't meant to say that, but it made him laugh. She was not sure if that was a good sign or not. He reached down and took her hand. She was in trouble.

"Then may I rescue you from this suffering?"

Mallory glanced at Mr. Trembill, who was still standing next to them. He nodded his approval as if she'd needed his permission. She may not have been a model long, but he did not own her. Had she known she was to parade around in "the Private Room," she would have faked sickness in his office. This was not what she had signed up for. Whatever happened to taking pictures and walking runways? This was borderline prostitution except in this case one might not even get paid.

"I should tell my friends that I'm leaving."

His smile was still tormenting her and not in a good way, yet not in a bad way either.

"I think Roy will inform them. I'm ready to leave now."

What was she getting herself into? Men like him could make or destroy one's career before they even knew they had one. She felt like she was being dropped in the middle of the ocean wearing half a cow around her neck.

"I guess I'm ready as well."

She tried to smile as he turned to bid his friend farewell. She was not ready for this man. Why couldn't she meet him when she had cemented herself in the business? They walked to the elevator, stopping several times to acknowledge one or two of his friends. She was sure he'd known every single person in the building. He moved quickly from one person to the next, smiling and shaking hands. He dragged her behind him, never introducing her to any of the people he stopped to talk with. When they'd finally made it to the open elevator, he stepped in and asked the operator to make it express. Mallory watched as the poor young man tried to keep his head straight. She had to lean closer to him to see if the poor thing was breathing. Trying to smother a giggle, she felt pressure as Richard gave her hand a firm squeeze.

When they stepped from the building, a tall sturdy man walked to a waiting limo and opened the door. His smile was probably the friendliest she had seen in a long time. She couldn't help but smile at him as Richard stuffed her into the car. He had stopped outside the door to speak to the man, so she scooted all the way to the other side and quickly fastened her seat belt—like that would stop someone like him from attacking her. She couldn't believe she was running off with this stranger. *Honey, if you make any more bad decisions, they are going to find you floating in that dirty river behind the agency.*

"Where do you live?" His voice was harsh as he entered the car, taking the seat on the opposite side to her left. She wanted to lie, but he had warned her not to. She didn't feel like testing her limits tonight.

"I'm staying in the company's apartment across from Studio Six."

The scowl on his face told her he knew exactly what she was talking about. It was not in the best condition and very crowded, but it was free, and that was all she could afford at the moment.

"You don't have your own place?" The words came out more like a scolding than a question.

She frowned and nodded. She'd only arrived in town three weeks to this day, and he expected that she would have all the accommodations he was used to?

"I don't think your headache will get much better there. If I try to be on my best behavior, would you reconsider coming with me?"

She was tempted though every atom in her told her to go home. "Where are you going to take me?" She wasn't looking at him for fear he would see how terrified she was of him.

"Don't answer my question with a question."

Her head flew up as she contemplated what she really should say to him. He was a demanding, rude, disrespectful ass, and this was not what she wanted. All she'd wanted was to go home and get away from people like him. His temper flared a bit, and she had to turn to look out the darkened window. She heard a soft throaty laugh come from his side of the car.

"I see you know when to fight and when to retreat."

Oh, so he thought she was retreating? If only she hadn't gotten in his damn car. Had they still been standing on the sidewalk, she would let him have it.

"You may speak freely when we are alone. You're safe with me."

She didn't want to look at him. Her emotions were probably on display like a neon sign on her face. "Like I said earlier, I won't be good company, so maybe you should take me home." A soft light suddenly lit her face. She turned to stare out the window as if there was something more interesting out there.

"Would you like something to drink?"

She nodded no and kept her gaze on the streetlights that seemed to race past the car.

"I would like to talk. Would you engage in conversation with me?"

She rolled her eyes in frustration. What could he want to talk about? Mallory wanted to ask him why he'd wanted to talk but suddenly remembered him telling her not to answer his questions with questions.

"Yes."

Well look at that. It only took him a mere fifteen to twenty minutes to train her. She shook her head and waited for him to speak again.

"Tell me about you and what brought you here. I want to know where you were born, who your parents are, if you have siblings, how you got here, and why you came."

Well, you aren't asking a lot of questions at all. She watched as he opened a bottle of champagne and drank straight from the bottle.

Raising it in her direction, he made a toast. "To me finding you tonight."

She didn't know what to say to that. "Do you want to know my cycle schedule too?" She was irritated. He was just too demanding.

He didn't seem bothered by her question. Taking another sip from the bottle, he glanced at her. "Not yet. Start with where you were born." He was enjoying her defiant attitude. It wasn't normal for women like her to act this way with him. They all knew who he was before they were introduced to him. Roy made sure to warn them about his role in their lives ahead of time. However, this one did not seem to know anything about him. "How long have you been with the company?"

She was fiddling with her dress. He hadn't noticed till now that he did not like the dress.

"I thought you wanted me to start at the beginning."

He lazily turned to her as if he was bored. She quickly turned to look out her window again.

"I've only been waiting in the apartment for a week. Mr. Trembill said I needed training. I'm assigned to one of the other model's classes. I like her."

He knew exactly why she hadn't been working. Roy intended to keep her for himself. Well, he should have left her at home tonight. "Now, you may start from the beginning."

She was about to speak when she heard his hand hit the seat. It frightened her so much she bumped her head on the glass window.

"I do not need to hear about when the sperm and egg met."

She frowned and rubbed her head.

"Are you all right?"

Would you be all right if someone scared you? She didn't feel like provoking him. From what she'd been told, he was not the kind of person you wanted to piss off. Her mother always told her to pick her battles wisely.

"You have no reason to fear me."

If she didn't know better, she would have thought he sounded hurt.

"I'm fine." Reaching up and unpinning her wig, she pulled it from her head.

Richard was in awe; he didn't think she could get any more beautiful than she already was. She was unwrapping her blonde hair that now fell to her shoulders. He watched as she ran her fingers through it. This was definitely the one. She was going to be his. If he had to kidnap and hold her hostage until she loved him, it would be done. Maybe nothing that drastic, but he would make her his.

"May I have some water, please?"

He reached for a bottle and passed it to her.

"You're even more beautiful than before." He gestured for her to move closer. He would learn what he could about her. Every piece of information he gathered would help in his conquest.

"My mother met my dad while on a family vacation in the Caribbean specifically in Montserrat, a tiny, little island paradise. She was ten years younger than him, so my grandparents did not want her around him. She decided to defy them and stayed with him. He was well off and promised her the moon. Since she was an adult, my grandparents had no choice but to let her do what she thought was right."

This was not what he'd wanted, but she wanted to tell him, so he listened.

"They were happy, enjoying their island lifestyle until my mother got pregnant with me. That's when she found out he was actually still married."

Well, that was interesting.

"He told her to stay on the island while he went home to take care of the whole marriage thing. She didn't like it, but what choice did she have?" She shrugged. "Well, he left her in the care of some friends and went back to where he'd left his wife. It must have taken some convincing because I was two by the time he returned."

Richard couldn't believe the woman had waited that long. She must have really been in love. Foolish woman. "Your mother waited all those years for your father?"

She smiled at him, causing him goosebumps. That was unusual. Women did not affect him in this manner. Well one other had, but she was a lost cause. This one was different though.

"She didn't have a choice. She had no money, no job, nothing. She was given only enough to care for us. His friends made sure she was taken care of, and she made sure I was taken care of. Anyways, he returned a different man. She was always happy when it was just the two of us, but when he came back, she drank all the time. I didn't know what was going on. I was happy I had a dad, so I didn't notice my mom's pain."

He took a sip of the drink he had forgotten he'd been drinking. "How would a two-year-old know what her parents were going through? Don't take that responsibility on yourself."

She knew he was right, but she had already blamed herself for her mother's misery.

"I was six when we moved back to the States with my dad. He moved us to New York to a small apartment in Manhattan, but he didn't stay with us. He would come over every day but leave after I went to sleep, so my mom told me he worked nights, but I knew she was lying. I'd heard them fight about it a few times. Anyway, I noticed my mother would wear lots of horrible makeup—I mean weird colors and lots of it. Kids would make fun of her when she'd drop me off to school, so our relationship got even worst. I would yell at her, tell her not to follow me to school because she looked like a clown."

Mallory was glad to be getting it off her chest. She had never spoken to anyone about her childhood. Sitting here talking to Richard felt right. She would be able to open up and let it all go. This was what she needed. She'd come here for a new beginning, and this was how it should have started.

She continued. "We stayed in New York until I was almost fourteen. My father came over drunk one night, and they had a big fight. After he went to sleep, my mother came to my room and told me if I wanted to go with her, I had to pack a small bag that I could carry with only clothes—no pictures, no jewelry, nothing that my father had given me. She said I could stay with him if I wanted, but she was leaving." She paused to take a sip of her water.

When she didn't continue, Richard reached over and placed a hand on her thigh. His touch sent chills through her entire body. Though it wasn't meant to be sexual, she was having trouble keeping her thoughts pure.

"Would you like to continue? You don't have to." He was concerned about her.

Looking in his eyes, Mallory could tell that he wasn't the monster they had made him out to be. He was caring; his eyes were now kind. She hadn't noticed this earlier, but now that it was just the two of them, he was different. There was a gentle side to him.

"Yes. I want to. I should have done this years ago, but I never really had a best friend that I could confide in."

Not that he was a best friend, but he was an eager ear. His hand was gone from her knee, and she missed it.

"My mom and I took off that night and left my drunken father in the apartment alone. That was the last time I saw him. I adored my dad, and my last memory of him was not great." She remembered how easy the decision to leave with her mother was when she's seen how angry he had gotten about something small. She'd wondered how many of those fights she had slept through. "We took so many buses that I lost track of where we were. My mom had nowhere to go, so we just chose a place off the map—a place she could blend in and raise me."

Richard couldn't imagine a place where she wouldn't stick out. Her blonde hair and blazing blue eyes were mesmerizing.

"I didn't like the town we settled on, but it was going to be home, so I had no choice. I lived in that boring one-horse town for seven years."

Richard's head came up so quickly that it startled her. "You're twenty-one?"

She didn't know why that piece of information shocked him. Most of the girls at the party were close to her age. Hell, a few of the ones in the apartment next door were way younger than she was.

"You look...younger." He leaned back in the seat. His gaze made her uncomfortable.

"Yes, I'm twenty-one. How old are you?"

He smiled and scratched his head. She wondered if he would lie.

"Does it really matter, sweetheart?" He didn't want to tell her his age, but he demanded she offer up everything about herself.

She would press this issue; it was a minor request. She tilted her head and looked at him through squinted eyes.

This only made him laugh. "I'm thirty-one, soon to be thirty-two."

She wasn't worried about the age gap. There was nothing between them.

"God, you're old."

He looked at her as if she had said something horrible. Then he laughed again. She was teasing.

"I mean you look younger, but you're old." She tried not to smile but failed miserably.

"Something tells me you won't mind my old age once you get to know me." He winked at her, causing her to reward him with one of her bright smiles. "Besides, it's not polite to make fun of the man you'll be spending the rest of your life with."

Mallory's hand flew to her face. Her mouth hung open in shock. Who told him that she would marry him? Was he even interested in anything but her body?

"Oh my god! You're going to murder me tonight, aren't you?"

His smile quickly disappeared as a concerned frown replaced it.

"I knew it. I knew I would die here."

He leaned forward and placed his hand on her thigh. "What in the hell are you going on about? I said nothing about hurting you."

She was joking, but he was truly concerned. She'd taken an acting class at the local library once, and it had helped her through some situations. This time she was really selling her fear.

"But you said I would be spending the rest of my life with you." She tried to sound terrified. Her body language, tone, and facial expression were all Oscar worthy.

"I meant as my wife, you lunatic. What is wrong with you? You automatically think I'm going to have you killed…"

She half smiled through the shock of his revelation. He realized at that moment that she'd been joking. She was genuinely shocked at his marriage admission now.

"You are going to be a pain in my ass, aren't you?" He gave her knee a gentle squeeze and sat back, shaking his head at her. The words registered and brought her out of her trance. He was serious. Not that he'd wanted to reveal that to her this soon, but he knew that no one else was good enough for her. She was his from the moment he'd decided to remove her from the party.

"What do you mean…"

He raised his hand to stop her. He wasn't going to get into it.

"We will discuss that later. Finish your story. What made you leave your mother?" He was not going to answer her.

She knew a deflection tactic when she heard one. It was the reason she had worn the wig tonight. "I'm sorry, but I don't think I can. I want to know why you said that."

He took a deep breath. He hadn't meant to say that. He didn't even know if he'd meant it. Yes, he did. Just the thought that another man had touched her, that Roy had thought he could keep her made him angry. He tried to relax, but she had already seen he was getting upset.

"I will tell you what you want to know after you finish your story. I have a few questions I need you to answer, and then you may ask whatever you like." He grabbed the bottle he had placed back into the ice bucket and took a drink. He turned to look out at the scenery. "Continue, please."

She knew he wouldn't budge. *Pick your battles, Mal. This one wasn't lost—yet.*

"Fine. I started dating a man after high school. He was a bit older, but I was working, and I guess my mother didn't want to be left alone, so she didn't bother me about it. I knew it pissed her off, so I kinda did it because I was mad at her."

He was watching her. His gaze was fierce, yet she saw it for what it was. He was concerned and jealous.

"My mother thought that if I went off to college, my father would find me, and then he would find her. So I was stuck with her in that shitty town." She had known how afraid her mother was of her father, but not letting her go to college because of her fear was too much. Their relationship was never great after they'd left her father. Her mother would always tell her she looked too much like him and so she thought her mother couldn't love her.

"How much older was the man you dated?" His question didn't surprise her. He was more interested in her former boyfriend than the fact that she was denied college due to her mother's paranoia.

"Clay was four years older. I didn't really care too much for him at first. He invited me out a few times, and I declined, but then my mother told me to stay away from him, and I ended up having a three-year relationship with him." She knew he would want to hear what had happened between them, but she didn't want to talk about that yet. "I came home one evening tired and too sleepy to even eat. My mother thought I was getting too thin and insisted that I had dinner. I tried to pull away from her when she grabbed me and tripped. I must have knocked myself out because I woke up to her screaming at the paramedics. They insisted on taking me to the hospital because of my bruises."

Richard was getting upset. He knew he wouldn't like the rest of this story, but he wanted to hear it.

"After I came home from the hospital, she packed a bag and gave me an envelope full of money. I was shocked. I had no idea what was going on. She told me to take her car and leave town. She didn't care where I went as long as I never came back. She would cover for me by telling everyone I went to visit family." She had skipped a lot of important information. She knew he wasn't an idiot, and he would ask, but that would have to wait. Telling a man like him who'd just declared he was going to marry you about your abusive past was probably a bad idea. People couldn't believe she had endured three years of abuse. They would always ask why she didn't just leave, tell her mom or the sheriff. It's easy for onlookers to make assumptions, but victims sometimes aren't able to overcome that easily. She had tried to end it a year after it started, but he had physically insisted that she reconsider. He had done all but kill to keep her with him.

"Did he hit you?"

The look on her face confirmed what he was thinking. Whoever he was would pay for it. He would personally make sure of that.

She felt ashamed sitting across from him. What would he think of her now? She should have kept her mouth shut. At least there was no pity in his eyes. Then again, pity would have been better than what she saw there. His facial expression did not match his body language. He seemed calm, but there was rage in his eyes. If Clay had been present, she was sure he'd be dead. Richard was nothing like the men she'd met before.

"Yes." She felt a strange feeling in her stomach as she saw the darkness in his eyes. He was beyond infuriated, yet he sat as he had before she had started speaking. Men like him were dangerous—that she knew. How could she be so careless? She was nervous.

"You have no need to fear me. I'm not like him." He tried to reassure her.

"No, Mr. Embers, you're far more dangerous than he could ever be." She shocked herself with the words that flowed from her mouth. What the hell was wrong with her? She wasn't the loose-mouth type. *Mallory, you need to learn to shut your damn mouth.*

Richard's gaze narrowed, causing her to retreat in the seat. "Not to you. I think you are more dangerous than I could ever be."

What did that mean? She'd never done anything for anyone to call her dangerous. "I've never hurt anyone. Why do you say that?"

His smile wasn't like the others she had seen tonight. This one was different—a bit sinister.

"You're dangerous because I might do things for you that I wouldn't do for others. For instance, I might relieve your ex of his life simply because he touched you."

She was utterly terrified. He would kill Clay for her? She didn't want Clay dead. Yes, he had beaten her, but she didn't want him dead. Did she?

"That's not what I want."

He waited for her to go on. She wasn't sure what he wanted her to say. The conversation had gotten scary, weird, and she wasn't ready for any of it. "That's in my past. I'm here to make a better future." He took another sip from his bottle. She would never again have to worry about her safety. He would protect her from the world around them.

"Aren't you afraid your father and that Clay fellow will find you once you become famous?"

She smiled at his comment. He thought she had what it took to become famous. Then again, maybe he was just saying what she wanted to hear. "You didn't really think this through, did you?" He licked his lips, and she wanted to taste them as well.

Jesus, woman, what is wrong with you? You're acting out of character tonight. She undid her seat belt as he watched her. She slipped closer to him before mustering up enough courage for what she wanted to do. She could see the curiosity in his eyes. She became even more nervous when a slow smile crept across his face, baring his beautiful teeth. Lord, he was beautiful. He reached out for her, and she complied.

"I'm not into playing games. I know what I want, and I usually get it." He pulled her to a straddling position on his lap.

"So what do you want? From me?"

He relaxed under her, the heat from his thighs setting her ablaze. His free hand ran up her leg, and she inhaled sharply.

"Everything." His eyes were dark with desire.

She'd never seen anything like it. She felt like a virgin about to be sacrificed to a dragon. He was hypnotizing her with his stare. She didn't know what to do, but she knew what she wanted. She didn't know how long it would last, but tonight he wanted her, and he would have her. She took his bottle and drank from it—something to settle the nerves. He gestured for her to placed it back in the ice bucket. She did.

"Once this begins, we won't stop until I tell you I'm done."

She gave him a deep frown. "I'm sorry?"

She was about to continue when she felt his finger slip inside her panties. She had no time to think, let alone protest. He knew what he was doing and doing it well. She held on to his jacket to steady herself. Holy shit! Her back arched, and she let a moan slip. Her eyes rolled back into her head. Jesus! I'm so sorry, Lord. I know this is wrong. She silently prayed, knowing she had crossed a line she could no longer see. "Oh shit."

Her body was moving to the rhythm he had created. Her eyes flew open as she felt his other hand on her breast. She instantly wished she'd kept her eyes closed. He was watching her like an eagle—an eagle of desire with magic fingers. *Eagles don't have fingers, you idiot.* She tried to hold his stare, but it was too much. She reached up and turned out the light. She couldn't let him see her face; she'd lost control of her body as his fingers expertly worked their evil magic. His hand left her breast, and the light was once again revealing her loss of control.

"Turn it out." She struggled through fits of moaning to plead with him.

"No." He was focused on her face. "I want to see how much you're enjoying this."

She tried to bury her head in his shoulder, but he gently pushed her back from him, never slowing down.

"Oh god. I'm…" She moaned louder as she neared the glorious climax she hadn't realize she wanted. She was no longer controlling her actions. She felt like a puppet on his lap.

"Open your eyes." He demanded as her body started to convulse. "Open them slowly." He didn't stop what he was doing to her. She couldn't hold on any longer.

"Oh shit. I'm gonna…"

The sound of a phone ringing somewhere behind her quickly reminded her where she was. Her head hit his shoulder as a wave of pleasure assaulted her. This time he didn't push her away, but he didn't stop his attack on her forbidden fruit either.

"You have to get that."

She prayed he would let her breathe. She felt like she was gonna have a heart attack. This was a first. Clay never made her body do the things it was doing now.

"Not important." She shook in his arms, moaning quite loudly in his ear as he continued to pleasure her.

"You have to…"

She could barely breathe now. "Not important."

As she continued to lose control, he whispered in her ear. "No one is ever to please you like this again—not even you."

She shook her head in compliance. *Whatever the hell you want.*

"I mean it. You will ask permission before touching yourself."

As he allowed her soul to return to her body, she sank her teeth into his shoulder, not knowing what else to do at that point.

He let out a soft moan that knotted her stomach. Shit. As she prepared for retaliation, the phone rang once again.

"Fuck!" He sounded angry as he reached for it. "What?" he yelled into the receiver.

She was both relieved and disappointed that his attention was elsewhere now. Mallory wished she could move, but after what she had just been through, she just relaxed and waited.

"Sir, we are here, but it looks like you have company. Would you like me to go around and drop you off at the cabin?"

The friendly voice that flowed through the car startled Mallory back to reality. She popped up, turning to see if they were discovered. The privacy window was still closed as Richard reached up and turned out the light. *Oh, now he wants to turn it out.* She returned her head to his shoulder as he continued to listen to whomever was on the phone.

"Yes, please." He didn't feel like dealing with anything else tonight. He had to make this woman understand she was his—completely. That was all he wanted to do—all he would do.

He returned to the call. "I do not wish to be bothered with any of this right now. I've just returned from a long trip, and I have an important engagement tonight. It'll have to wait." He listened to the man protest before he decided to end the call. "With all due respect, I need a fucking break. I've already given you my terms, and I will not change my mind. Now if you'll excuse me, I have something more important to tend to. Good night."

Mallory listened as he ended the call. She felt him relax once again.

"Are you ready to finish what you started?"

She tried to sit up when an aftershock took her by surprise, causing her to moan again.

"I'll take that as a yes."

She placed her hands on his chest and pushed herself up.

"What I started?" she asked, almost breathless. "All I wanted was to kiss you." She couldn't see his face, but she felt his hands tighten on her thighs.

"Is that all you wanted?"

She knew he was smiling. She felt his hand in her hair as he pulled her closer. "I think I can allow that." She would have given him a piece of her mind if it wasn't clouded by the heat he was generating in her yet again. Damn it. *I can't even kiss him without leaking.* She relaxed and let him possess her once again.

*****

The car pulled up to a large cabin dimly lit between a few giant trees. Mallory had no idea how long she was consumed by the sorcery he performed with his tongue, but she was disappointed it had been interrupted.

"I'll have Carletta bring the young lady a change of clothing in the morning. You know what to do if you need me. Try not to kill anything." Richard and the voice shared a laugh.

Mallory realized they were using the intercom and was happy for it. She was a bit embarrassed about what had happened in the car. Richard thanked the man and exited the car, pulling her behind him.

"Where are we?" She looked around frantically as they took the stairs hastily. He was in a hurry, and she could only guess why. They entered the cabin, but he never attempted to turn on any lights. "I can't see, Richard."

He didn't speak. He stopped and picked her up. She held on to him as he entered a darker room. She tucked her head into his neck and gently kissed his exposed skin. He stopped abruptly.

"I'm trying to be a gentleman. Don't push it."

She giggled before she realized what he had said. "Wait a minute. What?"

He continued in the dark toward his destination. When he finally stopped and put her on her feet, he pulled her close and whispered, "You're lucky I'm jet-lagged and a bit tired from my previous engagement." He kissed her forehead before turning on the light. "We won't have sex tonight. We'll wait—maybe a week."

She didn't understand. "What?" She let out a nervous laugh. He didn't want to sleep with her?

He placed her on the sink and stepped back. They were in a large bathroom. She glanced over at the miniature in-ground swimming pool that was pretending to be a tub. When she returned her gaze to his face, she thought she'd seen concern on it before that disappeared.

"I was with another woman maybe five hours ago. Had I known I would meet you, there would have been no need for her." He watched her reaction, and it darkened his mood. She looked shocked at the news. He would let her process it all before they discussed anything else, but he wasn't going to let her leave him tonight or any other night. She would have to get over it.

18

"What do you mean 'with'?"

He didn't want to explain, and he wasn't going to give her any details. She knew who he was. He took a seat on a hamper across from Mallory.

"I was on a very long business trip. I arranged for some company on my trip home."

Mallory's mouth flew open involuntarily. *Holy fucking shit. You kissed him. He touched you.* She sat staring at him as the words started to make sense. He had slept with another woman and still had the nerve to try to claim her?

"She didn't mean anything to me. I didn't kiss her."

She couldn't read whatever was on his face. Her temper was flaring. Well, so long, modeling career.

"Oh. Well then, I feel so much better. You didn't kiss her. You just stuck your dick in her and then you decided that you weren't satisfied with that—so what? Am I supposed to finish up where she left off?" She jumped from the sink and started out into the dark room they'd just come from. *How could you be so stupid. Falling for him? Him? The man is a whore and a damn gigolo.* She wanted to get away from him as fast as her feet would carry her. The light that was giving her some guidance disappeared as he turned it off. She fumbled around in the dark room, tripping over what she thought was a bed. "Damn it! Turn the fucking light on!" she yelled. She could hear him snickering in the bathroom. He was laughing at her.

"No. Come back and speak to me. I want to know why you're upset."

She could tell he was grinning. That fucking insensitive asshole was amused. She sat up on the floor. She wanted to crawl around until she found the door, but that would make him laugh at her even more.

"Come back to me."

If he could only see the death stare she was sending his way, he would shut that fucking sexy mouth of his.

"I want nothing to do with you. Just call your manservant to take me home." She decided not to give him the satisfaction of the response he was looking for.

"Last chance, woman."

His tone scared her. *Yep, you were right. He is going to murder you and bury your stupid ass out here—where the fuck ever out here is. You always fall for these jerks that treat you like crap. Why did you think he was any different? Everyone practically told you about him.* She felt like crying. She hadn't heard him approach her. The thoughts racing in her head had temporarily disoriented her.

"I told…"

The sound of his voice so close startled her. Mallory screamed and threw her hands and feet frantically as if she were being attacked. She felt her fist connect to his face and a foot hit something else.

"*Stop*, goddamn it!"

She froze at the sound of his voice. He was pissed. She was terrified. He grabbed her arm, yanking her to her feet. He practically dragged her around the bed she had tripped over. Richard touched the lamp next to the bed, lighting the room. He turned and threw the woman on the bed.

"I'm sorry."

She was scared. He could hear it in her voice. Mallory felt regretful as she saw the blood he licked from the side of his lips. His face was contorted with anger.

"I didn't mean to…" She trailed off when his eyes narrowed. Her heart was beating faster than a locomotive.

"Don't move." He spoke in a soft, steely tone.

She couldn't move even if she wanted to. She was frozen with fear. He turned and walked back into the bathroom, slamming the door behind him. She laid in the spot he had thrown her. *Cry. Cry so that he will take pity on you when he gets out of there. Look what you've done. Not even a month on your own, and you might have gotten us killed. I had a good life ahead, and now because of weakness, it's gone. No magazine covers, no movie deals, no nothing.* She chastised herself as the tears burned their way down the side of her face.

Mallory felt warm hands on her feet. She jerked as she came to. She had cried herself to sleep. Damn. How long had he been in the bathroom? She had lost track of time, lying there waiting on the uncertain. Her eyes were heavy with sleep.

"Relax. You can't sleep with your shoes on."

She laid still as he removed her shoes and threw them on the floor. He reached down and pulled a soft blanket over her before getting in the bed with her. She tried to roll away from him, but he wasn't in the mood. Richard turned her roughly to look at him.

"Look, I get it. You are clearly upset about what I told you, but understand this—if I didn't value you, I wouldn't have said a word. I would have done to you what I did to her and let you go in the morning when I was done with you." He stopped when he saw the tears in her eyes. She was really hurt, and he wasn't handling the situation well. He let out a frustrated breath. "Let's sleep on it. We can talk about it at breakfast." He kissed her forehead before turning out the light and pulling her close. "I didn't mean to hurt you. I'm sorry."

Mallory couldn't hold it anymore. She let her emotions take over. She felt his arms tighten around her as her sobs shook her. They laid tangled together until they both drifted off to sleep.

*****

Mallory woke to the smell of bacon and eggs. She stretched before rubbing the sleep from her eyes. Richard was opening some thick floor-to-ceiling curtains. He was wearing pajama pants and no shirt. Good god, he was sexy. She shook her head as she remembered the incident from last night.

"Do you wanna shower before you eat?" He turned to look at her.

Her eyes were still trying to adjust. "Yes, please." She almost didn't hear herself respond. She held her breath as he climbed into the bed next to her. She could see the bruise she had left on his face from her tantrum last night. "How's your…" His eyes narrowed, and he let out a groan.

"Better than my nuts." He groaned again when he heard her sharp inhalation. "Didn't realize you got them?" He seemed in better spirits than last night, but she wasn't going to test him.

"I'm sorry." She really was sorry. She had overreacted. He wasn't hers. She knew about his affairs. It was all the girls talked about—all of them, with the exception of Simone and Kat, would give their right arm to be where she was.

"You're not, but I haven't decided if I'll make you—yet." He threw the blanket onto the floor and helped her from the bed. "You'll find everything you need in there." He pointed to the bathroom. "That felt surprisingly good—despite the circumstances, of course."

She looked up at him. He was kinda smiling.

"What did?" she asked.

"Sleeping with you. I haven't slept next to a woman in a while." He watched her.

She knew he was waiting for a reaction. She wasn't going to indulge him. Mal started for the bathroom. She needed to shower. "I should get to the shower."

He watched her disappear into the bathroom. He smiled when he remembered her flipping over the bed. She was jealous or mad last night, but today was a new beginning. He would take her shopping and fix it. He had already planned their day. He grabbed the blanket from the floor and folded it nicely before returning it to the bed. He was tidying up when the phone started to ring, drawing him back to his reality. Work. Work was calling him. He answered it.

"Richard."

He listened as Ken tried his best to spit out everything he needed to say.

"Relax. I'm back now. I have a few things on my plate, but I can handle that." He knew that Ken could handle the tasks that he had given him, but the man enjoyed interrupting his tranquility with his whining. "Ken, relax. I told you I would see to it when I got back. I'm back." He listened before cutting Ken off. "Jesus Christ, dude, relax. You're gonna get a stroke. And no, you cannot come up here, but I'll see if Kat is free for lunch, and then you can surprise her with a little weekend getaway." He laughed at the excitement in Ken's voice. "I won't need the jet. Knock yourself out." He hung up the call then listened as the shower went off.

Looking over at the clock, he noticed six minutes had passed since she left him. She had rushed so he wouldn't have to wait. He quickly dialed Simone. She picked up on the second ring.

"Honey, I need a favor." He turned to see Mallory standing in the doorway. She was wearing the robe he'd left for her. Her hair was wet, half wrapped in a towel. He smiled before going back to the call. "You know you're my favorite, right?" He smiled before continuing. "I need you to get Kat out on a lunch date with Ken. He's having a hard time with a project. Probably gonna have a stroke if we don't intervene." He laughed at the caller, and Mallory felt a slight twinge of jealousy. She knew who he was talking to. "And you'll thank me one day when you're chasing after your nieces and nephews."

Simone. He was talking to Simone. Mallory walked past him and headed for the kitchen. She hadn't gotten a chance to see the place. She tried to ignore him, but her ears were trained on his responses like a hound dog on an escaped convict. "She is, and I'm gonna take good care of her. Thanks, baby. I owe you." He ended the call and followed her into the kitchen. "Have a seat, and I will serve you."

She unwrapped her head and started drying her wet hair. Taking a seat at a small table by the window, she was amazed that he could cook. He had people waiting on him hand and foot, but he could cook? The kitchen smelled so good.

"I would like to make a phone call."

She wasn't sure he had heard her because he didn't stop what he was doing. She watched as he filled their plates with food before coming to sit in front of her.

"Can it wait?"

She noticed the stack of bacon on his plate and the lack thereof on hers. What the hell did he think this was? There'd be no bacon eating if she couldn't partake in it.

"Ahh, what is this?" She looked from her plate to his before making eye contact with him. The amusement on his face annoyed her.

"Aren't you on a strict diet? Agency policy."

Damn them and their stupid diet. She wasn't going to gain any weight. She'd tried for years and nothing. A slice of bacon wouldn't be the death of her nonexistent career. She made a face that drew a laugh from him. Picking up her fork, she stabbed at the fruit on the plate while eying his bacon.

"Would you like a piece?"

She tried not to smile when she nodded a yes without deviating from her attempts to mash the fruit.

"I require payment for that." He placed a few strips of bacon on her plate.

"Thank you." She pretended to ignore his last comment.

He was watching her, waiting for something she wouldn't give him. If he wanted a show, then she would give him one. *Let's see how you like Mallory the pig.* Stuffing a few pieces into her mouth, she chewed wildly with her mouth open. "Mm, this is so good." She closed her eyes to keep from looking at him. A few pieces of bacon flew from her mouth as she spoke.

He didn't move nor speak.

She grabbed another piece and stuffed the whole thing in her mouth. "So, so good." This time she could hear him chuckling.

"You didn't ask where I got it from."

She froze as he spoke. Where he got it from? Why would she need to ask where he'd gotten the bacon? Her eyes grew as possibilities ran through her mind. It tasted like bacon—really great bacon. With her mouth still full, she adjusted the meat into her cheeks so she could speak.

"Where did you get it?"

He sat back with a huge grin on his face. "You sure you wanna know?"

No, she didn't. Well, yes—yes, she did. She nodded slowly.

He smiled. "There's this crazy woman who keeps little pigs in her house. I went by to discuss some business, and one of them got in my car. I didn't know it was in there until I was on the freeway. We scared the hell out of each other. I almost wrecked my car. I was pissed. I called to tell her about her little stowaway, but before I could, she went off on me about being a tyrannical money-hungry dictator." He watched the horror sweep across her face. "I hung up and drove home, took little Petey to the cook and asked him to carve me some bacon and pork chops."

Poor Mallory couldn't believe what he was saying. She sat with her mouth wide open.

"What you're eating, my sweet, beautiful lady, is the evidence." He burst into laughter as she spit poor Petey back onto her plate. "She has a five-hundred-dollar reward circulating for any information that may help find her little Petey." He couldn't stop laughing as she tried to clear all of Petey's remains from her mouth.

"How could you? I was eating a murder victim? Oh god, he tasted so good. Why would you tell me?" She got up and ran to the bathroom. He followed her, still laughing. "I can't believe you let me eat him." She was washing the evidence from her mouth.

Richard was propped against the door, practically dying.

"You know I don't think I want to spend the rest of my life with a pet pig murderer." She tried to push past him, but he grabbed her and threw her over his shoulder. Walking over to the bed, he threw her on it.

"You helped to dispose of the evidence, and that makes you an accomplice now." He tried to pin her under him. "This bonds us together forever." He winked at her.

"I had no idea what it was when I ate it." She tried to wiggle from under him but couldn't budge. He wasn't pressing his full weight on her, but she couldn't seem to escape.

"Guess who we're having dinner with this Sunday."

She froze. "No! No, I can't." The terrified look in her eyes made him laugh again. "Take someone else. I can't."

"Nope. You are my plus one from now until I take my last breath." He winked again.

She realized he was serious, but how could she go to that poor woman's house?

"Take Simone."

He frowned at her for a moment. She knew there was something between them. She'd overheard their conversation earlier. Though Simone and Kat were already the best female friends she had ever had, she felt weird now. Knowing that Richard may have been with Simone plagued her. They didn't live with the horde of women trying to be famous. They had been given a private apartment. She had been there just once when Simone invited her for a girls' night. It was against agency policy, but she figured they'd let Simone get away with murder as long as she stayed with them. She was amazingly beautiful in everything. Mallory loved how she could transform into almost anything with her wigs. She especially loved her natural afro.

"No. I'm taking you." He bent and kissed her.

She wasn't sure why the touch of this horrible man made her body feel like it was on fire.

He released her lips and sat up. "After last night"—he rubbed his jaw before covering his privates—"I realized that you do not appreciate the raw truth, so I will only offer information that you seek. Ask, and I will tell you. Now the question is, do you want the raw truth or a sensitive version that you can handle?"

She blinked up at him. What did that mean?

"There's only one truth."

He seemed to ponder the idea before pulling her to a seated position. "I am not used to softening the way I express myself. I am what I am, but with you I must be careful. You're not used to me yet. I am very demanding, and I expect things to go the way I want. I put time and effort into what I do." He stood and walked to a large window.

Mallory watched as he opened it and stepped out onto the deck. She hadn't realized it was a door. It looked like a window.

"Are you coming?" he called from outside.

She jumped from the bed and ran out to meet him. The morning was still a bit chilly, but the scenery was beautiful. She walked to the edge of the deck and found they were hovering above a pool. She tried to take it all in. Never had she seen anything so beautiful. She turned to see Richard leaning over the rail. He was observing her.

"This is absolutely beautiful. Everything seems perfectly placed—your garden, the trees, the pool, the birds—"

Richard cut her off. "Okay, woman, I get it. You're impressed." He shook his head at her.

Mallory was more than impressed. She felt as if she had entered some enchanted forest. She gazed out at the trees that sheltered the cabin from the outside world. She noticed in between the first row of trees there was the stump of one that had been cut down. Each stump was carved into some kind of seat. No two were the same. There were grass and flowers growing between most of them, but there was a graveled path that led off into the forest. She instantly became curious of its destination. What would she find at the end of this perfectly crafted path? She would find out.

"Do you like it?"

She tried to hide the smile that was overworking her facial muscles.

"Meh." She shrugged.

"Meh?" Richard was not fooled. He had seen her initial reaction. She was in love with his little hideaway. "Well, since you don't like it, I'll never bring you here again. Come on inside so we can dress and leave this horrid place." He turned and walked toward the door they had used to discover her new favorite place.

"Well, since I'll never come back here, I might as well." Before Richard could turn around, Mallory climbed onto the rail. He turned just in time to see her leap from it.

"Jesus Christ, woman! Are you crazy?" He ran to the stairs, taking them three at a time. He could hear Mallory scream. God, he hoped she hadn't hurt herself. He hadn't warmed the damn thing last night. He came around the corner to see her trying to swim toward the side. He went to help her.

"It's so cold." She could barely speak.

He stood waiting for her to reach him. When she finally doggy paddled to him, he reached down and dragged her from the cold water.

"Why did you let me do that?" She was shaking in the soaked robe.

He quickly removed the dreaded thing and threw it to the ground. "This doesn't help."

She was standing in front of him fully naked, wet, and freezing. "It hurts."

He picked her up and hurried up the stairs. "You're insane, you know that?"

Mallory held on tight to him as they entered the cabin. He took her straight to the tub and jumped in. The water inside was the complete opposite of the one outside. She welcomed the warmth of this one. Richard held her close. He ran his hand over her body, checking for any injury. His actions, though innocent, were causing her to overheat.

"Are you hurt?" He was worried.

"I'm fine now," she whispered.

When their eyes met, she saw anger. He was pissed.

"Why the fuck would you do that? Don't ever do anything like that again."

Mallory wasn't at all worried about his anger. For some reason, she had the sudden urge to tease him. She reached into his pajama pants and grabbed what she sorted. His eyes grew as she stroked him.

"Let it go, or you will regret it."

A mischievous smile adorned her beautiful face. He was not the type you wanted to tease. He would teach her the boundaries she wasn't allowed to cross. When she continued, he not so gently dunked her under the water. "I told you—one week."

She surfaced just in time to hear what he had said. When he turned to leave her, she stood and ran her hand over her breasts.

"I guess I better do it myself."

He turned and gave her a look that both frightened and turned her on. She wasn't waiting a week.

"I told you last night no one is to please you but me," he gritted through clenched teeth.

She narrowed her eyes and in a defiant move ran her hand from her breast down past her belly button, closing her eyes as she reached the core of her firepit. Someone would calm her blaze. She heard the water move violently, and before she could open her eyes, her hands had been captured.

"I warned you."

With one swift move, he spun her around and pressed her against the side of the tub. "I don't like that you think you can defy me." He raised one of her legs and placed it on the side of the tub. She closed her eyes and waited for the pain. From what she had felt earlier, this would be nothing like her previous encounters. As she felt him force himself inside her, she screamed. It was way more painful than she had expected.

"Good God, Jesus! That hurts." She wasn't at all prepared for that.

He whispered in her ear as he continued to thrust forcefully into her. "They won't be helping you right now. This is your punishment for your foolishness."

She hadn't expected it to hurt this much. This was nothing like what she had expected at all. She closed her eyes and tried to go back to the pleasure he gave her last night.

"I'm sorry…"

Her pleas went unanswered. He was in his own space now. She had no idea what to do except pray he would finish, fall asleep, and drown.

"You're hurting me, Richard."

He slowed down but didn't stop. "That is my intention. You will learn not to defy me."

She didn't like this. He was hurting her just because he could.

"Get off of me! I hate you."

To her surprise, he stopped.

"You're just like Clay. I hate you." She didn't want to cry. She was too mad.

He lifted her onto the floor before pulling himself out of the tub behind her. She sat, waiting to see what he would do next. Would he beat her like Clay? What had she done? She pulled her knees to her chest and look up at him. His erection was still ever present. She inhaled sharply at the sight of it. She was so focused on his priapism she hadn't looked to his face.

"I'm gonna take a walk. Don't be here when I get back." He left her sitting on the floor and went into the bedroom.

She sat there until she heard the door slam behind him. She stood and went to the shower, not noticing the blood she left on the floor where she had been. She hurried through a shower before rushing into the bedroom. On the bed was a yellow sundress, lace panties, and slip-on wedges. She looked around for her dress from last night, but it was gone. She dressed quickly and ran to the front door. Mallory didn't know what was on the other side of the intricately crafted door, but she knew her life was forever changed now. She would have to go home to her mother. There was no way she could stay after this. She opened the door to find the car and its chauffeur waiting for her.

"Good morning, miss." He stepped to the stairs and held out a helping hand. The small gesture made her want to cry, but she would wait until she was in a safe space. She turned and gave one last look at the cabin.

"Goodbye, Richard. I'm sorry." She took a huge breath of fresh air and stepped out. It was the end and beginning of something unknown.

"I have been ordered to take you home." His smile was gentle.

She nodded and went to him. He ushered her to the car, closing the door behind her. She knew the drive would be long enough for her to release the tears that fought for escape. She didn't deny them anymore as the car started to move.

The drive was surprisingly longer than she'd thought. She hadn't been paying attention to where they were going. She was curled up in the seat when the vehicle came to a stop. Mallory quickly wiped her face in her dress before sitting up. The door flew open, and she stepped out. This wasn't the agency apartment building.

"I will escort you to the elevator." The man, whose name she hadn't learned, handed her three gift bags. She absently took them and followed as he led her inside.

What the hell was this? Upon entry, she realized where she was. Simone lived here. Why had he brought her here? Did he think she was someone who could afford to live like this? She was nobody; she couldn't even afford her own place, let alone this luxurious establishment.

"I don't live here. I'm sorry I should have told you that." She tried to stop, but he pushed her forward.

"You do now. Don't worry."

What? What was he talking about? Richard had kicked her out of his cabin, out of his life. Why would he have this man bring her here?

"Richard asked me to deliver you here and give you the gifts you hold in your hand." He was still smiling. "I don't know what happened this morning, but you should go up and find comfort in your friends. I don't think you should brave this alone. I will have a chat with Richard later." He gave her a little shove as they came to the waiting elevator.

She was shocked. Things were moving so fast she couldn't get a hold of anything. He gently pushed her into the elevator then pushed the button for the penthouse. She turned and looked at him.

"Thank you. I'm sorry, I don't know your name."

He flashed another smile. "I'm Felix. If you ever need anything, you call me."

She didn't know what to say. The doors closed, and the elevator started its journey up to god only knew what. She had lost control of her life. What had she gotten herself into? When the doors started to open, Simone was standing there, waiting for her.

"Welcome home!" she yelled before taking in Mallory's depressed face. The happiness fell from her face immediately. "What happened? Are you okay?" She reached in and dragged Mallory into a hug. "Honey, what's wrong?" She rocked Mallory in her arm as she stroked her wet hair. "Do you want to talk about it?" She held Mallory in a motherly embrace.

"I don't know." She was bawling again. *Geez, she couldn't pull it together.*

What the hell was wrong with her? Simone released her and stepped back to observe her.

She couldn't look the woman in her eyes—she was ashamed. How could she tell anyone what had happened to her? Simone took her hand and led her into the apartment.

"Come, let's get you something to drink. You don't have to talk if you don't want to. I'm here when you need me."

They walked over to the couch in the living room and flopped into it. Simone pulled Mallory into her arms and held her while she cried.

"Kat!"

She frightened Mallory, causing her to jump.

"Sorry, baby."

Mallory heard Kat running down the stairs.

"What? I have to get ready for my lunch date." Kat took one look at the scene down in the sunken living room and ran to her sister. "What's wrong? What happened?" She climbed into the couch behind Mallory and joined in the hug. "Shh. It's okay." She had no idea what was going on, but her friend needed comfort. "Oh, Mal, I bet we look like a sexy Oreo cookie."

She was rewarded, as she always was, with a laugh from both women.

"You're so special. Go get us some wine."

Kat winked at her sister before running off into the kitchen. Simone placed her hands on Mallory's shoulders and turned her to face her. "You don't have to tell me what happened. It's okay, but if you want us to kill Richard, we're gonna have to do some planning. We have to cover our tracks well."

Mallory let out a tear-filled laugh. She was grateful for Simone and Kat.

"I don't want to impose on you and Kat. I have no idea why he sent me here. I'll head back to the apartment later if that's okay with you. I just don't feel like going back there right now."

Simone gave her an incredible look through squinted eyes.

"Sweetie, you live here now. Richard had your things sent over last night. You're roomie number two, and I am more than grateful for the tiebreaker. Kat and I can't agree on anything, so now you can be the tiebreaker." Simone flashed her one of her million-dollar smiles and a wink. "Besides, this is Richard's place. We're just squatting here until we're millionaires." She hugged Mallory again.

"What?" She didn't know how to tell Simone that all that might have changed over the last few hours. He had done all this before their incident at the cabin. She was sure he didn't want her in his apartment now. She had compared him to Clay. He had wanted to kill Clay last night when she'd told him about the man. He couldn't still want anything to do with her.

"All right, I know it's early, but I think we should go harder than wine. How about champagne instead? I mean we have reason to celebrate, right?" She took one look at Mallory's tear-stained face and frowned. "Okay, so maybe we have to plan a murder, but pink champagne goes with any occasion." She handed each woman a glass before seating herself on the floor in front of them. She gave the bottle a little shake before handing it to Mallory. "Here, you should open it. Just point it towards Sy's face and let her rip—knock out a tooth or something."

Mallory's and Simone's jaws dropped in shock. "What? Do you wanna get on the St. Thomas trip or what?" Simone's laughter jogged Mallory from her shock.

"So you both get on this trip, and I get stripped of my seat and a tooth?" Kat shrugged as she took the bottle back from Mallory. Simone quickly dove behind Mallory, who cowered in the couch as Kat attempted to pop the top of the champagne. Kat carefully pointed the top toward the ceiling.

"Here it comes." She pushed down on the cork, causing it to fly from the bottle. "Oh yes! Yes! Yes! Whew, was that good for y'all too?" She poured herself a glass as the other two handed her theirs.

"Are you practicing for later tonight?" Simone shoved her glass at her sister.

Kat filled the glass with a giggle. "I plan on doing more than that. I shall be dramatic tonight—Oscar-winning performance even." She held up her champagne toward the ceiling while covering her chest with the other hand. "I shall rock this man's world with sounds of pleasure like none this side of paradise has ever heard."

Simone and Mallory shared a look before setting aside their glass and applauding her performance. "Thank you, thank you. I have practiced the faces I shall make as well."

This caused Simone to spit the champagne she was sipping on her sister.

"Oh my god, yuck." Kat was not happy.

"Oh my god, I'm sorry." Simone ran to the bathroom to grab a few towels. On her way back, the phone rang. She threw the towels at Kat before answering the phone.

"Hey." She paused as she listened. "Yes, please bring them up." She hung up and returned to her spot on the couch.

"What was that?" Kat knew it was a delivery, but she'd always got a kick out of asking.

"Delivery." Simone pulled her feet into the couch and turned her attention to Mallory. "So, do you want to go on this trip in two weeks?"

Mallory knew what she was talking about, but it was for models that had been with the agency for a while, faces that had already been in magazines or gracing runways. She was still in class, for goodness' sakes. There was no way she was getting on that shoot.

"I'm still in class. I don't think I'm eligible." She looked from Kat to Simone, who were both smiling at her.

"What's in the bags?" Mallory realized she hadn't opened the bags she'd been given earlier.

Kat reached for one and handed it to her. "Open this one—it's the biggest." She smiled and did a little shake as if she was expecting a present for herself. "Open it, open it, open it," she chanted.

Mallory took the bag and removed the box. It was beautiful. She had no idea what it was. As she removed the peach bow that held the mystery intact, Kat cheered her on. She took the top from the box and revealed a key—not just any key but a car key. Richard had given her a car.

"Lemme see." Kat jumped into the seat next to her and took the box. "Get the other one."

She took the key from the box and twirled it on her finger. "Mercedes for the princess." She laughed as Mallory turned a shocked face to her. "Welcome to the crew, honey. Let's see what's in this one." Mallory nervously opened the second box.

"Well, it's official. You are now safe for private parties." Kat and Simone laughed at a private joke Mallory wasn't privy to. A jewelry box was inside the second package. She opened it to reveal a well-crafted diamond necklace. The little stone was secured in between two golden hands. It was beautiful.

"What does this mean?" She looked at Simone for clarification.

"It means you are protected by the great Richard Embers. No one at those awful parties would dare harass you. When you decline, they run for the hills. It works in those uppity stores too." Kat was smiling at her. "You can save the other one for later. I think it might be private."

Mallory didn't know what any of it meant. She was still worried that it was all in vain. He would ask her to return his gifts once he returned from his amazing cabin. She tried not to get too excited about the things she had been given.

"Let me help you with your necklace." Simone took the box and removed the thin chain that held the precious jewel. Mallory wanted to tell her no, but it was too late. She was already clasping it around her neck.

As she admired the necklace, the elevator signaled its arrival. A few young men stepped out, carrying large bouquets of roses. Mallory's eyes grew at the sight of the arrangements. They were the largest she'd ever seen. She was sure Simone was used to them, but she had never even gotten a daffodil, much less bouquets like these. They walked over to the large table by the giant windows and placed them gently on it. The older of the three men took the notes and brought them to Mallory. She frowned up at him before taking them. The man bowed and returned to the elevator. Mallory didn't bother to look at the little envelopes in her hand. She just passed them to Simone.

"I think these might be yours." She smiled at Simone, who was nodding at her with a brilliant smile. "That's not my name on them."

Mallory looked down and was shocked to see her name scrawled across the envelopes.

"Open them, open them." Kat was clapping and bouncing in the seat next to her.

"No, Kat. They might be private. Aren't you late anyway?"

Kat turned to check the grandfather clock in the corner. "Nope, I have time to read one of her private notes."

Mallory shrugged and opened the first one. It was from Richard. A phone number—his phone number. Mallory look at Kat, who was also making a confused face.

"Open the next one. That one was boring."

Mallory opened the other envelope that simply read "I'm Sorry." She shifted uncomfortably in the chair. She hadn't noticed

Simone's intense gaze on her face. "Open the next. Those two were boring."

Mallory didn't hesitate this time. She tore the note from the envelope and leaned toward Kat. As she unfolded it, the words that graced the expensive paper shocked both Kat and Mallory:

> Enjoy St. Thomas. I'll See
> You When You Return
>
> Richard

Mallory read the note again to make sure she'd read it correctly. She looked from Kat to Simone. Kat was obviously shocked, but Simone wasn't. She was smiling as if she had already known. "Is this real?" She couldn't believe it. She wasn't ready. She was nobody.

"I have two weeks to get you two ready. I want that cover photo, so we will be working hard." Kat almost killed Mallory trying to climb over to Simone.

"Oh my god, we are going to St. Thomas!" She had shoved a shocked Mallory out of the couch. They were going to St. Thomas. She was going to St. Thomas.

"Not if you smother me and kill Mal you won't."

This couldn't possibly be real. He was sending her on her first shoot all the way to St. Thomas. She hadn't finished her training. She wanted to call him, but she was afraid.

"This has to be a mistake. I don't think he meant that I was…"

Simone gave her a scolding look. "I was told right before you arrived that I had two weeks to get you two ready for St. Thomas. It's real." She reached out an arm to help Mallory from the floor. Kat scrambled to the floor and retrieved her drink. She gestured for the other two to join her in a toast.

"I told you. To St. Thomas!" She practically sang the toast. "Oh, and to big brother Richard"—she took a sip before adding—"and future husband to my new sister."

Mallory almost choked on the champagne. "You are now a Deveaux girl. We're triplets—the Oreo Deveaux triplets." She giggled at her own joke.

Mallory felt a warmth she hadn't felt before. She was a part of something important. She was a part of Richard's life. She felt her stomach churn as she remembered what had happened earlier. She prayed he would answer when she called him later. She would apologize for comparing him to Clay. She hadn't meant to.

Mallory and Simone spent most of the day going through her closet that was much bigger than the room she'd stayed in at the agency's apartment. They had packed Kat off to her lunch date and whatever else she was going to do. Simone tried to show her how to walk in her collection of shoes. They had been having such a good time together Mallory forgot about her situation with Richard.

"I love it here." She was excited about the future even if she wasn't sure what was in store for her.

"Give it a few weeks. You're going to love it even more. And here you don't have to follow those stupid house rules like back at club hell. No crowded showers. No catfights over assignments. No more disgusting diets." Simone threw herself across the giant fluffy pillow sprawled on the closet floor. "But I do insist that you go to the gym with me at least four times a week. We are going to work on that booty—no offense." She laughed when Mallory tried to look at her own butt.

"What's wrong with my butt?" She thought she had a decent one. Simone shook her head.

"That's just it. You have a butt. We are gonna get you a booty. You're a Deveaux now." She winked at Mallory.

"Well, I'm not genetically a Deveaux so don't get your hopes up." She flopped down next to Simone and started removing her shoes.

"Honey, my daddy is a certified bootyologist." Mallory scrunched up her face at Simone.

"What in the world is a bootyologist?" She had never heard the term before. Was that even a real thing?

"My daddy trains boxers. He also teaches women how to tone their bodies after childbirth, get the muscles back in tiptop shape. He came up with a few exercises that helps to grow your gluteus maximus—that and a daily addition to your meals. Family secret stuff."

They both laughed. Neither of them had heard the elevator arrive, so when Richard spoke, they almost had identical heart attacks.

"Sounds interesting. Can't wait to see the results."

Both women screamed before scrambling to their feet. He was leaning against the door dressed in a grey three-piece suit that was obviously tailored just for him.

"Jesus, Richard." Simone was the first to greet him. She walked over and threw her arms around him. Mallory watched their interaction. "You missed lunch. I expected you sooner." He kissed her cheek, pushed her back, and twirled her around.

"So that's how you keep this enticing body of yours? And here I thought you just woke up like this every day." They both laughed, seeming to forget about Mallory.

"Good God, no. You've seen my eating habits. I have to work out." She laughed as he released her. Mallory felt a bit jealous of the look he was giving Simone. It was blatantly obvious he admired her—maybe even loved her. She wrapped her arms around herself and waited for them to finish their banter. Besides, she was nervous about his being here. She watched Simone walk to the door before turning to Richard.

"Hey, Rich?"

He gave her a smile before answering. "Yes, ma'am?"

She looked at Mallory before turning her attention back to him. "You remember what you said the last time you watched me cook dinner?"

His smile faded, but there was still a hint of amusement on his face. He nodded. "Good talk."

She winked at him before exiting the room, closing the door behind her. Mallory had no idea what had happened, but she was even more aware that she was alone once again with Richard. Her heart was racing as if she'd run twenty miles in twenty minutes. She was sure he could smell the fear pouring from her. He walked over and sat on her bed.

"Come here." He waved her over and patted the space next to him. She hesitated but decided she would just do as he'd asked. Once she got close, he reached out and pulled her to him. She stumbled before coming to a seated position on his lap. Richard wrapped his arms around her and kissed her temple. She felt safe—safe in his embrace. How did he do it? One minute he's terrorizing her, and the next making her feel like he would move heaven and earth to protect her.

"Are you okay?"

She couldn't speak, so she nodded. He gave her a little squeeze before laying her back on the bed.

Dear God, not again. She was still sore from earlier. Her eyes displayed her feelings clearly enough that he understood. Her legs were still draped over his as he leaned over her.

"What happened this morning will never happen again." He ran his eyes over her body before returning his gaze to her face. "I wasn't sorry about what I'd done until I came back and found the blood."

Blood? What blood? She must have missed something. Had she bled on his floor?

"I'm sorry, Rich—" He cut her off before she could finish.

"Don't apologize to me." The command in his voice frightened her. "I'm the one who should be sorry. I'm not used to being in situations like this." He took a breath and gathered his thoughts. "Most people do what I ask of them, so I try not to be unreasonable." Had he thought his request that she not touch her own body was reasonable?

He sat up, turning his back to her. "I'm not perfect, and I get that I may not be for everyone. I don't try to be. I am what and who I am. However, after this morning, I realized that maybe the man I am is not the man you need."

Mallory felt a pain in her chest. He didn't want her anymore. She wasn't sure why she even cared if he wanted her; they'd met only last night. She had been with Clay for three years, and she never once felt the way she did now about him. "I told you before that I put work and time into the things I want. This is no different." He turned to look at her.

She was trying to keep the tears at bay. She would get through this just as she did with everything else.

"I won't change who I am for you, but I can make accommodations, and I need you to do the same. So you're going to have to be patient with me." He was smiling at her.

Was this really what she wanted? "What?"

He pulled her back onto his lap. "I need you to understand this won't be easy for you, but it will be worth it." He hugged and kissed her. "In the meantime, try to listen to Simone. I want you to stay here with her and Kat because I know they will look out for you. Simone is an amazing teacher. I trust her, and you can too."

Mallory nodded in compliance. She wanted to make this man happy. He hadn't made her any definite promises, but if she did what she was supposed to, things would work out. He'd promised not to lie to her, but sometimes people changed their minds.

"I have to leave you, and I won't see you again until after your trip. My parents are in town, and I have no idea when they're leaving." He helped her up and stood behind her. "Try to enjoy yourself." He turned her to look at him. She didn't look happy.

"I'll see if I can sneak away sometime next week."

She smiled, and he couldn't help it. He pulled her close and kissed her. She was his. He would show her that he was nothing like her fucked up ex. He would make her happier than she ever dreamed.

Simone was in the kitchen, chopping vegetables, when Richard and Mallory finally joined her. She usually cooked for herself and her sister. "Well, hello you two." She laughed when Richard pulled Mallory in front of him.

"See, she's fine." He gave Mallory a little shove forward. Simone started to laugh, but Mallory was lost.

"I can see that." She winked at Mallory. "So are you here to deliver our invitation?" She went back to chopping her vegetables.

Richard took a deep breath before answering. "I thought you were done with my family gatherings?"

Simone made a face. "I was—until Mal showed up. She needs to have the "Embers" experience before she decides you're Mr. Right."

Richard frowned at her. "Don't you think she should get a taste of what Christmas is gonna be like for the rest of her life?"

Mallory wondered how much Simone knew about her encounter with Richard. Had he told her everything? She could feel her cheeks burning red-hot. She was thankful Simone was too busy prepping the meal to pay her too much attention. She wanted to hide under the counter.

"Will you be accompanying her?" He was serious.

Mallory looked over her shoulder at him. His expression was scary serious. Why didn't he want her to meet his parents?

"Of course. Honey, I wouldn't throw my little sister to the wolves. You know that."

Richard walked around the counter to stand before Simone.

"She arrives and leaves with you." They were facing each other. "You'll take her shopping for something to wear on Friday after class."

Simone was tall, but standing before Richard, she looked so small. His six-foot-whatever frame towered over her. Mallory watched the two as he instructed her. Simone was not at all intimidated by him like she was. "Felix will be at your disposal." That made Simone smile.

"Will Kat be in attendance as well?" Richard ran a frustrated hand over his face.

"Yes. Ken will be bringing her." Simone started to giggle, leaning forward to rest her head on Richard's chest. Mallory felt like a fly on the wall. They were sharing a moment to which she wasn't invited. She wondered if she'd left the room they would notice. She watched Richard's face soften just before he started to laugh. He was extremely handsome. She watched these two beautiful people share something she'd never shared with anyone.

"I think I'll hire extra security." He shook his head as Simone almost slid to the floor with laughter. She was in his arms, laughing hysterically. Richard tried to calm himself when he noticed the look on Mallory's face. She seemed lost watching them. "Pull yourself together, woman. You're scaring Mallory."

Simone paused briefly to look at Mallory. "Honey, you had to be there. One of his guests got a little out of hand with Kat, and she cursed him and his wife straight to hell. They were so embarrassed they never made it back from the restroom. Missed the whole dinner."

Richard started to laugh again as he recalled Kat's words. "You tell her what Kat called them. I can't."

Simone was bent over the counter, laughing. Richard tried to regain his composure before waving Mallory over. She did as he wanted.

"She told the mayor his wife looked like a mangy sundried turkey wearing peacock feathers—badly." Mallory's mouth flew open in shock. "And that he looked like a half-boiled chicken in a cheap off-the-rack suit."

Simone ran to the sink to wash her face. Mallory couldn't believe what she was hearing.

"That is the edited PG version. She let them have it, honey, but they did deserve it." Simone was trying to calm down.

Mallory couldn't help but envy the way she looked fanning her face with her famous smile plastered across it. That was the kind of woman Richard needed on his arm—not her. Her thoughts had drawn her away from reality once again.

"I'm getting out of here. You two can gossip and do whatever you women do when you're alone. I have a plane to catch."

Mallory shook her head to clear her thoughts. She hadn't heard a word Richard had said. Simone came over and hugged him. She was still giggling when he let her go with a kiss on the cheek.

"I'll give you two some privacy to say goodbye." She wiggled her eyebrows at Mallory before heading out into the living room.

Richard lifted Mallory and placed her on the counter they were standing next to.

"I can see your little brain working overtime. It's not what you think. Our relationship is different. She and I are great friends and nothing more."

She knew she should trust him, but the way they interacted with each other was just beautiful. Their chemistry was amazing. He placed a hand under her chin and lifted it slightly. "I value Simone's opinion, and Simone thinks you're my soul mate. We just need a little work."

She was shocked. How could Simone think that when they had only met last night.

He smiled as if he could read her thoughts. "Ask her about her grandmother. You'll understand."

He bent and kissed her like he had earlier. She enjoyed his kisses. Her arms automatically wrapped around his torso as she pulled herself even closer to him. She would trust them. If he said they were friends, then that was what it was.

Richard reluctantly released her. "Let go of me, woman. I can only take so much of this torture."

She smiled when he stood back and adjusted himself. "Now, walk with me."

She did as he asked. They walked to the elevator with his arm firmly around her. When they passed through the living room, he winked at Simone, who returned the gesture.

"Don't let that one overwork you. She can be a dictator at times."

Mallory watched as he got into the elevator. He turned and mashed the button, closing the door. She felt a wave of loneliness standing there.

*****

Friday seemed to take forever. She hadn't seen or heard from Richard since he'd left her that Saturday. She knew he was busy and tried not to let her thoughts lead her astray. Simone had kept her so busy that she couldn't stay awake after dark. She worked her in the gym twice a day and even harder on the practice runway. Mallory quickly realized why Simone had risen to where she was. The woman was a natural at all of it. Other girls pushed their way into her training classes. Everyone tried to comply with her strict work ethic. By the end of the day, if you hadn't felt pain, you didn't work. They had all gotten a good laugh today when Roy came in and Simone made him walk the runway in a pair of heels. He'd wanted a few girls for a party he was throwing, but the Deveaux girls were exempt. She was happy for that. Simone was dealing with some of the other girls, so Kat and Mallory had to wait on her.

"My legs feel like they aren't there. I might have caught asthma today 'cause I can barely breathe." Mallory laughed as Kat sprawled herself across the couch they were in.

"I'm pretty sure I'm gonna drown today. I'm too tired to shower, and I'm gonna fall asleep in the tub."

Kat tried to laugh before declaring it too difficult. "I gotta go to the restroom. Don't leave me." She got up and made her way to the restroom.

Mallory hadn't noticed the women stalking her, but Kat had. She was finishing up in the stall when she heard two women enter.

"God, do you see how she follows Simone and Kat around like a lost puppy?" The women giggled. They were talking about her.

Mallory decided to stay in the stall. She didn't feel like confronting whoever they were.

"I don't think she realizes that Richard only dates the ones he doesn't think have what it takes." They weren't trying to keep their conversation private at all. The other woman snickered at her friend's revelation.

"Let the poor thing enjoy her days at the top. He always goes back to Simone. I mean she is a goddess among the women he takes to his bed—not that the others aren't pretty, but none can compare to his Nubian goddess."

Mallory sat there listening.

"Their relationship is kinda cool, though, him letting her pick his next fling."

Was that true?

"I'm sure she was the prettiest one in her one-horse town—the queen of all their parades." Both women laughed even louder. "Well, she should know that around here, she's just another regular in a crowd of regulars. There's nothing special about her here."

Mallory felt a knot in her stomach. She heard the door open but didn't move.

"Mal, your prince charming is looking for you. Are you in here?" It was Kat.

She hurried out of the stall. "He needs his Aphrodite to brighten up his day, girl, come on. Wash your damn hands first." She smiled at Mallory, who was trying to avoid the other woman.

"I'll be right out." She washed her hands and squeezed by Kat, avoiding eye contact with the others. Mallory pushed the door open with her shoulder when she felt Kat's hand around her wrist. She turned to look at her.

"Ladies, I don't think you've been properly introduced. This is my sister, Mallory. Richard's woman. So the next time you two wanna play your little gossip game, make sure neither of us are around." Kat took a step closer to the women, who retreat at the gesture. "Richard may end your boring-ass careers, but I will end you. And trust me, no one will ever find you. I'm from N'Orleans."

Mallory couldn't help the giggle that escaped her. They both turned to leave and found Richard standing before them.

"Oh shit! Richard. Hey." Mallory couldn't tell if he was amused of pissed. She avoided his eyes as she dragged Kat out behind her.

Richard gave the two women a slight nod before turning his attention to Kat and Mallory.

"What did you two do? I left you alone for five minutes."

Simone was coming to their rescue. "Richard." She walked over and stood between him and the girls. "What are you doing here? I thought we were going shopping after class." She tried to wave Mallory and Kat away as she attempted to distract Richard. She had no idea what had happened, but she could read her sisters like a book. They'd been caught doing something.

"I don't want those two in your classes anymore." He nodded toward the bathroom. "For their safety." He kissed Simone's cheek then stepped aside so she could check the restroom. Simone did just that.

"Ladies. You should have gone home today." She smiled before closing the door. "I think we better get going. We have an appointment." She cruised by Richard and grabbed her sisters.

They could hear him laughing as he followed them. He was happy Mallory was bonding so well with Simone and Kat. They were exactly what she needed. They would teach her how to be stronger and stand up for herself. She needed to learn to take care of herself—especially around him. He was trying to be more understanding, but he was no saint. He was glad to be back. He had some damage to repair.

*****

Mallory woke to Simone's usual banging on her door. She wasn't sure what time it was, but she didn't feel at all rested. They had spent the afternoon shopping with Richard before heading to dinner and then a club. Ken had joined them for drinks at the club. Mallory rolled over right into Richard's arms. When she stiffened, he groaned.

"Expecting someone else?"

She giggled and snuggled closer to him. "Maybe my maker. I don't think I like drinking anymore."

He chuckled and kissed her forehead. "Now you see why drinking is forbidden in the apartments. You women go crazy when you go out."

Another knock on the door sounded even louder than before.

"Come in!" Richard yelled.

The door flew open, and in walked Simone, carrying two mugs.

"I am not room service, sir."

Richard raised an eyebrow at her. "I told you not to let her drink so much. She looks half dead."

Mallory inhaled as she tried to bury herself in the covers.

"I might have contributed to some of her dishevelment." Simone laughed before turning to leave.

"Try not to kill her. I'm putting her on the cover of your magazine in a week. Everyone will have a chance to ogle all that hard work you're trying to destroy."

Mallory poked her head from under the blanket, and Simone winked before closing the door behind her.

"Wha...what did she mean?" She was sitting up.

Richard's attention was not on her question but her naked breasts.

"Richard!" she shouted when he pinched her nipple. "Stop that." She pulled the blanket up and covered herself.

"You're no fun sober."

Mallory's jaw dropped at his comment. What the hell did that mean?

He reached for the mugs, passing her one. He sniffed his before trading with her. "That's yours." He took a sip of the hot liquid and welcomed the familiar taste. He loved Simone's hangover remedies. They weren't as good as her other morning specials, but you were guaranteed rejuvenation with her hangover teas.

"Richard, did you tell Simone to put me on the cover? I'm not ready for a cover." She didn't want the other girls to think she was getting special treatment because of her relationship with him. She wanted to work for what she got. "I don't want to sound ungrateful, but I need to do this without your help. I do not want any special treatment because..." She stopped when she saw the mischievous smile on his face.

"What?" He sat up and leaned against the headboard. "That's a first. Most women welcome any opportunity they get."

She was frowning.

"I had nothing to do with your being chosen for the cover. Take that up with Simone. She chose you."

She didn't believe him.

He could see she wasn't buying any of it. "Do you wanna have a grown-up conversation that will change your life?"

She nodded, but he wasn't sure she was ready.

"Simone owns the magazine. She chooses whomever she pleases to put into it. I have no control over who she selects for whatever she selects them for."

Mallory's wide-eyed stare made him continue.

"She was the first Mrs. Richard Embers."

Mallory's mouth flew open. *What?*

"It was business. She said she could run the magazine better than I could since I had no idea what was going on over there. I made her a deal. I'm the puppet, and she the puppet master."

What the hell is he saying? "I'm so confused."

Richard reached for her mug and placed it on the nightstand. "Get dressed, and we will talk to Simone."

Mallory didn't move. She didn't know what to do. He'd told her that they were just friends, and now he says they were married. How could she believe any of this? Richard got up and headed for the bathroom. Mallory realized he had been naked the whole time. Her jaw dropped at the sight of his naked body. Jesus, he was perfect. There didn't seem to be an ounce of fat on the man.

He turned at the door to see her staring at him. "I'm glad you like it. I've worked hard on this—just for you. Now come enjoy your reward." He disappeared into the bathroom, leaving her confused and yearning.

She wanted to go in after him but sat on the edge of the bed, trying to process what he had told her. Was what the women in the restroom said true? Had Simone chosen her for his pleasure? She couldn't understand what she was feeling—betrayed by people she trusted. Was this what it was like in the business? He had told her to trust Simone, but how could she? They'd been using her from the beginning, pretending to care. Her eyes filled with tears as she realized these people hadn't felt one ounce of love for her. They'd all pretended to love her—especially him. She couldn't stay here. She had to get some fresh air and think, maybe clear her head. She ran to the closet and grabbed a pair of sweats. She needed to leave.

"I'm getting cold, woman."

She stopped when she heard his voice.

"Are you coming in, or do I have to come get you?"

She turned and opened the door. She could hear Simone and Kat talking downstairs. She quickly wiped her face as best she could then took off running down the stairs. She knew they would see her, but she would be on her way down before they realized what had happened.

"Hey, Mal. Are you coming too?"

She turned to see Kat walking toward her. She didn't stop to answer. She ran around the corner, plowing into Simone.

"Holy shit. Are you guys okay?"

Mallory tried to recover, but Kat was already there, trying to help her up. She pulled away from the woman she'd thought was her best friend. Simone was lying on the floor, holding her head. Mallory panicked. She backed up then turned to run again—this time into Richard, who was soaking wet in a towel. He looked around her and saw Kat trying to help Simone.

"Mal, what the hell?" Kat was looking worried.

Mallory tried to wriggle out of Richard's grip. He finally turned her loose and went to Simone's aid. This was her chance. She took off again.

Richard looked up and saw her bolting for the elevator. "Get her back here," he commanded Kat.

She didn't question him; she nodded and took off behind Mallory. The elevator doors were closing when she got there. Kat jammed her foot between the small space in the closing doors.

"What's wrong with you?" She realized Mallory was crying and stepped into the elevator. "What happened? Did Richard hurt you?" Kat was concerned.

Mallory stepped back away from Kat. The door started to close again.

"Let me go, Kat. I can't be here anymore." She pleaded with Kat. She knew she wasn't going to be able to leave now. Simone came around the corner, Richard in tow.

"Are you okay?" She was still holding her head.

Mallory tried not to look at Richard, who was obviously furious.

"You should come back in so we can figure this out. I don't know what it is, but you don't have to go through it alone, honey." She sounded so genuine that Mallory took a step toward her before halting. Simone turned to Richard. He was clearly upset. "Go finish your shower. We will handle this."

He reluctantly turned and headed back towards the upstairs.

"Please let me leave."

Kat couldn't take it anymore; she threw herself at Mallory and engulfed her in a hug. "You're not going anywhere. If he hurt you, we will make him sorry he was ever born."

Mallory struggled to free herself, but Kat was too strong. She felt the tears on her shoulder and was instantly aware Kat was crying too.

"You're his wife?" She felt weak. Her knees felt like mush.

Kat stepped back but didn't release her. "What are you talking about?" She seemed shocked at what she had heard. Did she not know her sister was married to Richard, or was she just pretending? Kat turned to Simone. "What is she talking about?"

Tears filled Simone's eyes as she swayed a little. "He wasn't supposed to tell anyone—not even you. Not yet."

Both Kat and Mallory watched in horror as Simone dropped to the floor, her hand covered in blood. She was bleeding.

Kat ran to her sister. Mallory ran to the stairs and screamed for Richard. What had she done?

"Oh my god. She's not waking up. What do I do?"

Mallory had no idea what to do. She held Simone's limp hand in hers and started to pray. Richard almost pushed her and Kat out of the way as he picked Simone up. He was barefoot and still wet from his shower. He was only wearing a pair of sweatpants. He rushed into the elevator, clutching Simone to him. She wasn't moving.

"Let's go. Move!" The harshness of his voice scared both women.

They did as he commanded and ran into the elevator.

"Press the Call button, and ask Joe to get the ambulance here now."

Kat complied.

"I'm sorry," Mallory whispered. She wasn't sure who she was apologizing to—Richard, Kat, or Simone. She had hurt them all today. Mallory felt Kat's shaky hands wrap around hers.

"She gonna be okay. You don't know Sy. She's strong. She'll be okay." She was trying to be strong just like her big sister.

The elevator came to a halt, and everyone rushed out. There were first responders waiting for them. Richard laid Simone on a gurney and stepped back to let the men do their jobs. He was worried.

"We are going to take her to the emergency room. Who's riding with us? Only one—"

Richard quickly cut the man off. "I am."

Looking Richard up and down, the man quickly regretted hesitating as he made eye contact with Richard.

"Yes, sir."

They rushed out the door and into the waiting ambulance. Bystanders were whispering in shock. They knew who she was. Mallory and Kat were quickly escorted to the waiting limo. Felix held the door open for the women as they hopped in. When he got in behind them, Kat turned and accepted his open arms.

"Simone is going to be all right. Richard will take care of her."

Mallory watched as Kat broke down. Felix extended a caring arm to her, but she declined, not wanting to get in the way. When he gave her a stern look, she felt her body moving as if he were controlling her actions. The man was warm and comforting as they sped through lights. Mallory could hear sirens blaring outside the car. They were being escorted by the police. She wondered how everything happened so fast but then remembered Richard was pulling the strings.

When they finally arrived at the hospital, they were escorted to a private waiting area. Richard was nowhere to be found. It was almost an hour before he made an appearance. He didn't speak to Mallory or Kat. Whatever was going on was relayed to Felix before he left. Mallory sat with Kat on a couch by the window, holding her. Her guilt was eating away at her. She had caused Simone's accident. Regardless of the situation, Simone had taken care of her. She was always supportive and reliable. Ever since they'd met, she was a friend. Her first week at the apartment had been horrible, but Simone made sure she had what she needed. When she was asked to join the party that night, she had told Simone she'd felt uncomfortable around Roy. She had suggested the red wig. Roy wasn't a fan of redheads. It had worked until Richard had shown up.

"She wants to see you now—both of you."

Richard looked so tired Mallory wanted to comfort him. His red eyes scared her. Had he been crying? Was Simone going to be okay? She had hit the ground pretty hard when they'd collided. She tried to ignore his angry stare as she helped Kat out of the room.

Richard walked past them and led them to Simone. "Try not to upset her." He turned and left them.

Kat rushed into the room to her sister. Mallory was afraid of what Simone would say, so she took it slow.

"You can come in, Mal. I'm not angry with you." She was sitting up in the bed, hooked up to a few different machines. A slow IV drip hung behind her.

Mallory wiped her tears in her sweatshirt.

"Please come here?"

She walked over to the other side of the bed and took a seat in the chair.

"Are you okay?" Simone seemed genuinely concerned. *How could she be worried about anyone else at a time like this?*

"I'm all right. I'm sorry I hurt you." She was crying again. Simone held out her hand in comfort. Mallory took it and held on tight.

"I'm fine. It wasn't really the fall that has me stuck in this bed." She tried to smile as Kat jumped up.

"What do you mean?" She knew her sister was hiding something—something that was going to hurt forever. She knew the look on Simone's face. It was the same look she had gotten from her mother almost ten years ago. "What the hell is wrong with you?"

Simone tried to smile.

"Just tell me." She sat on the bed and held her sister's hand.

"I have a heart condition."

Kat jumped to her feet.

"I found out I had a defective heart over a year ago." Simone tried to blink her tears away. She had to be strong for Kat and Mallory.

Kat stood with her jaw hanging in shock.

"They don't know how long I can go without a new one, but that's not an option." She knew the risks of any heart surgery.

"Are you crazy? What do you mean it's not an option?"

Simone knew Kat was not gonna take any of this well. She had tried to shield her sister from the truth.

"You can't leave me. You're all I have, Sy." She crawled into her big sister's arms and cried. She felt physical pain at the thought of losing Simone. She did not have enough time with her. There was so much she'd wanted them to do together.

"I'm not leaving you alone, Kat. You have Richard, Mallory, and Ken." She tried to comfort her sobbing sister, but it wasn't working. Kat was too stubborn.

"I don't want them. I want you." Kat turned to look at Mallory. "No offense, Mal, but you can't replace Simone. None of you can."

Mallory could barely see through her tears.

"Katherine Ann Marie Deveaux! That is not very nice."

Kat sat up to look at her sister. "Simone Quinnetta Deveaux, you're an asshole."

Simone knew she hadn't meant it.

"Stop, Kat." Mallory didn't want them fighting. She didn't want Simone getting upset.

"You shut up. Both of you shut up."

Simone and Mallory watched as Kat stormed out of the room. She was pissed and hurting.

"Should I go get her?" Mallory knew she wouldn't be able to bring Kat back, but she would try if Simone needed her to.

"No. She needs time to process the hurt. She's not very good at accepting bad things." Simone gave Mallory's hand a gentle squeeze. "You shouldn't let her talk to you that way. You're older than her."

Mallory gave her a sad smile. It was all she had for now. She felt as if her heart had been ripped from her today. A few hours ago, she was angry with Simone and Richard for lying to her. She wanted to leave them both and run as far as she could. Now she was sitting here, wishing she had more time with them both. Richard was angry with her. She had hurt Simone—his wife, his real true love. Mallory felt her throat tighten. She couldn't think about those things right now. Simone needed her. Her sister needed her.

"I don't wanna come between you and Richard." As the words flowed through the air, she regretted setting them free. This wasn't the time.

Simone raised their entwined hands to her warm cheek. Mallory could feel her tears between their fingers. "You're not coming between anything. It really isn't what you think. Richard can explain it to you later." Simone took a deep breath before continuing. She was too tired to explain, but she would assure Mallory that she was where she needed to be. "I love Richard, and I want him to be happy. You have no idea how happy it makes me to know that you are the woman who will make him happy. I love both of you. I hope you know that."

Even though they hadn't known each other that long, Mallory believed her. "I love you too." She got up and hugged Simone.

"Stop all this crying. You're gonna get boogers on me."

Just then Mallory snickered and blew a little snot on poor Simone's chest.

"Oh yuck. I told you not to get that on me."

Mallory pulled back in horror. She quickly wiped the slimy liquid from Simone's gown.

"It's not boogers. It's just snot."

They both lost it when Mallory accidentally blew a snot bubble from one of her nostrils.

"Oh my god!" Simone tried leaning away from Mallory as she flopped back into the chair, neither of them aware of Richard's presence.

He had to clear his throat to announce himself, shocking both women. He was dressed in jeans and a polo shirt.

"Richard, thank god you're here. Mallory is trying to drown me with snot."

The laughter erupted again as another snot bubble grew in Mallory's nostril. Simone let out a small scream as it popped. Mallory quickly covered her face with her hands as she laughed.

"Where's Kat?" The question ceased all laughter.

"She needed to blow off some steam." Simone was smiling.

Richard could tell she was in some pain but trying to be brave. He walked over and pressed the button for the nurse. "You need to rest." He turned to Mallory. "Felix is gonna take you home. Stay there."

Mallory was about to answer when she noticed the look Simone was giving her. It was one of those "stand up for yourself, or I will" stares. Mallory took a breath, plastered her most defiant look on her face, then turned to Richard.

"I'm fine right here. I'll go home when I'm ready." She shocked herself with how firm the words sounded coming from her. "Thank you for your concern, but my sister needs me here." She decided that was enough. She didn't know if she could handle it if he were to yell at her. He looked pretty angry. She looked down at her fingers to avoid his stare.

"Now you give him the dreaded death stare like this." Simone turned and gave Richard one of her icy stares. When a smile finally lit the man's face, she turned her attention back to Mallory, who was smothering a smile. "Like that. Now you go." Simone nodded in Richard's direction.

"I'm gonna go find Kat." Richard shook his head at both women before exiting the room. He could hear Simone congratulating Mallory for standing her ground. He was proud of her even if her defiance was aimed at him. A nurse almost ran into him. "It's okay. She'll buzz when she needs you." The woman turned and left.

"I shouldn't have done that. He's upset with me."

Simone brought her hand down on the bed, making Mallory jump.

"So what if he's mad? You're allowed to have those feelings as well, Mal." She wished she had time to help Mallory realize her true potential.

"I'm not you, Sy. I'm not strong like you."

Simone gave her a stern look.

"No, you're not, Mal. You can never be me, but you can be the Mallory you need to be." She smiled at Mallory before continuing. "You're made of sugar and spice and very nice lady parts, but me—I'm made of sugar and spices, hot sauce, and awesome lady parts with a dash of angel tears." She smiled again when Mallory started to laugh. "Mal, I'm not like anyone else. I'm Simone Quinnetta Deveaux-Embers. I am the only one—just like you're the only one of you. I may not live to see another tomorrow, but honey, I'm grateful for all the todays and yesterdays that I've had, for all the people I've met and loved, for Richard and you. I love you both very much, and I'm so happy I got a chance to see you fall in love."

Mallory got up and sat on the side of the bed. She held Simone's hand in hers and silently prayed. They needed more time.

"I know you two will be happy, Mal. You just have to love him—love him for the both of us."

Mallory leaned forward and hugged her.

"And my bratty little sister."

They held each other tight.

"You better not blow any more snot bubbles on me."

How would she ever be able to let go? Simone was right—there was no one else in the world like her. She was an angel.

Simone and Mallory sat talking about all the places she wished she had time to visit. She even shared with Mallory her dream for the magazine. It was different but interesting. Simone's ideas seem to get better the longer they spoke. It was well over thirty minutes before Richard returned with Kat.

"I see I wasn't missed." Kat came in first and sat on the bed. Richard stood at the door. He didn't come in. "Did she convince you to stick around?"

Simone nodded no.

"Then what have you two been babbling about?" She rolled her eyes at Mallory and then Simone.

"I think it's time we left. You can check in with her later." Richard was talking to her.

Mallory looked at Simone before responding. Without looking in Richard's direction she rolled her eyes at Simone.

"I'm not ready to go yet, so maybe you should come back later when I am."

Simone covered her mouth to hide her smile. Kat, on the other hand, sat staring from Mallory to Richard. She couldn't believe what she had heard. Mallory could barely believe what she was saying. She waited patiently for Richard to explode, but nothing happened.

"I'll be back around dinner. Be ready then." He was absolutely pissed, but she was proud of herself.

Kat sat with her eyes almost falling from her face, mouth agape, still looking at Richard. That was not the response she was expecting from either of them.

Richard turned to leave. "Take care of your sister. The nurses were instructed to make sure you're comfortable. Felix will keep unwanted visitors out." He winked at Simone before leaving.

"What the fuck just happened? Did you just grow balls? Giant balls?" Kat was shocked at Mallory's newfound confidence.

Simone hi-fived Mallory, who was still shocked at her boldness. "She's learning to stand up for herself." Simone sounded so proud that it made Mallory smile.

Kat frowned at them both. "Well maybe you should have told her to try swimming with minnows before sharks."

Mallory and Simone shared a laugh at Kat's reaction.

"Keep messing with Simone. She's not the one who'll have to deal with the consequences or the wrath of you know who."

She was right. Richard would be mad later, but she would have to deal with it. Right now she wanted to spend time with her sisters. She wanted to know more about them both.

"Enough about Richard. I can handle him." Both Kat and Simone gave her a look before sharing one with each other.

"What?" She giggled.

"You told me not to let anyone steamroll me, and I won't. If I can stand up to Richard, then everyone else will be a breeze." She plastered a confident smile across her face.

"Well damn. Look at the glass half full. I hope you feel as strong as you sound, honey, cause men like Richard will drink you dry."

Simone gave Kat a nudge with her leg. "Stop it. She's doing fine, and she will feel just as strong once we're done with her."

Kat made a noise that made Simone shake a fist at her.

"What would you like to talk about, Mallory. We will ignore Katherine and her bitter little heart."

Kat laughed and gave her sister the finger.

"Will you tell me about you and Richard?"

Simone didn't seem shocked at the question. She smiled at Mallory as if she was waiting for that question. "That's a long story that happened in a short time. However, it would literally take forever to tell you about us—but I'll give you the important parts." She adjusted herself in the bed.

"Ahh, is this good for your bum ticker 'cause I'm not about to watch you give up the ghost. You're not haunting me." Kat made a serious face that only made Simone laugh.

"Are you still married?" Kat wanted answers just like Mallory, but her sister's health was more important. She didn't want Mallory's inquisitiveness causing Simone any discomfort.

"I doubt he would be parading you around Sy if they were." She got off the bed and went to retrieve the vacant chair.

"No, Mal, we're not." She held out her hand for Mallory's. "I knew there was no future for us. I didn't wanna ruin his life. When I met him, I'd already known I didn't have much time in this world." Kat dragged the chair across the floor so loudly a passing nurse stopped in to see if all was well.

"Is everything all right?" The short stocky woman looked mean.

Simone smiled and nodded at her. She gave Kat a stern look before leaving.

"I don't think nurse Dracula likes me."

They laughed as she took her seat.

"Why didn't you tell me about all this before? I'm your freaking sister." She knew Simone had her reasons, but she didn't like not knowing.

"It was easier not to tell you. You wanted to be a model so bad, and I needed you to focus on that."

Kat gave her a disapproving look. "So your plan was to come here, meet the richest man we've ever met, make him fall in love with you, marry him and divorce him then become super popular, plaster your smiling ass all over his magazine, and live my dream right in front of me." She rolled her eyes and turned to look out the window. "Thanks."

Simone knew she was just trying to be dramatic. "That is not what happened. I came here to make sure you didn't end up naked in front of some jerk promising you a world he didn't own. So you're welcome."

Kat was scowling at her sister. "Thanks!" She knew what Simone had done for her and the others. She wasn't as naive as everyone thought. Simone had gotten doors open for her and others that looked like her. "Get back to your stupid story. I'll tell her all the good ones when you're not around."

Simone snickered. "Anyway, I met Richard last new year's. We were both not wanting to be at the company get-together. I was volunteered as eye candy, so I made everyone who spoke to me miserable. I told them I had cramps and those that didn't care I told I had an itch. It worked on most people, but this one creepy old man said he didn't care. They had penicillin for things like that."

She fake gagged at the memory. "I convinced him I needed to run to the ladies' room before we could leave. Unfortunately, he went to stand by the door, so I climbed out a window onto a fire escape." She avoided the stares she was getting. "I figured I would climb down seven flights in my heels. Thankfully, I didn't have to. Richard was sitting out there, trying to avoid others as well."

Mallory recalled he had saved her too from a dreaded party.

"We talked for a while, then he offered to rescue me from the rest of the wolves—granted he was probably the most dangerous of the pack."

Kat found that funny since that's pretty much what she thought as well.

"Anyway we left, and he drove us to his house. I wasn't a fan of being kidnapped, but I knew exactly who he was. Everyone did."

This all sounded so familiar to Mallory.

"He made me a proposition. I declined. He was pissed, but he didn't give up. I told him what I thought of him and the way he used the poor girls who just wanted to make their dreams come true, how he and Roy treated us like their personal prostitutes. That didn't go over very well. He told me that if I spent the next thirty days with him, I would see him in a new light. I knew what that meant, but I had a plan."

Mallory's curiosity kept her gaze on Simone. She wanted to know everything, but she would have to settle for what she could get.

"I told him I didn't think I could form an honest opinion if he made me sleep with him. He informed me that it would be a great tragedy for him to have me so close and not touch me, but he could and would control himself. I doubted it, but what I wanted was more important than my virginity." Simone paused at Mallory's shock. "What?" She knew what was coming.

"Wait a minute. You've never?" Kat was also shocked at this.

"No, Kathrine, I haven't."

Both Kat and Mallory stared at her, hoping she was kidding.

"Why are you guys so shocked?"

Mallory didn't think anyone could resist Richard—especially when he felt the way he had about Simone. How did she manage to keep him away from her?

Simone shook her head in disbelief. "I told you, he has great self-control, and so do I."

Kat shook her head at her sister. "I'm sorry, but if I spent a month in Richard's house, he would be pregnant. Have you seen the man? This whole time I thought you had given up the golden fruit. I mean he practically jumps when you speak."

Mallory tried to pretend what Kat had said didn't affect her. She had been with Richard twice already, and they'd only known each other for a short while. She tried to hide her discomfort.

"Like I said, I didn't want to cause him any pain. I knew I had limited time and I needed to focus on you and the others. If I could get him to see how they really treated us, then maybe he would do something about it." She had been prepared to use whatever tactics she had to in order to secure a future for her sister. She'd vowed not to leave this world without some stability for Kat.

"After a few weeks, he started making changes. They knew I was his little spy, but I didn't care. Roy started pulling me to the side and offering me all kinds of assignments if I would shut my mouth. Apparently, Richard wasn't aware that we were forced to attend parties we didn't want to. There was a lot he didn't know. Roy was using some of the girls to blackmail clients into staying with the magazine. He would overcharge them and keep some for himself."

60

This was shocking news to Mallory and Kat. "It was probably the third week I was there. After dinner I was tired, so we decided to go to bed early. On the way up, I passed out. Thankfully, Richard was with me and caught me before I bruised my beautifulness." She tried to laugh but saw her eager audience's worried expressions. "I was fine. He had the doctor come over and check me out. The little snitch made me get a full physical. Then he told Richard without my permission about my condition. He instantly became overprotective, fired me and threatened to keep me hostage at his new cabin if I didn't seek treatment, even threatened to tell you when he found out I hadn't told you."

She smiled at her sister, who wasn't finding any of this amusing. Kat was trying to keep it together. She couldn't believe Simone had kept all that from her. They were sisters, and she should have been told.

"We talked about a lot after that. I told him why I was here and what I was hoping to change before the inevitable. I didn't expect him to understand, let alone go out of his way to do the things he had." She gave Mallory's hand a little squeeze. "He told me if I married him, he would give me creative control of the agency. I would be Roy's boss. He wanted to teach him a lesson, and I would be perfect for this task. I could change things for everyone—not just Kat but all the girls. I didn't even think about it. I said yes."

Mallory knew Simone had a good heart; she didn't think she would have wasted her short time doing what Simone had. "The first month we were married, he took me all over the place. Everywhere he went, I had to go. I barely got to see my bratty sister, but she was taken care of so that I wouldn't worry. He moved her into our apartment and had Felix stay with her."

Kat started to laugh when she remembered how Felix had stalked her. He wouldn't let her go anywhere without him. He'd called and told on her when she decided to walk around naked in the apartment. Simone had chewed her butt for messing with poor Felix.

"She made poor Felix want to quit with her shenanigans."

That made Kat laugh even louder.

"Anyway, I took him to see Nanan, our grandma, the old voo-doo lady in the bayou."

Richard had mentioned something to her earlier about Simone's grandma. She was sitting on the edge of her chair.

"She told him that we were never meant to be more than friends. That he would meet his forever one the same way he'd met me. She would make him feel everything he was feeling for me, but she would be able to give him everything I couldn't. This woman would change him but for the better. She would give him children and the family he wanted."

Mallory tried to wipe the tears before they fell. Her heart hurt for Simone and Richard. They loved each other and deserved to be together.

"Good ole Nanan. Can't put a little sugar in her fortunes. At least this one was spot on." Kat knew her sister was happy Richard had found Mallory, and now she knew why. "Don't feel bad, Mal. Nanan believes that everyone has a path they have to travel. Now if you so choose to pick up the wrong hitchhiker on your path, you might end up like Richard's parents."

Simone snatched her sister's hand. "Kathrine! Stop it."

Mallory wanted to know what that meant but knew Simone would never let Kat tell her.

"What? They hate each other. They act all lovey-dovey in public and—"

Simone halted her again. "Kathrine Ann Marie Deveaux!"

Kat wasn't fazed by her sister's tone. "It's Mrs. Jones to you, heifer. Mrs. Kenneth Marion Jones." She rolled her eyes at the women when they both looked at her like she wasn't being honest.

"I'm sorry, what? And Marion? Really?"

Kat shook her head and gave both women the finger.

"I tell you I'm married, and you make fun of his middle name? He happens to be a good man and I love him—and he loves me." She added harshly. "He asked me to marry him and move in and I said yes. Well, that was before I knew you were at death's door beating it down."

Simone was shocked. "You're not serious, right? I mean he's like thirty-eight."

Kat became furious. "So!" The look on her face scared Mallory a bit. She had never seen Kat angry.

"You're twenty, Kat. He's taking advantage of you." This made Kat even angrier.

"No, he's not! He is the most amazing person I've ever met. He's loyal, gentle, kind, educated, and in love with me! I don't care what the hell you or anyone else thinks about us. We are getting married." She got up and walked to the window.

Simone was happy her sister had found someone. She decided to poke at her a bit before congratulating her. She turned and winked at Mallory.

"Yeah, but have you seen him. He's short, fat, hairy, and old. He looks like he should be guarding a bridge and killing goats."

Mallory held her breath as Kat almost exploded.

"Bitch! Not everyone can look like your Richard. He is perfect just the way he is, and if I have to help him chase goats, then you better believe I will, Billy Bitch. At least Ken is mine and mine alone."

Simone was smothering a smile as she watched Kat exit the room.

"She'll be back. She hasn't finished cursing me out yet. It gets worst." She smiled at Mallory.

"You really feel that way about Ken?" Mallory wasn't sure what the hell had just happened. Simone was not like this.

"Of course not. I love Ken. He's a sweetheart. If he wasn't, Richard wouldn't have let him anywhere near Kat."

Kat came around the corner in time to hear that. "I hate you sometimes." She walked over and hugged her sister.

"Congratulations on your marriage, engagement, or whatever you have going on."

Kat sat back with a smile. "Well, after our last getaway, I might not be able to do this anymore."

Simone frowned at her sister. "What do you mean?"

Kat turned away with a giggle. "He says after what we did, there might be little seedlings growing in my garden."

Mallory couldn't hold in the laughter. Simone's facial expression was priceless.

"Oh dear god, I think I'm gonna be sick." Simone rolled her eyes back in her head and fanned herself dramatically.

This made everyone else laugh even more. Mallory knew that losing Simone would hurt both her and Kat. She didn't know if she could handle it, but times like this she would cherish forever. They spent the rest of the day laughing and talking about whatever blew their way.

*****

It was almost nine when Richard returned to the hospital. Simone and Kat were asleep. Mallory was resting her head on Simone's thigh when she felt a hand on her shoulder. She turned to see Richard dressed in his tailored tux. She inhaled at the sight of the man. He placed a finger over his lips and almost made her slide from the chair. He did things to her that she didn't even know men could do—all without even touching her.

"We should go. Let them rest."

Mallory stood but didn't move. "Should we wake Kat?"

He shook his head. "No. She will stay here tonight. I don't want Simone in this place alone."

He took her by her arm and led her from the room. They walked in silence to the elevators and then to the car. He had driven himself. She didn't think he drove himself around. He had said he did, but she'd never seen it—not that they were together enough for her to know. He opened the door for her, and she got in. She wished she knew what to say, but nothing made sense in her head. It seemed every time they were together, she would do stupid things that made him angry. She decided silence was her best option at the moment. If he wasn't going to speak, then she wouldn't either. They drove back to the building in silence—no music, nothing but the sounds of the city around them. The drive back to her apartment wasn't very long, but it felt like forever. Richard pulled the car up to the building, and a tall man walked up and opened her door.

"I don't wanna stay here." She hadn't meant to blurt that out, but she had.

He turned to her with a dark look.

She couldn't stay here without Kat and Simone. "Please take me back to the apartments."

Richard took a breath to steady his anger. "This is where you live. You will stay here." His tone was even and icy. He didn't care what she wanted; he was still angry with her. She started to get out of the car when he stopped her. "If you try to leave after I'm gone, Gus will lock you in the storage room until I see fit to come back and let you out." His hand left her arm, and she felt lonely. She was alone again. She turned and accepted the hand that was being offered to her. She exited the car and walked with the doorman into the building. She wished she had the strength to tell him what she wanted to, but it wasn't there.

"Don't worry, miss. I would sooner lose this job before I held you against your will."

She smiled up at the man escorting her to the elevator. "If you feel it necessary to walk away from whatever ails you, it is your right. It is quite illegal to own human beings in this country."

She felt the tears. Did he think she was his slave?

"Let me know if you need a taxi. I won't ask you where you're going. I do suggest, however, that you take it to an airport or bus station then get another to your actual destination."

Mallory let a giggle slip. Gus's voice was calming. She liked him.

"Would you like me to ride up with you?"

She felt the sudden urge to hug him. She turned and hugged the man, shocking him. He didn't seem bothered by her impulsive gesture. He held her until she loosened her arms. He pulled a handkerchief from his pocket and handed it to her. With a smile, he ushered her into the elevator. "You are stronger than you think, young lady. You have a superpower that you aren't using. You are in control. Don't forget, but if you do, ole Gus will be here to remind you." He winked at her, making her smile.

He was right. She was her own master. The elevator doors closed, and she ascended to her prison.

Gus turned and went back to his post. He had meant every word he had spoken. He stepped out to see an angry Richard leaning against his car.

"What did Gus the motivational speaker have to say to her?"

He had known Richard for many years. He was the one who had hired him. "Nothing but the truth, Mr. Richard." He smiled at Richard. He didn't scare him. Gus had encountered worse than him many times.

"Must have been some speech. Got you a hug and a smile."

Gus chuckled and tilted his head to the sky. "The stars are beautiful tonight, aren't they, Mr. Richard?" Gus knew how much Richard hated him calling him Mr. Richard. He looked to the clouded sky.

"It's cloudy." He knew what the man was doing.

Gus stepped closer to him and whispered, "Yes. But we have both seen them. And remember how beautiful they are regardless of the clouds. Their beauty is in our memories eternally." The old man smiled at him then turned and went to open the door of a taxi that had just arrived. As Gus escorted the older couple to the door, he turned to Richard. "Try honey. It works better than vinegar."

Richard knew seeing Mallory right now was a bad idea. He decided he'd come back in a few hours when he was in a better mood. A few drinks would calm him down. He knew exactly where he would go. The party at his house would keep him longer than he wanted to be, and there were people there he hadn't wanted to talk to. He got in the car and drove to the parking lot. He would drink in private. He had an apartment below the women—not that he'd ever mentioned it to any of them. He had gotten it to be closer to Simone. He wanted to be close if anything had happened to her, but he'd never needed to use it before now.

*****

Mallory knew what she needed to do. She wouldn't wait for Simone to get home. She needed to leave before anyone knew she had left. Going home was risky, but she needed her mother's help. Simone needed her mother's help. She quickly packed a bag with enough clothes for a few days. She would leave a note for everyone before she left. Checking to make sure she had everything, she grabbed her bag and headed downstairs. It was extremely late, and she was a bit tired, but she had to leave now.

"Running away again?" The voice, though familiar, frightened her, causing a scream to escape. It was the one person she had hoped to avoid. How the hell had he gotten into the apartment without her knowing?

"Richard?" She dropped her bag and stood waiting for a response. He didn't sound happy, but she would explain.

"Why did I expect anything else from you?" He turned to look at her. The room was lit by the lights that snuck through the bare windows. "Every time the going gets tough, Mallory gets going." She heard him place his glass on the coffee table. He stood and walked toward her.

"I'm not..." She stopped when he got too close.

"You're not sneaking out like a thief in the night?" He placed his hands in his pockets as if to restrain himself. "Was this how you left Clay? Did you sneak out in the middle of the night then too?"

She felt a sting in her heart. Why was he acting like this toward her? She had done nothing to him.

He shook his head when she didn't answer. "I guess I don't deserve an explanation either. I mean he knew you for years, where I've only known you what, two weeks?"

She felt like killing him. "One week." She didn't care if he was mad. He had no right to talk to her like this.

"Right. So how much do you need for your escape?"

She didn't know how well he could see her face, but she was furious. She wanted to rip his head off. What did he think she was?

"I do owe, but that's not why I'm making the offer. See, if Simone finds out that I let you leave with nothing, she'll kill me. I don't want that on her conscience." He walked past her to a painting of a safe behind her. She turned to see him punching buttons. When the painting opened, she inhaled sharply. She'd thought it was a painting the whole time she'd been there.

"What's it worth to get rid of you, Mal?"

If he was trying to hurt her, he was doing a hell of a job.

"I don't need anything. I'm grateful for everything I was given already, and I do have some money of my own, thank you." She prayed she didn't sound as helpless as she felt.

"Ten thousand?" Mallory couldn't believe him. "I mean, I don't know how far you plan on going, and I don't care. Just as long as you stay far away from her."

She felt that more than anything else he had said. Her eyes filled with angry tears.

"I find it funny that you just said you were grateful because I don't think you've ever been. Take your mother for instance."

She froze. The tears seemed to freeze in her eyes.

"You show your gratitude by treating her like shit, never telling her thank-you for saving you from the monsters in your life, for her sacrifices. Just took what you needed and ran off." He knelt and placed a few stacks of money in her bag. She didn't move.

"Then there was Simone. She took you in, cared for you, made you family. Then you run her over and run off without so much as a thanks bitch, I appreciated the love."

Mallory's knees gave out from under her. She hated him. She wasn't trying to leave Simone. She wanted to help her. Sitting on the floor, she tried to wipe her tears and control herself.

"Oh no. Did I say something hurtful? I forget Mallory doesn't like the raw truth. She'd prefer the fairytale version. Guess I'm fresh out." He zipped her bag closed and threw it at her. "Don't forget your keys." He stood and started toward the elevator.

"I don't want it."

When Richard stopped, she closed her eyes. She didn't think he would hit her, but his words had hurt just as much as some of her beatings. His chuckle made her hold her breath.

"Are you gonna return all my gifts?"

She didn't answer him.

"I have a strict policy about returns, but for you I might make an exception. I mean if you're gonna return everything I'll gladly accept the ones I gave you in private as well."

Her anger dried any tears that threatened to show her weakness. "Fuck you, Richard." Her voice was barely above a whisper, but he had heard her. He came over and squatted before her.

"I'd love to."

When her head came up and their eyes locked, the angry flames that burned in her gaze made him laugh. "I did enjoy fucking you, Mallory. You were much better than most of the others, and I hope you learned some things. Might help to ease Clay's anger when he sees you again. I'm sure he'll enjoy the things I've taught you." As the words left his mouth he regretted them. He hoped she didn't say something that would put him over the edge. He needed to get away from her before he ended up behind bars. He started to reach for her but stopped himself. "You should go." He stood and stepped back.

"I almost believed you." She got to her feet, picking up her bag as she did.

"Believe what? That I love you?"

She didn't want this to go on. She needed to leave.

"I don't chase women, Mallory. I have enough chasing me to not have to chase you. It's not worth the trouble." He nodded toward the elevator.

Mallory walked past him to the key rack and took her keys. She wouldn't argue anymore. It was over. She would not come back here—not to this place. She got into the elevator and rode it to the garage. No more tears. Get as far away from Richard Embers as humanly possible.

Richard watched Mallory disappear behind the closed doors. He felt sick to his stomach. He walked over to the phone and dialed a number. It rang a few times before it was answered.

"Follow her. Make sure she gets where she needs to go safely." He paused for a moment. "If Clay so much as breathes in her direction, *put him down permanently.*" He hung up. Now he had to deal with Simone and Felix. They wouldn't be happy with what he had done. He would wait until they had discovered her missing before he'd mention any of this. A tear ran down his cheek, startling him. He wiped it quickly from his face.

"Fuck."

He walked to the elevator and stood, almost wishing she would be behind the doors when it opened. She wasn't. She was gone. He had chased her away—far away from him. He rode the elevator to the lobby and went in search of Gus.

"Mr. Richard, you look like shit, sir." Gus was sitting across the street from the building. He was taking his break where he always did.

Richard took a seat next to him and accepted half of the tuna sandwich he was offered. He didn't think he would be able to eat anything, but he took a bite.

"Best tuna in town though I don't think you'll appreciate my hard work in your state." Gus chuckled and fished another cola from his bag. He tried to hand it to Richard, but he declined.

"You're gonna have to eat. You sure gon' need all the strength you can muster when that little one gets back." He shoved the drink at Richard.

"She's not coming back." He hoped it wasn't true.

Gus's laughter made him regret coming out to sit with him. "You know I bet you wouldn't be laughing if she was the one sitting out here with you." He sounded like a jealous sibling, and he knew it.

"No, I would not, but I laugh because you are your worst enemy, and right now you're looking for someone to blame, but that someone is you. What will you do?" He turned to look at Richard. He almost felt sorry for him.

"I had to let her go. I can't give her what she wants right now."

Gus made a grunting noise. "Young man, I have been around for quite some time. I watched the Father create the stars—that's how long I've been around—so I know a thing or two."

Richard tried not to laugh but couldn't help it.

"Thing one, I know that you love two women—two women that you locked in the same cage."

Richard was serious again.

Gus continued. "Thing two, one you love and the other you are in love with. There is a difference. Now, the question is, do you know which is which?"

70

Richard slouched in the bench. He knew what Gus was saying, but it didn't help him. He loved Simone, and even though she seemed happy he was moving on, he knew she still loved him. He didn't believe that shit her grandmother had said. He went along with it for her, but Mallory made him think about a solid future without Simone. He felt guilty—guilty for loving them both but not being able to let go of one for the other. How could he hold on to Mallory when half his heart still belonged to Simone?

"You know what I think? I think that it's gonna rain in the morning—I mean pouring like the great flood."

Richard loved talking to Gus because he made him think. He never answered anything.

"How the hell do you do that?"

Gus turned to look at Richard. He was smiling.

"What?" He knew that Richard valued his opinion.

"Every time I come to you for advice, you go off on some bullshit about stars and clouds and fucking rain." He waved his hand in frustration. "Fuck!"

Gus patted Richard's knee and stood.

"I have to let them both go."

Gus shrugged then helped Richard to his feet. "Gonna be one hell of a storm." He collected his things and started toward the building. "They'll be all right without you because they have each other."

Richard watched the man walk back to the building before walking in the direction of the hospital. He had to see Simone.

*****

No one stopped him when he stepped out of the elevator—they all knew who he was. Richard made his way to Simone. He knew what he had to do, but the closer he got to her, the harder it got. He had lost Mallory; now he had to let Simone go. He noticed Kat was fast asleep in a couch in the corner of the room. He didn't recall seeing the uncomfortable-looking contraption when he was last in the room. He walked over and took a seat next to Simone on her bed. She was asleep too. He didn't want to wake her, but if he didn't do this now, he didn't think he could. He picked up her hand and kissed it softly. Her eyes opened slowly. He waited for her to wake.

"Hey, you."

She adjusted in the bed and stretched like a fancy cat in a sunny windowsill. "Hey, what time is it?" Simone looked around the room as if she were looking for someone else.

"She's gone." He spoke in a whisper so that he wouldn't wake Kat.

"I thought she'd come back with you. What time is it?"

He watched as she turned on her bedside lamp. He waited for her eyes to adjust to the new lighting.

When her gaze fell on his face, she knew. "Richard?" He couldn't hide his emotions; everything was displayed on his face. "What happened?" She was whispering too.

"I let her go."

The shock on Simone's face made him look away.

"What? Why?"

He could hear the sadness in her voice. He didn't know what to say. There was so much to say, but he just couldn't find the words, so he just opened his mouth and let his brain do what it did.

"I was trying to do it your way, but I can't. I can't pretend that I don't still love you."

Simone could hear the pain in his voice. She knew he was hurting.

"When I'm with her, I don't think about you as much. I want to give her everything that you wouldn't let me give to you. Then as soon as I'm alone again, I feel guilty for not trying hard enough with you, for letting you go without a fight, for trying to be happy when I know that you're not."

She tried but couldn't stop the tears. She thought that he'd moved on, but now she realized it was killing him. He had been the one to initiate their divorce. He wanted her to try to enjoy her life without him hovering. They'd been divorced for over three months, and he had been with others, but Mallory was different. He was in love with her. She could see it when they were together. She was the one—the one he was meant to be with. She didn't understand why he couldn't see that. Nanan had told him what she'd seen for him. Why couldn't he believe it?

"It would have been much easier for me to watch you fall in love with someone else than it is for me to love another." He had to do something that he would hate himself for. "You still have my heart, Simone, so I'll make you a deal. You get yours fixed. I've already paid for it. You get it done, and I will move on."

She didn't like this. "No. I can't. Please don't..." She could barely speak through her crying.

He took a breath before he continued. He had to do this. He felt the hot tears accumulate in his eyes. "I will always love you, but I will not come back until after you do this. Take care of your sisters." He got up and kissed her.

She couldn't speak. She wanted to, but the words couldn't make it past the lump in her throat.

"Goodbye, Simone."

She tried to hold on to him, but he gently pried her hands from him. He was crying as he turned and walked out. Simone couldn't believe he would leave like that. What had she done?

Kat had been catching up on some well-needed sleep when she heard her sister's crying. She jumped from the horrible couch the nurses had brought her to sleep on. Not that she wasn't thankful for it, but the springs in the damn thing had been assaulting her in her sleep.

"Sy, what's wrong? Are you in pain? Should I call someone?" She was worried when she saw her sister's face. Why was Simone so upset?

"He's gone. He said if I don't get the surgery, he's not coming back." She sobbed.

Kat had no idea what she was talking about. She pulled her sister into a hug. Who the hell was she talking about?

"Who's gone?" She needed to calm her sister. Where the hell did Mallory go?

"Richard."

Kat pulled back to look at Simone. Had she heard correctly? Richard would never leave Simone like this. He loved her.

"What? What are you talking about? Where's Mal?"

Simone was too hysterical to explain anything. She was worried about Mallory. Richard had said he let her go, but where had she gone?

"I don't know. She's gone."

Kat's eyes grew as she tried to understand her sister's words through her sobs. Mallory wouldn't leave either. Maybe Simone was having a nightmare.

"Mallory wouldn't leave you, honey. She's one of us, and you know Richard would never leave you. You probably just had a nightmare."

Kat hoped that was it. She was scared. What if Simone had a heart attack? She couldn't handle this. She needed support. She reached for the phone and dialed the apartment. She would call Mallory and Richard and clear up everything for Simone.

*****

Mallory had been driving for hours. She decided to make the trip without stopping. She needed to keep moving. If she stopped, then she would think about what Richard had said, and she didn't want to deal with that right now. She had a mission and wouldn't let anything get in the way. She would be home in less than five hours. She would explain everything to her mother and convince her to come back with her. She would find them a place of their own—definitely nothing as fancy as the penthouse but something nice, something she would work hard for. She would take care of her mom. It was time she repaid her for all her sacrifices. She tried not to recall Richard's words, but she did. She had never thanked her mother for the things she had done for her. He was right about that. She had saved her from her father and Clay. Shit. She didn't know how she would avoid seeing him when she got there. Maybe she should call someone, but who? The sheriff maybe. He would make sure they got out of there safely. He had told her he was glad she had decided to leave on her way out of town. She was worried. Had she paid attention to the silver Audi trailing her, she would have known she wasn't alone on her trip.

Bryon Slaughter was a former marine. He was hired to keep Mallory safe when Richard wasn't around. He hadn't expected any excitement with this detail at all, but then he remembered Richard giving him the green light to take lethal action to protect this woman. That excited him. She hadn't noticed him following her even when they almost bumped into each other at the last gas station. She was beautiful, but she was off limits to him. Richard wouldn't have asked him to watch her if she wasn't important to him, but he was starting to fantasize about being with her. He took another sip of the nasty gas station coffee. He hoped he got to carry out his orders.

The sun was rising; she was almost home—just a few more hours. Mallory was tired but determined not to stop. She was speeding and hoped she didn't get pulled over. There were a few cars on the lonely road with her. She pulled over and decided to put the top down on her overly expensive gift from Richard. She loved the car; it was fast and completed with all the luxuries. She never tried the phone to see if it worked. She decided to call her mother. As she picked up the receiver, she realized there were a couple of voicemails. Who had called her? She played the first one and was shocked to hear Richard's voice. It must have been an old one because he was asking that she drive safely. His voice sounded so sweet in his message, but she remembered the difference in it last night. He had sounded so angry. The next message was also from him. This one must have been old as well because he said he'd called to tell her he loved her. She felt her chest tighten and tried to steady her breathing. The third message was from a hysterical Kat. She was begging Mallory to come to the hospital. Something about Simone having to be sedated. She quickly dialed the number for the hospital. She waited to be connected to Simone's room. Kat answered promptly.

"What's wrong? Is she okay?" She listened as Kat tried to explain what had happened. She sat staring into space as she listened. "Richard is gone?"

What did that mean? Why would he leave Simone alone like this? Had it been because of her? She had to explain to Kat that she had left only for a few days. "I'm on my way home to get my mother. She's a nurse. I was going to bring her back to help us with Simone."

Kat was crying. She wished she had stopped by the hospital to make sure Simone was okay before she'd left. She couldn't turn back now. She was too close to home. She had to continue on, but how could she when Simone wanted her by her side?

"Kat, the nearest airport is in my hometown. I'll get my mother and head back on the first flight. Please take care of her. Tell her I love her and I'll be there as soon as I can. I'm so sorry. This is all my fault." She listened to Kat as they both cried on either end of the line. She needed to get back fast. She couldn't bear it if something horrible happened to Simone while she was gone. She loved them both and would do whatever it took to make sure they were okay.

"I love you, Kat. I'll see you tonight. I promise." She hung up and dried her tears. She had to get back on the road. She had to get home fast.

Byron watched from his hiding place as Mallory conversed on her phone. She was sad. Something must be wrong. She was crying. He didn't know who or what had caused this beautiful woman pain, but he wanted to end them. She should never be unhappy. He would never let her suffer like this if she was his. Who was he kidding? A woman like her would never be his—not when men like Richard took an interest in her. They had money and luxuries he could only dream of. She was getting back on the road. He would let her drive ahead. He had to check in anyway. He decided to do that before getting back on the road.

Mallory wanted to call Richard before she took off but decided not to. He was angry with her so she didn't think he would listen. He had blamed her for Simone being hurt. Not that she didn't understand, but why would he leave her when she needed him? Why couldn't these two people who obviously belonged together not see what others could? She wouldn't worry about that right now. In three hours, she would be home. She might have to kidnap her mother, but nothing or no one would stand in her way. She wished she wasn't alone on this trip, but who would she have brought with her? Simone needed Kat, and Richard was angry with her. She pushed the loneliness aside. She had driving to do. She decided to let the morning sun rejuvenate her as she sped to her mother's.

*****

After hanging up from Mallory, Kat dialed Richard. She waited for him to answer, but like all the other calls, they went to voicemail. Why wasn't he answering? She was getting frustrated. She took one look at her sister, sleeping, and decided to use her resources. She would take charge of this situation. She was going to fix this just like Simone would have. She would get Mallory back as soon as possible, and they would figure out what the hell was going on with Richard. She quickly dialed Ken. He would help her.

*****

Mallory pulled over right outside the town. The butterflies were present now. She was terrified of what was waiting for her there. She picked up the phone and dialed Richard's number. She didn't think he would answer, but she needed his help. The phone rang twice before it was answered. Her stomach clenched at the sound of his voice.

"Are you okay?"

She hesitated. She'd called but now she was at a loss for words.

"Mallory!"

She jumped at the sound of her name. "Yes. I'm okay." She took a deep breath and closed her eyes. "If you aren't too angry with me, I need your help."

There was a long silence. She almost hung up when he didn't respond.

"What do you need from me?"

She slumped forward, resting her head on the steering wheel.

"I'm just outside my town, and I need a fast way out of here. I'm gonna pick my mother up, and I need a flight for us out this afternoon." She swallowed the lump in her throat. "She's a nurse. I'm going to ask her to help Kat and me with Simone." She waited for his response.

"The jet is waiting at the airport for you. Felix will meet you at your mother's."

She sat up abruptly. How?

"I read your letter."

She smiled and tried to relax. "I wasn't running out on Simone… or you." She waited for his response. When she heard nothing, she interjected. "I know you're angry with me, but I never meant to hurt either of you. I just don't understand our situation. I know that you both love each other, and yet you keep pushing each other away." She was frustrated with it all. "I want to love you, Richard, but I feel like I'm in the way. Like if I wasn't there, you two could work on what you have. But I'm not going to abandon Simone or Kat." She meant it all. "I feel guilty for loving you and Simone. I feel like I'm betraying both of you, and I don't know what to do." She sat waiting for him to say something—anything.

"Now you understand how I feel."

She didn't expect that response. What did he mean?

"I can't be around either of you right now. You need each other more than you need me. She won't focus on her happiness if she's trying to make sure we're working out. If she won't let me save her life, then I need to let her live whatever life she can. She should be happy, and she won't be as long as I'm around."

Mallory understood. He was hurting. Why didn't she notice that before?

"I'm sorry about last night. I shouldn't have said those things. Take care of yourself, Mal."

She didn't want the call to end—not yet. "Can I still call you sometime? Just as a friend?" That's not what she wanted to say, but it was out there.

"You won't need to. Work on your dream, and live your life. Work hard for what you want."

She felt a surge of courage. "Tell me again."

He knew what she wanted to hear. She waited silently.

"I love you, Mallory."

She placed her hand over her mouth before wiping the tears that were washing down her face.

"One year." It was her turn to give out ultimatums.

"What?" He wasn't sure what the hell she was talking about.

"You owe my mother grandkids, so you have one year to get your shit together. In the meantime, take care of yourself." She couldn't believe what she was saying. She heard him chuckle and decided to end the call before he got the upper hand. "Thank you for everything. I love you, Richard." She quickly hung up.

It was time to get back on track. She wiped her face and decided to face her demons head on—no more running. If she could stand up to Richard, then Clay was child's play. She laughed nervously when she realized how crazy all this was. She decided to call her mother and talk to her as she drove. She'd take the back roads, though, no use looking for trouble. She would put the top back up and pull her hoodie over her head. No one would recognize her until she was home.

*****

Mallory was almost home when she saw the flashing lights and heard the sirens. She wasn't speeding. Why was she being pulled over? She quickly retrieved her driver's license from her purse and waited.

"Well, if it isn't Betty Blue Eyes."

She looked up at the familiar face of the sheriff. He was smiling as he leaned into her car. "Now whose baby did you steal? This can't be yours."

She was almost happy to see him. "It actually is mine—a gift."

The sheriff's expression turned to one of concern. She hadn't realized how that sounded until she saw the look he was giving her. "From work." That didn't make it much better. His eyebrows almost pushed his hat from his head. "I work for a modeling agency. They make sure we keep up appearances." She was just making it worst.

"Do they send jets for you too?"

She frowned at him. "What?" She knew that Richard had said the jet was waiting for her, but she hadn't realized anyone knew it was for her.

"Over at Mac's Airfield. There's a jet waiting for you—very nice."

She was shocked. Mac's Airfield was private. It was where they kept the crop-dusting fleet—if one could call the three little Cessna planes a fleet.

"Oh. There's an emergency with my boss. She was hospitalized yesterday. I thought I had time to come home and get back before I was needed."

He smiled again. "So, your boss is a woman?"

She frowned at the smiling man.

"Never heard of a woman named Richard before." He laughed as her jaw unhinged. How the hell did he know about Richard? Was he here? "Come on, supermodel. I'll escort you home."

She sat anxiously, waiting for him to pull off. She needed to get home. If Richard was here, she hoped Clay was nowhere around. If the sheriff knew she was coming then, half the town, if not all, knew she was coming. She felt her heart accelerate as they started down the road.

Mallory could see the limo sitting outside her house. Why did he have to be so flashy? Now people were sitting outside their homes, hoping to see what was going on. She didn't like these folks in her business, and to make matters even worse, she was being escorted by the damn sheriff. She pulled into her driveway and tried to hurry into the house. The door was unlocked as always.

"Mom?" She called as she hurriedly closed the door. She wasn't surprised to see Felix sitting in the kitchen, enjoying a huge slice of cake. He stood to greet her with a hug and kiss on the cheek.

"You made it." He was always so welcoming she held on a bit longer. She knew he didn't mind, but she stepped back and apologized.

"Sorry. I just really needed that. Where's my mother?" She had more hugs to share.

Felix took his seat and started eating his cake again. He nodded toward the backdoor. She gave his shoulder a squeeze before running to the backdoor and disappearing through it.

"Honey." She stopped abruptly when she saw who her mother was talking to. Her heart raced with excitement—an excitement that quickly turned to fear when the back gate was thrown open. Just when she thought she could have a smooth transition, in walked Clay.

Richard turned to see who had caused the excitement to melt from her face. He knew as soon as he saw the man.

"Miss Jenna. I see your little runaway has returned." He stalked toward Mallory as if he hadn't seen Richard standing there. Mallory was frozen in place.

"Clay!" Her mother's voice jolted her from her nightmare.

Mallory stepped back involuntarily. Clay stopped before Jenna, who was standing in front of her daughter. "I told you, you have no business here. My daughter is off limits."

Mallory didn't turn around when the backdoor opened and closed, causing her to jump. Her focus was on the scene in front of her. Her little mother was the only thing keeping Clay from her.

"I just wanna talk to her."

Mallory felt herself dragged to one side. She looked up at a furious Richard. She started to panic.

"I see you've moved up to the big city boys in suits." His smile was scornful. Why was she so afraid of this idiot? He wouldn't be dumb enough to hit her with all these people around. With a dash of shaking courage, she stepped away from Richard and stood with her mother.

"I think we've said all we ever need to say to each other. You should go."

Clay laughed as if she amused him. She wasn't known for standing up to him. He pushed Jenna out of the way. Everything seemed to move slower. In her peripherals, she could see movement. What would Kat do? What had Simone taught her over the last week in the gym? Use your hands to protect yourself, and never forget men have nuts. She breathed as Simone had taught her then took a small step forward and punched as hard as she could. Her tiny fist connected with Clay's throat. *Follow through, Mal.* She heard Kat cheering her on in her head.

She quickly grabbed his shoulder and swung her foot between his legs pushing him back as she did. *Don't stop now, Mal. You have to make sure he doesn't get up.* Simone's words came through clearly over the blurred voices that were shouting at her. She planted her foot and swung the other into his stomach. She hadn't heard what the other voices were saying. Simone's instructions were all she concentrated on. Clay was down and moaning in pain.

Payback, Mal. Make him pay for every time he hit you. She was about to let loose another wave on the man when she felt herself lifted into the air.

"Enough." Richard was restraining her.

She turned to see her mother's shocked expression as Felix protected her. The sheriff was staring at Clay's crumpled body rolling on the ground. She had done it—protected herself. No, Mal. It was her mother she was trying to protect. He had touched her mother. The thought of him pushing her mom brought back memories of her father doing the same to her mother. She wiggled fiercely in Richard's arms. She wasn't done. He had to pay.

"Relax, little one. He's down." Richard's voice sounded amused.

"Did you teach her that?" Felix smiled proudly at little Mallory still struggling in Richard's embrace.

"No." He was shocked and proud of his little woman. The anger he felt had dissipated by what he'd just witnessed. He'd still make sure Clay never came anywhere near Mallory again, but in the meantime, he would let her enjoy her victory. He hadn't seen that coming. When the man came too close, she was terrified. Whatever Simone and Kat had taught her had given her the freedom she'd needed.

"Hell, I'm not sure what the hell I should do right now. I wanna laugh, but I think I'm supposed to arrest you. That poor man was…" Had the sheriff not doubled over laughing at the joke he hadn't gotten out, he would have noticed the angry looks from Felix and Richard.

"Good lord, Dell. Get him out of my backyard." Jenna turned to walk back into her house. Her heart was still racing. She couldn't believe what she had seen. Mallory was gone a little over a month, and here she was now fiercely defending herself. Jenna wondered if it was these men who had taught her daughter those moves. She was proud of this new Mallory.

"Get inside, the rest of you. These people around here are probably peeping through the fence. These so-called privacy fences are a joke."

Richard didn't hesitate; he half carried Mallory into the house, leaving Felix to help the sheriff. They carried Clay to the cruiser that was parked out front. The man was still wheezing and groaning in pain.

"Thanks, son." He closed the door and called for someone to retrieve Clay. He wanted to talk to Felix. He had meant to speak to him earlier but hadn't gotten a chance to. "So you're Felix Masters Jr." He wasn't asking. He could see the resemblance.

Felix nodded suspiciously. "You knew my father?"

Sheriff Dell smiled and gestured for them to head inside. The neighbors had gathered in groups and were whispering. They walked into the house and headed to the kitchen where Mallory was icing her hand.

"Lord, how hard did you hit him?" Felix tried not to laugh when he saw Richard sitting with a hand over his mouth to hide his amusement. Jenna had gone to her room to finish some last-minute packing.

"Where's Miss Jenna?" Felix took a seat next to the cake he had abandoned when Clay had made his entrance into what he was sure was the man's last moments. He was sure Richard would kill the man. He knew what Clay had done to Mallory. Richard had told him on their way over. Though it was his job to keep Richard from committing crimes of the sort, he too wanted Clay out of this world. He was glad Mallory had been able to take care of it. He knew it wasn't over by far. Richard would fix Clay, but right now, he was just proud she had found her courage.

"I don't think Jen will mind if I help myself to a piece of this cake." Felix watched as the sheriff cut himself a healthy slice of cake. He wondered how many times the man had done this. He seemed to know where everything was. After collecting his cake and a beer, he took a seat next to Felix. "You know, I think I might be your godfather. I knew your father when he was in the army."

Everyone stopped what they were doing immediately and turned their attention to the sheriff. Felix was intrigued. He had never met anyone from his father's army days. He had tried to distance himself from anyone who reminded him of his Vietnam years. He'd taken up law enforcement in their small slice of paradise after returning.

"I almost shot your father once." Sheriff Dell laughed when everyone turned a curious eye to him. "I ran into him one evening at our makeshift chow hall. He was looking at a photo of this very beautiful woman." He paused to take a sip of his beer. "I was a troublemaker back then. I snatched his picture to give it the once-over. I had no idea at the time that she was his, well, woman."

Everyone waited patiently as he stuffed a piece of cake into his mouth.

"I heard a few whispers and decided to let it feed my sorry little ego." He stopped again to drink his beer. Richard was losing interest in his story. The man was eating like a slob. "Well, since he didn't seem interested in indulging me, I carried on. I decided to poke fun at him. I asked him if she wasn't the wrong shade for his kind."

This got Felix's undivided attention. The woman he was talking about was his mother.

"Yes, I was an ass. I went on and on, but he said nothing. He just extended his hand for his photo, didn't even make eye contact with me. That was when my mouth decided to write a check my ass was not ready to cash." He shook his head in regret. "I said if you give me this photo, I would damn sure make use of it. Hell, when we get back, I'll even teach you how to show her a good time." He gestured with his hands. "The whole table cleared within seconds when he stood, but I didn't take a hint. I was about to pocket the picture when darkness took me." He rubbed his face in frustration. "First time in my entire life anyone ever gave me two black eyes with one punch. At least I was only conscious for the one I barely saw coming."

The whole table was snickering.

"I woke up in the infirmary, my sarge standing over me, asking if I knew who the hell I was? He told me next time I stand on the tracks, make sure I know when to get off, or I might get hit by the Masters Express again."

Felix knew his father had a temper, but the man had rarely ever lost his cool.

"I told everyone to tell him I was gonna shoot him if I ever saw him again." He seemed awful proud of his story.

"My father wasn't really into violence. He loved boxing and martial arts but only as sport."

The sheriff nodded. "He was a damn medic. Big as he was, he was there to patch people up. I couldn't believe it." He shared a laugh with Felix. "He and I eventually became friends. I told him that when I got out, I would come home and bring order to my little town, clean up some of the messes."

Felix never understood why his father had decided to work in law enforcement. He never liked carrying a gun, but he did.

"In his twelve years in law enforcement, he may have used his service weapon three, maybe four times at the most. He always tried to talk first, show compassion. Drove my mother crazy."

Felix and Dell sat talking about his father. They barely noticed Mallory and Richard's departure.

"What is your mother gonna do about the house and her things?" Mallory flopped down into the couch. She had almost forgotten how comfortable the old thing was. Richard took a seat at the other end, pulling her feet into his lap. Mallory had no idea what she was gonna do. She hadn't thought about it.

"I don't know. She can have one of her girls house-sit until we figure it out. I just want to get out of here and get home before Simone is released." She didn't make eye contact with him. She didn't know how he felt at the moment, and she wasn't sure she could handle another Richard tantrum.

"I will get you home before then." He was glad she thought of the apartment as her home. He hoped that living with Simone and Kat would help her find her strength. He was proud of the way she'd handled herself with Clay. He hadn't expected it and was shocked when she took charge of the situation. Felix had warned him not to touch Clay until he'd put his hands on Mallory. His lawyer had concurred.

"Thank you for being here. I know you didn't have to come. I appreciate your time." She was thankful he had come.

"I won't be staying when we get back. I was on my way to New York when I read your letter." She tried not to seem disappointed. He was serious about leaving.

"Will you visit Simone before you go?" She waited for an answer, but he said nothing. "Kat said she had to be sedated earlier." She was sure he'd known. He seemed to have known everything else.

"I know. I've already said everything I needed to the last time I saw her."

Mallory let out a heavy sigh. She wouldn't push. She didn't know what else to say.

"All right, children, I think I'm all packed."

Mallory sat up when her mother finally interrupted the awkward silence. She was ready to get the hell out of town and back to some sort of normalcy. "I'm sure I have all that I'll need for now." She had packed two suitcases and a small travel bag.

"I guess you're ready then." Richard stood and grabbed the suitcases. "Shall we?" He started for the door.

When he left, Mallory decided to take one last trip to her room. She needed to retrieve something she had left last time. Everything was just as she'd left it. Her mother hadn't changed a thing. She dug into the closet, removing the jewelry box she had hidden ages ago. Inside was a locket her father had given her. She had kept it secret from her mother all these years. She quickly pocketed the jewel-encrusted locket.

It was nearly three o'clock when they arrived at the airfield.

Jenna had made a detour to drop off her keys at the hospital to a friend. "I'm not really a fan of flying."

Felix smiled as he watched Jenna slowly climb the stairs to the jet. "You have nothing to worry about. We have the best pilot, and it's only a short flight."

Jenna wasn't at all comforted. She just needed to get to her destination and back on solid ground. "I'm afraid your words aren't comfort enough for me. This has always been a fear of mine."

She walked into the cabin and was awestruck by the luxurious setting. Never had she seen anything like it. Everything looked new and comfortable. The seats were equally spaced and perfectly placed.

"Wow, this is beautiful." Jenna walked to one of the chairs and took a seat. "I might like this after all. Is this how you always travel?" The fancy leather was soft to the touch unlike the seats of the commercial jets she had flown previously.

"I go where the big guy goes, so yes." Felix took the seat next to Jenna.

Richard and Mallory took the seats further in the back of the aircraft.

"I think Felix likes my mom."

Richard chuckled at Mallory's reaction. "She's in good hands. You don't have to worry about Felix's intentions. You'll be the first to know if he develops feelings for your mother." He sat back and watched Mallory as she eyed the interaction between her mother and Felix. "I hope you don't mind, but I have some contracts to look over. Feel free to entertain yourself."

Mallory turned to look at him, but he was already digging through his briefcase. She didn't want to entertain herself. They had two hours to talk about whatever she wanted to.

"I think I do mind."

Richard didn't seem bothered by her comment. He continued to remove his paperwork.

"I think we should talk."

He stopped and turned to her. "About?"

She didn't care what they talked about. She just wanted to talk. He was leaving her, and she didn't know when she would see him again. New York was worlds away. Hell, anywhere away from him was worlds away for her.

"I don't know, Richard, anything. I just don't want to sit here and watch you work. You can work when you get to New York." She found a button on the inside of her chair and pressed it. When the chair reclined, it made her breasts bounce, catching Richard's attention.

"I can think of several things, but your mother is present."

Mallory's head whipped around so fast it made him laugh. His eyes fell on her breast as his hand started toward them. She quickly slapped his hand.

"Stop that. My mom is right there." She giggled when he frowned and folded his arms like a child. "I'm sure you can wait two hours." She wiggled her eyebrows at him.

"I'm not staying. I have a meeting tomorrow." She felt a strong sense of defeat.

He could see the disappointment on her face. "I think you and Kat have a shoot tomorrow as well. Did Roy tell you?"

She nodded. "Yeah, I was excited, but now I don't know."

He reached over and spun her chair, so she was facing him. "Why not?"

She looked around, amazed that her chair was able to spin. Had she known that, she would have annoyed him by spinning in circles until she got sick. She smiled at the thought. She tried to turn away, but he was still holding on to the chair.

"You're going to learn that for every job you turn down, that's one less you get offered next time. As beautiful as I think you are, others may not see what I do. Until you've solidified your status in this business, you will take your assignments. I won't let Roy send you on anything I wouldn't approve of—not that Simone will let him."

She understood what he was saying. Simone had told her the same thing.

"So you think you're the only man that thinks I'm beautiful? I bet there are lots of other men who find me absolutely amazing." She tried not to smile at the deep frown on his face.

"What?" He was squinting at her.

"I bet there are many men who find me attractive. I'll prove it to you." Before he could lose his temper, Mallory swung her chair forward. "Hey, Felix? Do you think I'm beautiful?"

Felix gave her an approving smile. "I think you're absolutely gorgeous."

She turned her chin up at him before waving her hand in victory. "See. I told you."

He shook his head and laughed. "I pay him to lie to you. He thinks you have a big shiny forehead." The look she gave him made him double over laughing. He was enjoying every moment with her. The captain finally announced their departure. When the aircraft started to move, Mallory became nervous. She couldn't remember the last time she was on a plane.

"So when do they serve the peanuts and liquor?" She watched as Richard leaned forward, opening the top of a small table she had planned to use as a footrest. It was a little refrigerator unit packed with drinks. He took a small bottle of champagne, opened, and passed it to her. She was joking but took it anyway.

"I'm not a fan of peanuts, but I think we have some other snacks onboard. Felix knows where they are." She took a sip of her champagne and handed him the bottle. He took a long sip. "The last time we had champagne together, you were sitting on my lap. Remember?"

Her mouth flew open as she checked to make sure no one else had heard what he had said.

"Or did you forget? I can remind you right now."

Her hands flew to her face as she felt her cheeks heat up. The memory of their drive to his cabin brought back the heat to her entire body.

"I would let you remind me, but you have to be in New York." She didn't look at him. "Seems I might need some riding lessons. I'm starting to forget if I actually like that or not." She tried to keep the smirk from her face when she heard him sigh.

"You have two hours after we land. If you're not at the cabin within that time, you'll wait three months."

She felt a rush of excitement. *Poke at him. Don't do it, Mal.*

"I can wait. Can you?"

He chuckled, stretching his hands in front of him palm up. "I'm not afraid of them."

Her eyes grew as she caught the meaning of his gesture. "You're not allowed to if I'm not." She gave him a stern look—or at least what she thought was a stern look.

"How will you know what I do when you're not around?" He was smiling one of his mischievous smiles.

"You'll tell me. Richard doesn't lie, remember."

As they were lifted into the air, she reached for his hand. She did not like flying after all. She closed her eyes and tried to relax.

"You'll get used to this, and the next time we fly together, I'll induct you into the mile-high club."

She squeezed his hand as the jet leveled. She had no idea what this mile-high club was, but if he wanted her to be a part of it, then she would join.

The landing was surprisingly better than the takeoff. She was happy to be back, but that meant her time with Richard was almost over. Everyone prepared to disembark, but she had some things to tend to before she could.

"Richard, can we talk."

He raised an eyebrow. "We've been talking this whole flight, chatterbox. What have you forgotten?" He was teasing, but she was serious.

"I really wanna see you later, but I have to get my mom settled and check on Simone. Kat might need a break, and I doubt that I'll have enough time to make your deadline." She was disappointed, but she knew she had more important things to take care of. "I don't want to waste your time, so maybe you should just head to New York, and we will see each other soon."

He took a step closer to Mallory. "Miss Sweet, are you dismissing me?" He knew that wasn't what she was doing, but he enjoyed messing with her. "I have never been turned down before. I don't think I like this."

She didn't want to disappoint him, but he had given her limited time. There was no way she would be able to get to the cabin in time.

"Of course not. I just don't see how I can get to you in time."

As much as he wanted to accommodate her, he didn't want her to think she could push him around. "Well, Miss Sweet, I shall see you soon." He pulled her close and kissed her cheek.

"What the hell was that?"

He tried not to laugh.

"You won't see me for God knows how long, and that is it?"

He almost crushed her in a heated kiss. When he finally released her, she was damn near gasping for air.

"That's more like it, sir." She swayed a bit as she stepped back and adjusted herself. "I look forward to our next meeting." She gave him one of her brilliant smiles before turning and exiting the aircraft.

He watched as she left him. He was proud of her. She was learning how to make better decisions, but he was still going to make sure she had every advantage. He decided to start with Roy. He knew Roy was aware of his interest in Mallory, but he needed to make sure the man was clear on the boundaries. He instructed the flight crew before making his calls.

*****

Kat and Simone were sitting quietly, watching TV, when Mallory and company arrived at the hospital. She was greeted with a huge hug from Kat. "Where the hell have you been? I've been worried." She squeezed Kat before letting go.

"I needed help from a professional." She turned and waved her mother over. "This is my mom, Jenna Sweet."

Kat politely greeted Jenna as Mallory went to Simone.

"Hey, you." Simone's eyes welled up with tears as they embraced. "I'm sorry, Mal. I didn't think…"

Mallory shushed her. Simone knew Richard had told Mallory he was leaving, but did she know it was her fault? She hadn't expected Mallory to come back.

"You have nothing to be sorry about. Richard and I spoke, and we will see each other in three months."

Simone dried her tears with the sheet that was draped over her legs.

"I hope you don't mind, but I would feel a lot better if my mom was around."

Simone agreed with a nod.

"She's the best nurse ever and not just because she's my mom either."

They both shared a laugh.

The girls spent the next few hours talking and making plans. Simone shared her plan for a new travel review in the magazine with everyone. She would put together a team of girls that would travel around, bringing attention to vacation destinations people should visit. They would spend a few days in each location taking photos of sites and lodgings. Then Simone would write a review of the location. She had been planning this new addition for months. Kat and Mallory were excited to get it on the way. They sat quietly in the couch, making a list of other girls that would join Simone's travel team.

*****

It had been a long three months. Mallory and Kat had been on every location with Simone since the second week after her release from the hospital. The woman was brilliant, but she drove her crew with a passion that scared the weak. She made sure her team of models was treated with respect, dignity, and compassion. Almost all the younger models were tripping over each other to join the team. There were fifteen girls in total, and they were all slowly making their way into the limelight. They had become a tight-knit group. Simone was fair with the jobs and made sure they were paid well.

Even Roy was impressed with the way she handled herself. She didn't let anyone abuse her girls. He'd send flowers to their locations to thank her for her contribution to the company. The magazines had been flying off the stands since they'd added the travel section. He found that more companies were trying to advertise with them since the addition. This made his job a lot easier though he would never admit that. He had to hire an extra secretary to keep up with all the new business they were getting. He loved the contributions he was getting from all over. The girls were happier, and his pockets were heavier. Designers offered free merchandise for a discount on advertising while others would lend, if not donate, their products for the same.

The girls practically flew for free to and from their destinations—all of which were chosen by Simone. Once or twice in the last month, they had been able to use a private jet from an up-and-coming vendor. This made it easier for them to complete their assignments. It wasn't always the exotic, expensive destinations that were featured but sweet little gems in small-town America that were usually overlooked. The girls would sometimes split into two groups in order to cover several destinations at once. The three issues that had featured several must-visit American towns had done extremely well.

It was finally their relaxation time before their next trip. Mallory had gotten a chance to talk to Richard on several occasions, but their conversations were usually short due to his work. She had no idea what he really did, and it was starting to plague her. He would only tell her where he was and that it was business—never what kind of business.

Kat came running into the hotel room with an opened envelope in hand. "Bali, bitches." she yelled as she dove into the couch. "We are going to Bali."

The room erupted in celebrations as the women jumped on couches, screaming at the top of their lungs.

"Wait a minute!"

Everyone stopped and turned to Sylver. She was the one in charge of the second team when they were split.

"Are we all going, or is this a split assignment?"

Kat shrugged. She hadn't read the whole document. Simone came just in time to answer the question. Everyone waited patiently for her to seat herself.

"No, it's a split assignment. The rest of you are going to the Caribbean."

The room was silent as they waited to hear who was on which trip. Simone took a seat next to Mallory on the couch and pulled the list from her folder. She read the names for the Bali trip first. Kat was pissed when she didn't hear her name called. She knew Simone would be upset if she threw a tantrum in front of the others.

"Excuse me, but the Caribbean is very large, so where exactly are we headed?" Monica was the second youngest model on the team. She wasn't going to Bali, but she didn't care. As long as Simone kept her on the team, she would go wherever she was sent.

"Saint Thomas and Saint Croix. We have a double assignment that needs to be completed in a week. So, those of you on the Bali trip, consider this a mini vacation. You'll have two weeks—one for work and the other if you want to explore." Simone set her paperwork aside. "I do not need to scold you on behavior. You mess up—you'll be replaced. You don't follow the rules or you try to ditch the bodyguards—you will be sent home and removed from my roster. This trip is very expensive, and the vendor wants specific, detailed pictures and information. While I understand this is a privilege for us to have gotten this assignment, your safety is of the utmost importance. No one is to go anywhere alone."

She was serious. She worried when she wasn't with her girls. "I need everyone to make sure they give their passports and other important documents to Sylver once you clear customs. Mark is in charge of security, and before anyone bellyaches about how strict he is, that is exactly why he's going. Please try to enjoy yourselves and be safe. You leave tomorrow night." She clapped her hands, and the Bali team got up and left the room. The remaining girls gathered closer to her.

"You look tired, boss. Are you okay?" Mallory was concerned about Simone's health. She had been very tired lately. Even though her mother was hovering over Simone like a new mother, they could only do so much to keep her healthy. She was taking her meds, but they seemed to contribute to her lack of energy.

"I'm fine—just tired actually. Today's sun was a bit much." She tried to smile, but everyone had already seen how she was really feeling.

"You know, you can go home and get some rest. Kat and I can handle this one."

Simone gave Mallory a look of disapproval. "Yeah, I don't think so."

Kat inhaled sharply, covering her chest with her hands as if she was appalled at the lack of trust. "Whatever."

Simone tried not to smile as she remembered why she hadn't trusted Kat and Mallory with the task. "May I remind both of you of the Florida incident?" She looked from Mallory to Kat.

"What happened in Florida?" Monica wasn't around very long. She hadn't known of the trouble Kat and Mallory had gotten themselves into. Mallory tried to hide her face as the poor girl waited for an update.

"Well, Nica, before you joined the dark side, we had already been around." Kat sat on the edge of the couch and started to tell the tale. "Sy used to trust us, but Mal demolished all that trust with one punch."

Mallory folded her arms over her chest and gave Kat the stink eye.

"You see, sweetheart, not everyone cares for people that look like us. These days it's kinda hard to tell when talking to people on the phone. Anyway, we had an assignment outside Jacksonville, Florida—a tiny town that had some great sites." She cleared her throat then continued. "We had booked a bed and breakfast to stay at for a few days. Little did we know the proprietor did not like people of color. So when Mal, Sylver, and yours truly showed up ahead of everyone else, this is what happened." She giggled, took a deep breath, then went on. "Mal had to pee, so when we pulled up in our limo, she jumped out and was greeted by a sweet-looking old lady. However, when Sylver and I disembarked the vehicle, said old woman was shocked. She asked Mal if the n-word women would be staying with her."

Kat started to laugh, confusing poor Monica. She didn't think any of that was funny at all.

"Well, it took about two seconds for Mal to realize what was asked, two more seconds for her to reach back and plow this old woman in the face, sending her flying into her prized rose bushes." Those who knew the story were snickering. Monica and Simone were the only two not joining with them. "Honey, I was proud and scared. There was a deputy there, and I swear I thought he was gonna throw us in jail. I had to cover my mouth to keep him from seeing my grinning. Poor Sylver started having a panic attack. So instead of help old Margaret out of her bushes, he ran over to grope Sylver."

Everyone was practically sprawled out on the floor, laughing.

"Oh my god, I had to go help the old Betty out of her bush. I was like 'Ma'am, I'm Black. May I assist you out of your predicament?'"

The laugher had drawn a larger crowd who recognized the story immediately. They were all laughing as an animated Kat tried to reenact the situation. "The whole time, Mal is cursing this poor lady out. She forgot she had to pee and hopped her happy ass back into the limo. She refused to stay there, not that any of us were going to, but she went from sweet Mallory Sweet to Darth Vader in a snap." Kat fanned herself as if she was overheating. "We ended up staying at the mayor's house for the three days we stayed there. Oh man, was Simone mad. They practically begged us to stay and complete the assignment. Apparently she wanted to sue, but big brother Rich had a chat with her, and all we had to pay for were her rose bushes."

Simone knew better than them the trouble they had caused. Richard was furious when he found out what had taken place. He was there within hours of the incident. After working his magic, the woman had agreed to accept payment for her damaged roses and their cancelled stay. She was sure there was more to what he had done than the others had known. He had pulled Mallory to the side and had a talk with her about her temper. The old lady had sent them an apology before they'd left for their next destination. She had found that very weird, but she hadn't shared that with anyone else. Richard wasn't as sweet as he pretended to be; she had seen the other Richard a time or two when they were married. She knew him better than any of these girls did.

"Ever since that day, Mal and I haven't been able to go anywhere without Sy. She doesn't trust us."

Just then, Jenna came looking for Mallory. She had a phone call in the other room. She jumped up and went to take her call.

Mallory knew who it was. She closed the door behind her before taking the call. "Good evening, Mr. Embers, how are you?"

Richard's voice made her feel warm inside. "Better now. How are you?"

She took a deep breath but didn't answer.

"Are you okay?" He waited for her to respond.

"I don't think I'll be able to make our rendezvous." She held her breath and waited.

There was a long pause on the line. "Why is that?"

She wanted to see him, but she needed to be there with Simone. She was hiding something, and she wouldn't leave her side until she knew Sy would be okay.

"I need to go on our next assignment. Simone isn't feeling well, but she won't take a break." The long pause made her think he was upset. "I really wanna see you, but—"

He cut her off. "It's fine, Mal. You don't need to explain. I understand." He didn't sound like he understood. In fact, his tone suggested he wasn't very happy at all that she had chosen to stay by Simone's side instead of his. "Take care of her, Kat, and yourself. I know Miss Jenna is doing an amazing job, but she can only do so much."

She didn't know what to say to him. He would never admit that he was disappointed that she wouldn't come to him.

"I promise to take you somewhere special for Christmas."

She felt a little excitement since Christmas wasn't that far away. She would have to get through these next few weeks, and then he would be with her.

"Thank you, Richard. I look forward that." She heard him groan in frustration.

"I better let you get back. I'm sure you need to pack. Will you tell everyone I said be safe and stay out of trouble?"

She laughed because she knew he was talking specifically to her and Kat. They were the problem children.

"I love you, Miss Sweet."

She enjoyed hearing him declare his love for her.

"I hate saying that name." He ended the call.

She hadn't had a chance to tell him she loved him. Why the hell did he all of a sudden hate her name?

*****

Mallory had been moping around the hotel all day. Everyone was preparing to go out to dinner at Victor's Hideout on the hill near the airport for dinner. It was their last night on the island of Saint Thomas. Everyone was having an amazing time, even her mother. She had worn a two-piece on the beach that morning, turning heads as she shyly took a walk with Simone. Mallory was shocked that Simone had talked her into putting on the revealing garment. They had been all over the island, and tonight they would take their last set of pictures at the restaurant during dinner. She tried to forget the date she had been anticipating for months, but she wished she could have gone to see him.

"So are we gonna have to deal with Sourpuss Sally tonight, or will you try to enjoy our last night here?" Kat was hugging her from behind.

Mallory relaxed and accepted the comforting embrace. "I miss him. Don't you miss Ken?" She had almost forgotten that Kat was probably going through the same thing she was. Ken had come to see her once while they were in Connecticut almost three weeks ago, but that was the last time they had seen each other. They spoke every night unlike her and Richard.

"Of course I miss my bear. I wish he was here to share this place with me, but this is my job. When we get married, things will be different. Hell, who knows, maybe I'll quit and become the stay-at-home wife and mother he wants me to be."

They giggled at the thought of Kat being a homebody.

"Entyway, we are ready to go break dinner rules. You ready?"

Mallory gave herself a once-over in the mirror. The dress that was sent for her to wear was an orange thigh-length spaghetti-strapped wraparound. It wasn't meant to hug the body, but as she turned, Kat started to cheer.

"Look at that booty, booty girl! Shake it, baby, shake it! That's a Deveaux booty right there."

Mallory couldn't help but laugh. She started out the door ahead of Kat, who was still cheering her on.

"Lord, we gon' have to get you security for this ass."

They walked out to meet the others, who could hear Kat's cheers down the hall.

"Can you two ever behave?" Simone ushered everyone into the elevator and pressed the Lobby button. She laughed when Kat and Mallory shared a look before nodding no. "Just try to stay out of trouble for a few more hours. We leave in the morning."

Tonight they would get their pictures. She would write her review then head back to the States. Kat and Mallory would have to continue on without her. She didn't want to tell them until they were done with their assignment. She didn't want to spoil the mood.

Even though it was mainly for work, the girls thoroughly enjoyed their dinner. The view from the rooftop at the restaurant was amazing. The staff treated them like royalty, and the food was amazing. They were allowed to order what they wanted though everyone had to order something different. They shared their meals with each other as they gushed over how great everything tasted. A few tourists recognized them and wanted photos. It was an evening to remember. Now that they were back at the hotel, everyone busied themselves with packing. Simone and Jenna had retired to bed, so Kat and Mallory made sure everyone was situated.

"What's with you, Mal? You look like you're sad." Monica liked Mallory. She was like a big sister to her. She had helped her get on the team.

"Mal is upset because she missed a dick date."

Mallory had no idea why anything that came out of Kat's mouth shocked her anymore.

"Really, Kathrine?" Everyone snickered as Mallory's face turned beet red.

"What? I miss my man too." Kat made a sad face. "I can't wait to get home and rape him."

Mallory had to shush everyone to keep from attracting attention from Simone or her mom.

"You know what we should do? I hear that a walk on the beach can cure whatever ails you." Everyone turned to look at Monica. She was so quiet, and now here she was suggesting they break curfew.

"Nica!" Kat tried to quietly yell. "I love the way your tiny little mind works." She tiptoed to the door and checked the hallway. "I think we can make it. Everyone, grab a robe. We are going skinny-dipping."

Two of the girls instantly declined.

"What? The others are in Bali enjoying themselves. This is our last night here. No one will ever see us again except in the mag. Who cares if someone sees us? It's dark out. We will have a story to tell those Bali bitches." Kat ran into the other room and retrieved a few robes. She handed them to each girl. "Let's go." She grabbed the room key and silently closed the door behind them. Sneaking out was the easy part, sneaking in would be the tricky part. How would they explain why they were wet? Kat laughed as she ran down the hall behind the others.

The night sky was a little cloudy, but it was fairly clear. The girls walked a good five minutes away from the hotel before they found their spot.

"This is it." Kat threw her robe in the sand and removed her shoe.

"Wha...what if it's cold?" Monica was having second thoughts.

Kat didn't like last-minute doubters. If you were in, then you were in. It was too late now.

"You're already out here. Just get in the damn water. The sooner we get in, the sooner we can get out."

She shook her head at poor Monica. Mallory was already undressing when she noticed a car parked on the road behind them.

"Oh shit. There's a car back there." She snatched her robe to cover her half-naked body. Everyone followed suit. Kat tried to see if she could see any movement in the dark car, but it was useless. She couldn't see a thing.

"It's fine. If we can't see them, then they can't see or recognize us." She continued to remove the last of her clothes.

Monica was still a bit worried, but she did as the others did. They piled all their belongings in a little stack and took off running into the water. It was refreshingly cool—not too cold but not warm either. They were going to enjoy their last night on this island paradise. Who knew if they'd ever get to come back?

"God, this feels good." Monica swam by Mallory, splashing her as she did.

The girls were enjoying themselves so much they forgot to leave a look out. They were highly unaware of the two figures that had crept up during their game of water tag. Simone watched as her girls splashed around chasing each other.

"Maybe you should join them." Jenna knew that Simone wanted to enjoy her last night with her family before returning home. She had planned to give them a little treat before she'd discovered them breaking out. She hadn't told them that she was leaving them yet, and it was eating at her. She didn't like not being close to her sisters or the girls she was so protective of.

"This is so dangerous. They don't even know we're here." She worried too much.

"This beach is semiprivate. No one here holds any malice toward these girls. There's also security around. You know Richard has that covered. Try to relax, honey." Jenna tried to comfort Simone. She had grown extremely protective of her in the last few months. She loved her and Kat as she had Mallory. They were her daughters, and she would do what she could to help them enjoy what time they had together. She had spent too much of her life hiding. She wished she had done more with her life after leaving Mallory's father. She had stayed in that little town, trying to run from a man that wasn't even chasing her. "Well, if you won't join them, I will." Jenna got up and started to undress. Simone couldn't believe her eyes.

"Miss Jenna, what are you doing?" She watched as the woman she had come to love as a mother stripped down to nothing.

"Living."

Simone sat staring with her hands over her mouth as Jenna ran into the water. The damn girls were so into their game it took Jenna's announcement to draw them back to reality.

"Hey, ladies."

All splashing ceased as they turned to see a naked woman wading toward them. It took only a second for them to realize who it was.

"Oh my god, Mom?" Mallory and Kat were the most shocked of the group. "You're naked!" Mallory started to make her way to her mother.

"Yes, I am. What's wrong with that?"

The other girls were crouched down in the water as they realized they were caught.

"Wait a minute—if you're here, where is Simone?" Kat was worried. She knew she was in trouble.

"On the beach. She's being a prude." Jenna waved toward the shore where Simone sat laughing.

"Is she mad?" Kat was sure she would get an earful once she walked up on the beach. She hadn't even noticed them before Jenna startled them. Simone had asked them to stay alert, and of all the people that could catch them being anything but, it was her.

"Don't worry about her. She knew you would make a break for it." Jenna giggled as she moved past them. "So, who's it?"

The girls didn't know what to make of the situation. Were they busted, or was it safe to play?

"Well, I guess I am since no one wants to be." Jenna lunged at the closest person to her. "Now you're it."

Everyone seemed to snap out of their trance as Monica yelled, "Wait a minute! Don't you have to count?"

The game was back in full swing minus one. Mallory decided to sit with Simone. If she was out here, she would keep her company. She walked over and dropped down next to Simone.

"You too sexy to get naked?"

Simone laughed as she handed Mal a robe.

"I can't believe my mother is skinny-dipping." She shuddered at the thought.

"What's wrong with that? She's living her life for a change."

Mallory turned to look at Simone. What did that mean? Her mom had always lived her own life. She had gone to nursing school like she always wanted and bought herself a house. Well, the bank still owned it, but it would be hers one day.

"What about you?" Mallory covered herself with the robe. "Shouldn't you be living your life like that too?" She nodded toward the water, where everyone was having an amazing time.

"I'm fine right here keeping an eye on you troublemakers."

Mallory laughed, but she felt a bit sad for Simone. She should be having fun like the rest of the girls. She thought for a second before deciding to take matters into her own hands. She turned to Simone with a devilish look she was sure Simone was unaware of. Without a word, she sprung on Simone. Straddling her, she tried to wrestle Simone's dress off her.

"Mal, what the hell?" Simone hadn't expected her to jump on her.

Both women wrestled around in the sand for a minute before Mallory was victorious. Simone was lying in the sand, trying not to swallow the sand she had scooped up in her mouth during their tussle. She barely saw a naked Mallory waving her dress above her head in triumph.

"You are crazy." She laughed.

"Ha! Now in you go." Mallory grabbed a tight hold of Simone's legs and started to drag a screaming Simone toward the water. "You're gonna skinny-dip tonight, woman…"

Just as she reached the water's edge, a set of headlights illuminated the beach. Mallory froze as her head shot to where the blinding lights were coming from. "Oh shit!"

Simone and Mallory quickly rushed into the water in an attempt to hide their naked bodies. Everyone was crouched down into the water with barely their heads visible. Someone had been watching them. The shock and sheer terror of not knowing who was out there was overwhelming.

"Simone, go get the robes." Kat pushed her sister forward a bit.

"What? No!" She wasn't getting out. If she had to swim back to the safety of their hotel, then she would do just that.

"But you have panties on. The rest of us are bare-assed."

Realizing Kat was right, she knew she would have to. She was about to move when Miss Jenna grabbed her.

"There are two men walking this way."

The lights were still shining brightly in their faces, making it hard for them to recognize anyone. They watched helplessly as the men walked over to their clothes and collected the robes. It must be hotel security. The men walked to the shoreline and stood, offering cover to them. Simone wished the damn car would turn the lights off. She could barely make out anything but the silhouette of the bodies before them. Their faces were shrouded in the dark now that the damn cloud had decided to cover the freaking moon. She wasn't going out to them.

"You can drop them there. It's okay." One of the men bent his head, and she could tell he was laughing. Did island murderers wear suits to the beach to kill women who were careless?

"Out—now!"

Holy shit. Everyone knew that voice. Mallory immediately lost all her courage and hid behind Simone though she wasn't the most frightened of the group. When no one attempted to move, they were once again ordered to remove themselves from the water.

"Now, ladies!"

This time no one hesitated. Simone was the first to reach the men, Mallory and Kat in tow. Richard handed them each a robe, but Simone only passed it back to one of the girls.

"I didn't bring one, thank you."

The man next to Richard quickly removed his jacket and handed it to her. She politely took the gift she was offered and put it on. The man then raised his hand and snapped his fingers twice, and the lights that had blinded them disappeared. Simone stepped aside so that the others could get their robes. She watched her girls hurriedly slip into their robes then half hid behind her. Mallory had been pulled to Richard's side. She watched as Miss Jenna proudly snatched a robe from Richard, whose head was bent. She could tell he was amused.

"Miss Jenna." Richard sounded way too amused for Jenna. She liked him, but he was ruining their fun.

"Party killer."

A few snickers were heard among the group.

"Wait, mom, take my robe. Monica needs hers." Mallory didn't think about what she was doing. She just removed the robe and handed it to her mother.

"Honey, you're naked again."

Again, the snickering overtook the group. Richard grabbed Mallory's wrist as she turned to find her clothing in the pile. He removed his jacket and handed it to her. He wasn't happy, and she knew it. He had come to see her, but not like this. She wasn't in the mood to deal with his anger tonight. She was having fun, living her life. He wasn't going to change that. She wouldn't let him.

"Is everyone covered?" Richard turned and gestured for them to return to the hotel.

"Wait, our clothes." Monica tried to get back to the pile on the sand but was halted by the giant man that was standing before her. Richard made her feel small when she stood in front of him. She looked up and caught a glimpse of the serious face that peered down at her. She slowly turned and ran after the other girls who had already started speed walking back to the hotel. Mallory, witnessing their encounter, started to laugh at what she had seen.

"You scared the poor girl." She giggled as she walked next to Richard. His friend had walked ahead, leaving them to walk alone.

"Then she has more sense than you. At least she knows not to piss me off."

Well, so much for a smooth night. Mallory rolled her eyes and decided she would just shut her mouth—a task that became increasingly hard as she realized what he had said.

"You know, if you want a woman that fears and does everything you want, then have at Monica. I'm not her, and I won't be." She was pissed now. How dare he? She didn't want to walk next to him anymore. How did she miss this jackass when he wasn't around? All he did was insult and make fun of her. She started to walk faster to catch up with the others who were getting too far ahead. She didn't get far. Richard grabbed his jacket and yanked her backward. Mallory hadn't expected him to snatch her and was temporarily rendered unbalanced. She just knew she was going to eat sand when he swept her up.

"Must you always make everything difficult?" Straightening her in front of him, he continued, "If I want Monica, that wouldn't be an issue. The fact that I've been celibate since I last touched you should tell you everything you need to know about who I want."

She didn't know what to say. Her stomach knotted, and she felt a sudden surge of warmth. She bent her head to keep from revealing her happiness. He was infuriating, but she loved him. She shook her head as she wondered if there was anything he could do to change that.

"May I return you to the hotel so that you can get cleaned up?"

She nodded and turned to continue their walk. She had forgotten she was wearing his jacket until she felt a hand caress her butt. The action caused her to jump. His hand was a bit cold, but she welcomed it. Richard pulled her closer to him as they walked back together. Everyone else was way ahead of them and almost back at the hotel's beach entrance. She watched them disappear as she strolled with her man. Yep, he was hers, and she intended to make sure he stayed that way.

Mallory wasn't surprised that Richard had taken her to his room instead of back to the one she had been in previously. He escorted her to his shower where he ran a bath for her. She watched as he threw bath salts and whatever the hell else were in the jars in the sunken tub. It wasn't as large as the one in his cabin, but this one was pretty huge. She sat on the sink and watched him check the temp before starting to remove his clothing. Lord, this man was beautiful. He undressed as if he was used to her being present as he did.

"Get in."

She was still covered in sand and clad only in his jacket. When she didn't move, he turned to her. "Come here. Please." She noticed how tired he looked and jumped from the sink.

"You look drained."

He smiled as he collected her in his arms. He removed his jacket from her body. "And yet you continue to make me work harder than I want to." He lifted her and stepped into the tub.

The memory that she had suppressed of their last tub encounter came back as if it had just happened. Mallory tried to push it to the back of her mind once again. She didn't want to ruin tonight. He had come to be with her, and she was grateful. She would show him just how grateful she was for him. Having been with the traveling women had taught her a lot. He was in for a treat tonight.

*****

Mallory stretched as the rays of sunlight peeked through the sheer curtains. Richard was sleeping peacefully next to her. She sat up to admire his beautiful face. They had spent the better part of their night making love. He was impressed with her new tricks but wanted to have a discussion about her new knowledge since he hadn't taught any of it to her. She ran her hand over his chest before moving a little further south. He quickly retrieved her hand.

"Unhand me, demon woman. You should be tired, sore, and aching after what you did to me last night." He tried to stretch, but Mallory nibbled at his neck. "Damn it. Enough, Mal. I think I might be pregnant."

Mallory burst into laughter.

"Keep laughing, and I'll drag you through the worst custody battle you've ever heard of."

She couldn't stop laughing.

He turned to her. "I'm afraid to kiss you after what happened last night." He groaned when she finally snuggled up to him.

"I aim to please you and only you." She kissed his chest before he pushed her back from him.

"Which brings a few questions to mind."

She tried to hide her smile but was unsuccessful.

"Where the hell did you learn your new tricks, ma'am?" His face was semiserious.

"Are you sure you want to know?"

He frowned at her. "I absolutely do." He tried to sit up.

"Okay. Porn."

Richard froze as her words registered. What the hell did she just say? He blinked rapidly as he turned to her in shock. "I beg your pardon."

Mallory knew she had to explain quickly before he jumped to conclusions.

"Some of the girls found out I had never seen a porn movie before." The look on Richard's face amused her. She tried not to laugh at his shock. "They found one and made me watch." She held her breath when a myriad of emotions flashed across his face. "Apparently it's a thing girls do in high school, but I didn't have any real friends in high school, so I never did. I missed out on a lot."

Richard wasn't sure how he felt about the news. "So, did you watch this by yourself?" His curiosity was getting the better of him. He knew she wouldn't lie, but he didn't know if he really wanted to know.

"No. We watched as a group." Mallory watched in amusement as Richard's hands covered his face. He was shaking his head. "We had wine and bananas."

His head whipped around so fast she couldn't hold her laughter. "Oh goddamn. Bananas and wine?" Then he remembered last night. "Oh shit." He sucked in a deep breath. "Well then. I'm impressed and worried."

Mallory was happy he had enjoyed her performance. She didn't think she would like it, but she had—and so did he. She couldn't wait to report back to her instructors. She wouldn't give too much detail, but she was proud of herself. Last night she had taken control of their lovemaking and was successful in her conquest. Watching the smile on his face now empowered her. She felt freer. First she skinny-dipped—with her mother! Oh shit.

"Oh my god." She couldn't believe what had happened last night.

"What?" Richard was a bit concerned.

"My mother was skinny-dipping last night."

Richard let out a hard sigh. "And the fantasy is ruined." Then he remembered not recognizing Miss Jenna until she was actually standing in front of him. She hadn't cared that he had seen her. "Although your mother does have amazing—"

Mallory's hand came down over his mouth, cutting off his last words.

"No! You get that out of your filthy mind right now."

Richard chuckled behind her hand. His eyes suddenly went to her naked breast. Desire and lust flashed in his sexy blue eyes, and she was more than ready for him.

"No. Shit. We might be late for breakfast."

Mallory frowned when he jumped from the bed.

"I promised Kal we would have breakfast with him this morning, and he is not a very patient young man."

Who the hell was Kal? She watched Richard walk to the bathroom and was shocked at the marks on his back. They were deep red as if some had bled. She could hear the shower, and when he got in, she heard him groan in pain.

"Are you joining me, werewolf woman?"

She laughed as she hopped from the bed and bolted for the shower. "Just so you know, you'll be hearing from my lawyer when we get back to the States." He pulled her into the shower and kissed her.

*****

Simone was attempting to grab a piece of bacon when someone pulled it from her grasp. She dropped the tongs she was trying to use and snatched the bacon from the plate it was dropped on. She hadn't even looked up to see who had the audacity to take her bacon.

"That is mine." She looked up at the figure standing next to her and gasped. He was even sexier in the daylight. Who in god's name was this perfect being? His smooth chocolate skin rivaled even hers. His eyes were a beautiful shade of gold, and the man was built to perfection. His sandy brown curls fell to his shoulder like a cascading waterfall. She blatantly gave him the once-over.

"You shouldn't eat that. It is considered unclean." What the hell did he just say? She hadn't really heard a word that escaped that pretty mouth of his. When his lips parted, a brilliant smile lit his face. She thought she would faint.

"What?" She didn't like that she sounded like a breathless fool. Men did not make her lose her train of thought. Who was this damn magician that had fogged up her head?

"The bacon. It's not good for you." She heard that.

"Well, neither is the air we breathe, but no one is holding their breath now, are they?" She bit her lip when he laughed. He was making her poor defective heart race. Only one other man had ever done anything close to that. "I'm Simone by the way." He bowed politely and took her hand.

"I know exactly who you are, Miss Simone." Of course he did. She had plastered herself all over the damn magazine the last few months. He kissed her hand, causing heat to rise in places she hadn't felt in a long time. "I am Kalu, but you can call me Kal." He stepped closer to her. "Or anything you want."

Holy hell. Was this how Kat and Mallory had felt about their men?

"Have breakfast with me."

Simone wanted nothing more than to run off with this estranged Olympian god, but she had priorities.

"I'm sorry, but I'm having breakfast with my family." She smiled what she hoped was a brilliant and not awkward smile.

"Lunch?" He was way too close. She swore she could feel his heart pounding against her chest.

"Sorry. I won't be here for lunch either. I guess it's bad timing."

Kal raised an eyebrow at her. "Only if one cannot do anything about it."

What the hell did he mean by that? He leaned close to her ear, and she swayed.

"But I can."

She had to get away from him. There were people staring at them. People were walking around them to get their food. Kal seemed to notice the inquiring gazes around them.

"I think we should get back to your family." As soon as the words registered, she snapped out of her fantasy.

"No. You shouldn't. Not that I don't want you." When he smiled, she realized she needed to finish what she was saying quickly. "What I mean is my sister is very mouthy, and she asks a hundred questions."

He raised a hand to stop her. "I can handle your sister. If it gets me an audience with you this beautiful morning, I would fight a shark."

Good god, he's crazy. She shrugged, threw a few more pieces of fruit on her plate, and turned toward her table. Kat was going to have this poor man for breakfast. Richard and Mallory needed to hurry the hell up.

*****

"You went to get pancakes and came back with chocolate cake." Kat wasted no time at all. Jenna almost choked on her juice as she recognized the young man with Simone.

"Kathrine, stop it." Usually, Kat would listen, but who the hell was this guy? He was sexy, but he was with her sister.

"I just wanna know who he is?"

Simone took her seat and gestured for Kal to sit. "This is Kal. You met him last night on the beach."

Kat's mouth dropped before forming a huge smile. "Oh, this is the owner of "the jacket"?" She made air quotes with her hands. Simone tried not to make eye contact with anyone—especially Kat. "So, where are you from, Kal?"

Simone placed a frustrated hand in front of her face. "I warned you."

Kal didn't seem at all impressed with Kat's questioning. When he didn't answer, she continued to grill him.

"Cat got your tongue, or are you just dumb behind all that sexiness?"

Jenna reached over and popped Kat on her arm.

"You know, if we were back in my country, my father would have you beheaded."

Everyone shot him a look of shock. What the hell?

"What?" Simone covered her mouth as she realized he wasn't security at all. He was Richard's friend—the fucking prince. Before she could warn Kat, she heard her sister respond.

"Well, we not in your damn country now, are we? And around here, women like me can whoop your ass."

Simone raised a hand to stop her sister. She knew exactly who he was now—not that Kat would care. Her mouth was lethal when tested. Simone was so thankful when Kenneth finally walked over to the table. Kal's face was dead serious as he shot Kat a steely glare—a glare that was returned by her sister. Do something, Simone, before your sister loses her damn head. She was about to apologize when a smile crept slowly across his face.

"I can handle her. She's all mouth." He turned his attention to a shocked Simone and winked.

"What's going on?" Kenneth had no idea what he had walked in on.

"Where's Richard? He's not one to be late." Kal ignored Kat's icy stare. He would have fun with her later, but right now he wanted to hang out with Simone. He needed Richard to cancel her plans for him.

"He's on his way." Kenneth leaned over and kissed Kat, who was staring at Kal, on the cheek. "So, you've met my fiancée and her family."

The shock on Kal's face made Simone giggle. He looked terrified. "What?" He looked from a confused Kenneth to Kat. "That one is your fiancée?" Kat was about to give him an earful. "Oh my god. Are you okay? Blink twice if you need help."

Kenneth and Simone burst into laughter. Kat did not care for this. She did not like anyone making fun of her Ken.

"I mean it. If you're in danger, let me know. There's still time to save you."

Everyone at the table was laughing except a pouting Kat.

"What did we miss?" Richard pulled out a chair next to Jenna for Mallory before taking a seat next to Kal.

"Man, why didn't you warn me about the baby dragon you're letting Ken marry?"

Richard threw his head back and laughed. He knew Kat was furious, but she would behave now that he was here. "Don't worry, Kat, he's a friend. This is Prince Kalu." Richard knew how she felt about Ken. Even though he was much older than her, she never hid the way she felt about him. No matter the stares or whispers, she was proud of her Ken Bear. He was one of the kindest people she had ever met, never had she seen his temper—if he had one. He was always smiling especially when she was around.

"He's just jealous that I have you." Ken placed a kiss on Kat's hand. She tried not to blush, but she couldn't help it. A huge smile spread across her face.

"It's okay Pooh Bear. I'm not worried about him." She placed a kiss on Ken's cheek that made him smile. Kal and Richard shared a look.

"Pooh Bear?" Kal whispered to Richard. "A Pooh Bear and a baby grizzly—what a fairytale."

Miss Jenna spit all the juice she was trying to consume onto the table. She broke into laughter at the comment. She tried to apologize through fits of laughter.

"I'm sorry." She was practically crying with laughter. Everyone else joined her after making sure she was okay. "I'm going to my room before I choke on my breakfast. Oh good lord." She stood and excused herself.

Kal stood and walked over to her. "It was a pleasure meeting you—and just between us, you looked amazing last night." He winked and placed a kiss on Jenna's blushing cheek.

"Thank you."

The girls couldn't believe he had been so bold. Miss Jenna was blushing fiercely as she headed for the elevator. Kal took the seat Jenna had vacated next to Kat. "So, Baby Dragon, friendly question—why do you want to marry the old man?"

Kat's eyes grew as she turned to Kal. He tried to keep his expression blank. From the look in her eyes, he knew she was protective of Ken. Everyone sat silently, waiting for the explosion.

They were shocked when a smile crossed her face. "Not that it is any of your business, but I happen to love my Pooh Bear, and I get that your tiny little heart has never loved anyone but yourself, so you couldn't possibly understand what we have. But I am not about to let my soulmate get away because you care about how much younger I am. I was never trying to please you or anyone else."

Before she could continue, Kal stopped her. "So it's not his millions in investments or his future inheritance that you're after?" His face was cold as he stared into Kat's eyes. She was boiling. No one at the table moved. Kat had no idea what he was talking about. What millions? He worked for Richard. Ken was a working man with a good job.

"Excuse me?" Kal realized she had no idea what he was talking about. She was actually just in love with Ken. He couldn't believe it. Kat stood to walk away. She didn't want to embarrass Ken or Richard by cursing out the arrogant asshole that sat next to her. Prince or no prince, he was an ass hat. "Please excuse me. I think I'll take a walk on the beach before we leave. Have a wonderful breakfast, everyone." She looked down at Kal. "Don't forget to choke on yours." So much for peacefully walking away.

Kal reached up and dragged her back to a seated position. With the swiftness of a cheetah, Ken grabbed Kat's free hand.

"I sincerely believe he's lucky to have you." He gave her a smile and wink. "I look forward to your smart mouth gracing our conversations from here on."

Ken slowly released Kat's hand. She seemed more relaxed now that she knew Kal was only joking, but he had some explaining to do. He never told her that he was wealthy. She had thought he only worked for Richard. He needed to tell her everything.

"Well, now that you two are done getting acquainted, I think we should take that walk now." They stood and excused themselves from the table. "I'll make sure she's ready when you are." With that, he led Kat toward the beach entrance.

"You think he's in trouble?"

Richard shrugged in response. He had no idea what was about to happen, but he knew they would be okay. Ken wouldn't give up his Kat that easily. She was his everything now.

"They'll be okay." Simone smiled at Kal. She hadn't known about Ken's secret wealth either. She wondered why Kal had brought it up, why Richard had never told her about it.

"So, Miss Simone, what are your plans for the foreseeable future?" Kal moved closer to her. He wanted to speak with her privately, but he didn't mind that Richard and her friend were still around. Richard knew what he wanted, and Kal always got what he wanted.

"Like I said earlier, I'm heading home today. I have some important business to attend to." She didn't make eye contact with him.

Mallory was a bit taken back by Simone's response. She hadn't known about any business. They were scheduled to be in Saint Croix this afternoon—all of them.

"What are you talking about, Sy? I thought we were heading to Saint Croix this afternoon."

Simone wished she had told Mallory and Kat what her plans were. She didn't want to talk about it in front of Kal. She didn't know him.

"It's okay. I just need to see my doctor for some new meds, that's all." She knew that the girls had noticed her slowing down. They had seen how worn out she was these last few days. "I'm fine, Mal."

Richard sat quietly listening. He had told her that he wouldn't come back until she had made a decision, yet here he was. He tried not to show how pissed he was, but Kal knew. They'd been friends for too long. He could almost tell what Richard was feeling from one look.

"I'll come with you."

Simone knew how much Mallory cared for her, but she needed her to finish the job. "No, Mal. I need you and Kat to finish this assignment. It's only a few days, then you'll be home, and we can take a break." She tried to smile, but Mallory wasn't buying it. Now she just wanted to leave.

"No! I'm going with you. If you're going home, then so am I."

Simone knew she had to go, but she needed them to finish their assignment.

"Listen, this is what you get paid to do, not take care of me. That's your mother's job." She wasn't making eye contact with anyone. "If I ask you to finish an assignment without me, then that's what you do. This is what you signed on for."

She got up to leave, but Richard stopped her. He was standing before her, blocking her retreat. There was more to whatever was going on than she wanted them to know.

"Kal will go with you."

This made Kal smile. Not that he liked Richard volunteering him without asking, but for Simone, he would gladly go. This is what he wanted—to be alone with her so that they could talk.

"Richard, I don't need a babysitter. I have Miss Jenna. I'll be just fine." He could hear the hurt in her voice. She was always trying to hide the way she felt from him.

"I'm not asking." He nodded at Kal, who stood at the silent command.

"At your service, ma'am." He was amused but concerned. He wasn't used to this, but if he wanted her, he would have to learn quickly how to take care of her. She was important to Richard, her sister, and her friends. They were important to her as well, but soon she would feel the same for him.

"I'm sure Kal has other things to do other than stalk me." She felt the moment he came closer to her.

"No, I don't. It would be my pleasure to stalk you," he whispered.

She tried not to laugh but couldn't help it. Kal was different to what she had expected. He wasn't as uptight as Richard was. Maybe it wouldn't be a bad idea to keep him around. Besides, she owed him for messing with her sister.

"Fine, but I'm not the easiest person to deal with, and I will be working. You will not get in my way." She turned to look at Kal, but he was too close. She felt her body heat rising as she looked up at him. He was causing fires inside her, and she was sure he knew that.

The sexy smile on his face was doing things to her body. This was a very bad idea.

"As you wish, my princess." He winked at her. Lord, this man was trouble. She would have to make sure Miss Jenna didn't leave them alone too much. Simone didn't feel like eating anymore, not that she could now.

"I think I'm going to head to the room. It was a pleasure meeting you this morning." She backed away from Kal. His narrowed gaze made her smile. She wondered what was going through his head. She turned to Mallory. "I'll see you after breakfast." Mallory was mad. She could see that. Richard had taken his seat next to her once again. "Richard." There wasn't much to say to him. He had gotten his way as always. He nodded at her as she walked to the elevators.

"I'm not hungry, Richard." Mallory wanted to chase after Simone, but she didn't want to leave Richard since she had no idea when she would see him again. She was sulking at the table.

"She's cute when she's pouting." Kal was smiling at her. Had she not been mad, maybe she could have appreciated the beauty that was this man. Since she'd met Richard, no one really made her look twice, but Kal did. Even last night when they thought he was a security guard, he held his own next to Richard.

"Aren't they all?" Richard's mood had changed. Simone's news had put him in a bad mood.

"You can go after her if you'd like. I can keep him company." Richard gave Kal a look. He wasn't pleased that he was dismissing Mallory.

"Are you sure?" She saw the look on Richard's face and wished she hadn't asked. He was giving poor Kal a death stare.

"It's okay. Kal can cuddle with me while you're gone."

Kal almost choked on his orange juice.

"I'm sorry?" Mallory laughed at the exchange between both men. Their facial expressions were hilarious. "Nope, last time you wouldn't let me be the big spoon. I wanted to be the big spoon."

Richard's laugh could be heard throughout the dining room. Kal was shaking his head. It was very refreshing to hear Richard's laugh.

"I'm taller." Kal gasped and frowned at Richard.

"By about half an inch."

They were laughing again. She could just sit there watching them interact. She had never seen Richard like this. She liked him like this. He turned to her with a smile.

"It's okay. You should go check on Simone." He stood and pulled her into his arms. "I'll be okay with this idiot."

She heard Kal grunt behind them. "I resent that."

Richard kissed her like no one was watching. She was almost breathless when he let her go. She was sure her face was cherry red when he ushered her toward the elevators.

"I'll see you later." He sent her off with a pat on the butt.

Kal chuckled at the way Richard stared after Mallory. "Does she get to be the big spoon?"

Richard snorted. He watched Mallory disappear into the elevator.

"So, what do we do now that you've chased all the women away?"

Kal chuckled. He had never been accused of chasing women away. "Talk. We talk about what I want." He smiled at a frowning Richard.

What he wanted was Simone. He always had—from the first time Richard had shown him her photo. Never had he been jealous of Richard until that very moment. When he had found out their marriage wasn't what it seemed, he was relieved. He convinced Richard to divorce her. At first Richard was skeptical, but after a very long night of drinking and heartfelt conversation, he had agreed. If anyone could talk some sense into Simone, it was Kal.

"I did my part. Now it's up to you. I don't know what the hell you're walking into, but I wish you good fortune."

Kal made a weird noise that made Richard laugh.

"Just try not to give her a heart attack. I saw the way she looked at you."

Kal smiled and winked at a few women sitting several tables behind Richard.

"What can I say? This chocolate goodness is hard to resist."

Richard rolled his eyes and grunted. He loved Kal as a brother, but sometimes he wanted to bop him over the head. He wondered if that's what he had sounded like before Simone and Mallory. "You're not bad yourself, Rich, but you're no Kal."

Richard made a face and snickered. "I mean even your lady was giving me the side eye earlier. I think she might like what she sees too."

Richard's demeanor instantly changed. He did not like that at all. Mallory was his—his.

"Let's not cross that line." He was dead serious.

Kal knew when to poke him and when not to, but he had a purpose. "What? It's not like you're invested in this one. She's just another Kim."

Richard's hand clenched into a fist on the table. Kal knew he was hooked. Now all he had to do was reel him in. "The sex is amazing, so you think you're in love, then she gets rid of your kid, and you find yourself another Simone. These women don't want what you want. They want their faces on magazines and strutting runways. If you wanted the forever wife type, you should have gone after Kat."

Richard's fist struck the table, scaring almost everyone in the vicinity. The silence in the room was deafening.

"Enough." His voice was soft yet steely. The people around them watched, not knowing what was going on. One man looked furious and ready to explode while the other smiled a brilliant smile. Kal waited for the normal sounds of socializing before he continued. Goading Richard was always fun even when it ended in a fight.

"Seriously. She's beautiful, but she's in this for a career. I could see it in her face. Just be honest with yourself. You don't really have the best of luck with these women."

Richard was furious. "Thanks for the advice. This one is mine."

Kal tried to keep a serious concerned look on his face.

"She knows it, and so will you."

Kal shrugged. "I just don't wanna see you go through it again."

Richard realized after his outburst what Kal was doing. His family had taken him in as one of theirs, loved him, treated him like a prince when he was with them. He knew how Kal felt about him.

He was the overprotective little brother—insufferable at times—but he loved his brothers and would do anything for them. Kim had done a number on him, and if it hadn't been for Kal and his family, he may not have made it through. His drinking almost drove him to suicide. She had betrayed him, hurt him. He hadn't been in love with her, but what she had done was unforgivable.

"Make sure you're right." Kal stood. "I'd hate to kill this one too." He was serious. "I kinda like her."

With that, he left Richard sitting alone. "I know," he whispered, sitting back in his chair.

When he had told Kal what Kim had done, he was only trying to make sense of it. He had no idea the man would take the woman's life, but he had. She'd taken his son from him, his unborn son. All of it was just to spite him. He wasn't ready for any loveless marriages, but when she announced her pregnancy, he'd offered her almost everything. Six months, and he had finally decided to give in. He wasn't going to let her raise his child alone. However, he was a whole week too late. She had terminated the pregnancy without telling him—no remorse whatsoever. She had done it to hurt him, and Kal made her pay for that. It was like the news had hurt Kal as much as it had him. He hadn't been his loving understanding self during that time. His father's monster had finally seeped into him. His mother had made them both come home so that she could help them heal. She had worked her motherly magic on them—something he would never forget.

*****

Kal and Simone had taken the day to relax and enjoy the weather. It had rained the last two days, and she had turned into a workaholic. The woman was driven like none he'd ever met. She was always busying herself, trying to negotiate assignments and payments. He would never admit it to her, but he loved watching her work. The way she chewed her bottom lip when she was deep in thought was quite possibly the sexiest thing he'd seen in a long time. Everything about her was amazing. He had caught her peering through the window at him after a swim and teased her about it. She acted offended, but he knew she wasn't.

"There's a cute little chicken shack down here. The girls and I sneak down here a lot." She was excited to share her secret with him.

"Does that mean I'm one of the special ones now?"

She gave him a deep wink as she parked. The neighborhood wasn't like the ones he was used to. This wasn't like the places they had gone to before.

"I'm mulling it over." She never waited for him to open doors for her, and she was too independent to let him pay when she took him out. He hated it but loved being with her. They'd spent time together every afternoon since they returned three days ago. He had spent the whole flight back trying to convince her that staying with him at Richard's house was a better idea than them trying to stay at her apartment, but he soon regretted it when she announce that he would have had to stay with her because there weren't any spare rooms. She would have gladly shared her bed with him if they didn't have the luxurious mansion at their disposal. He wasn't sure if she was messing with his head, but he kicked himself for not letting things play out. The smile she had given him almost made him lose it. Now every afternoon he tried to get her to move back to her apartment. "You are gonna love this place. Mal and Kat always choose this as our go-to cheat spot." She waited as he came around to meet her.

"Does Richard know about this?"

She took his hand and half dragged him toward the counter. "Yeah, he does."

He was certain she wasn't telling him the truth. He could tell by the tone in her voice. "Oh? Well then, I guess we can all come here for lunch when your girls get back."

She stopped and turned to him. With a mischievous smile, she said, "Fine. He doesn't know, but if you tell him, I'll let Kat finish you, then Mal and I will drive you back to Louisiana and feed you to my uncle's gators." She squinted at him as if to intimidate the giant standing before her.

This only made him laugh. Pulling her into a hug, he kissed her forehead. "You are borderline crazy, you know that?" He released her.

"I like it—not the feeding me to the gators part, but I like the way your evil little mind works."

She gave him the reward he sorted—a smile that did more than warm his heart.

"Your secret is safe with me, my little evil genius workaholic princess."

She started again toward the counter with a laugh. She would never admit it, but she loved it when he referred to her as his princess even though she always made a face when he did.

"Come on. I'll order for us."

They took a seat at the counter and waited for the heavyset man in the apron to attend to them.

"Hey, Sy. Where are the girls?"

She gave the man a brilliant smile. Kal was a bit jealous, but he was in observation mode.

"They're on an assignment in Saint Croix." She waved at a woman in the back. "Hey, Momo."

The woman placed the pan she was carrying down and hurriedly cleaned her hands.

"Is that my Monie out there?" She exited the little shack and snatched Simone into her arms. "Hey, princess. How have you been?"

Kal made a groaning noise that got the gentleman's attention. He did not want anyone else calling her their princess. She was his.

"Don't worry, young man. Sy is like the daughter we didn't have."

Kal turned his attention to him.

"I'm Bobby, but everyone calls me Bobo." He seemed like a good person.

"Kal." He gave the place a once-over. "How long have you had this place?"

Bobo walked to the fridge and grabbed a drink. He pulled a straw from a container and handed them to Kal. Leaning on the counter, Bobo started to talk. Kal listened even though he wanted to spend time with his princess instead of this man.

"I've had the place for several years now. My wife and I usually move on after a while, but this spot has been pretty good to us." He looked around Kal at the scenery. "The park gets busy sometimes, and busy people get hungry. They smell the food and come running especially in the afternoons." Bobo laughed.

Kal looked up at the menu board that was hanging behind Bobo.

"Damn near everything we make has chicken in it."

Kal noticed something called chicken butter. "What exactly is that?" He pointed at the words next to the picture. Unwrapping his straw, he absentmindedly opened his drink and placed it in it.

"Yeah, like I said, we make almost everything with chicken."

Kal looked down at the drink he had in front of him. Quickly checking the label, he looked back at Bobo suspiciously. They laughed a hearty laugh.

"Not that one, but we do have a chicken flavored drink."

Kal made a disgusted face. Who the hell would want a drink made from chicken?

"What is this?" He asked as he took a cautious sip.

Simone was next to him, taking her seat. "Sorrel. It's so good." She rolled her eyes as if she'd just orgasmed. Her reaction made both men laugh. "I ordered for us, shouldn't take but a second."

Bobo watched Kal as he stared at Simone. He knew that look. The poor boy was smitten. He hoped that he was a professional already or at least had a decent job because their Simone deserved everything.

"So are you a model too?" Bobo asked Kal. He was quite confused when both Kal and Simone burst into laughter.

"Nah, he's just a regular smegular guy." Simone wiggled her eyebrows at Bobo.

"I definitely resent that." He didn't know what the hell a regular smegular guy was, but he damn sure wasn't one. "I think I might be insulted." He turned away from Simone in mock hurt.

"Actually, he's Prince Charming, but to those who know him, he's just regular old Kal."

He knew she was teasing.

"I can see that. When I first saw him, I thought he must be the most beautiful man I've ever seen." Bobo laughed at his own joke.

Kal shook his head in amusement. He wondered what they would say if they knew he really was a prince. He liked when people didn't recognize him. Most showed their true identities when he was just regular Kal. He had embarrassed a few people who talked about his family in front of him not knowing who he was. Richard loved it when he confronted people about their ignorance. They used to go places and cause trouble all the time back in college. His protection detail hated every moment of it.

"I'm afraid I'm more of the corporate type. I don't walk runways or grace magazines as often as your Simone." He winked at Simone. She was smiling at him. If only she knew what that damn smile did to him. He was close to kissing her when their food was delivered to them by Momo.

"Here you go, sugar—your favorite, fried wings and French fries." She placed two baskets in front of Kal and Simone.

As Kal pulled his basket closer, he had to wonder where the hell did they get the wings. They were quite possibly the largest wings he had ever seen.

"What are these?" he asked, curiously staring at his food.

"Chicken wings and fries." Simone was confused.

"Well, I know these are fries, but what in the hell are these?" He lifted a wing and swung it gently between his finger. Everyone else stared at him.

"You're joking, right?" Simone gave him a shocked look. "Have you never had chicken wings?"

Kal shook his head. "Of course I've had chicken wings—regular chicken wings." He replaced the wing in the basket. "These look more like pterodactyl wings than chicken wings."

Simone laughed hysterically. She leaned against Kal to keep from falling from the stool.

"These things are the biggest damn wings I've ever seen. I think your chickens have been lifting weights or something."

Bobo and his wife were practically dying with laughter. Though his face was quite serious, they knew he was just joking.

"Do all the wings look like these?" he asked.

"You are a mess. I can't take you anywhere."

He didn't wait for her to calm down. He pulled her in and kissed her. He was a bit surprised when she wrapped her arms around him. He had to pull back to keep from going too far.

"Just in case I get taken out by these dinosaur wings." He decided that he would try them. He crossed his heart before taking a bite. The first bite rendered him speechless. The wing was full of flavor. It was well seasoned, crunchy, and delicious.

"Mm. This is amazing." He took another bite and noticed everyone was staring at him. "What?" he asked, still chewing. He looked at each person, noting the proud and satisfied looks on their faces. "I still think it's pterodactyl, but it's delicious." He decided to ignore them and enjoy his pterodactyl wings.

The afternoon seemed to get away from them. He sat talking to Bobo as Simone and Momo served customers. She seemed to fit in anywhere. That was a quality he admired in her. She would fit in perfectly in his life. He would make sure of that.

It was a bit after seven when they returned to the house. Kal had a container with his stash of dinosaur meat. She couldn't believe how amazing the day had turned out. Kal and Bobo spent most of their time conversing while she helped Mo with the customers. He had convinced Bobo that he could open a small restaurant and expand once more people started talking about his amazing pterodactyl wings. She loved watching him interact with the people he met. He was royalty, but today you couldn't tell. He was just a regular sexy man-god hanging out and playing basketball with Bobo and the kids. She had done the other team a disservice when she started cheering for them. Kal did not appreciate it and made them pay. At one point, the guys started asking her to stop cheering for them. He was a monster on the court. His shirtless sexiness drew a crowd of women all cheering him on. It was the reason she had started cheering for the other team.

"I had a great time today. Your friends were amazing people." He swept Simone into his arms and started up the stairs. "Though I didn't appreciate you turning on me." She threw her head back and laughed.

"It didn't stop you from bringing your A-plus game. Those poor boys hate me now."

He kissed her cheek. "That was your fault."

She wrapped her arms around his neck. "Well, what did you expect? All those damn hussies cheering you on. I had to do something."

He stopped at the top of the stairs. "Wait a minute. Were you jealous?"

She gave him a side glance. "I might have been."

He placed her on the ground. She tried to walk away, but he pulled her back.

"It wasn't my intention, but I hope you know that I am all yours."

She searched his face and found he was serious.

"I want something from you."

Simone frowned up at him. He was serious, no smiles in sight.

"Do you now, Prince Kalu? I'm sure I have nothing that you want or don't already have." She waited for his response.

"I want you to take some time and think about what I'm about to ask of you. I don't want an answer now—three days."

She was nervous. Had Richard put him up to this? She hoped he wasn't about to ask her about surgery. She had already fought these battles and couldn't take on another opponent. Miss Jenna was the last of the battles she had fought, and it had taken a lot for her to tell her no.

"Please don't ask me about my…"

His hands cupped her face as he placed his thumb over her lips. "I want you—all of you."

Her eyes filled with hot tears.

"I know about your illness, and it's okay. There's a lot I need to tell you, but first, I want you to know that I have been in love with you since the first time I saw your likeness in a picture. Richard showed it to me, and for the first time ever, I wanted to be him."

She pushed herself into his chest and sobbed.

"I want you to be happy. If you only have another three days, I want you to be happy."

126

There was no way she could take up any of his time on a wasted adventure such as herself. She was a lost cause.

"Kal…" She didn't know what to say. In a different situation, she would have jumped at the chance to be with him, but she was on borrowed time. Her last appointment hadn't gone as well as she'd expected.

"I'm not asking you to fix it. I'm asking you to let me take you somewhere special and just try to enjoy the time that we have— whether it's a few days, months, years or a few hours."

She was shaking from her crying.

"Kat and Mallory can handle this without you. They're both happy, but the fact that you're not makes it hard for them to enjoy their happiness. I'm sure you've realized by now that they feel guilty for finding love knowing you haven't."

She knew he was right. The girls were very protective of her. Kat hadn't been trying to run off with Ken on their off days. Mallory wasn't really bothered by the fact that Richard hadn't been around the last few months. However, she'd seen how happy they were when they had finally seen their men. He was right. Kat had given in way too easily when she'd found out Kal was going to be spending the week with her.

"I don't want you wasting time on me." She was trying to protect him.

"I'm a big boy. I can handle it."

She looked up at him. He was so serious she wanted to give in.

"Just say yes. Trust me, I'll make it worth it." He hoped she would give in. He had already mapped out a plan. All he needed now was her approval. "Say yes, Simone."

She wanted to. "I thought I had time to think about it?" She tried to back away, but he didn't let her.

"You do." Kal watched Simone's movements and knew he had won this battle. A few weeks at home with his mother, and she would give in to what everyone wanted. His mother would convince her. "I want to take you home with me. My mother's birthday is around the corner, and I want you with me." He gave her a little space. "I'm sure you're gonna love her."

Simone thought for a second. "I'll go, but you have to promise not to tell them about my condition, and Miss Jenna has to go with me."

Kal gave her a brilliant smile. That had seemed too easy, but he was excited. "I promise I won't say a word about it."

She loved how happy her decision had made him. Kal turned her and started for his room. He'd made her a promise not to tell her secret, but he hadn't told her they had already known. Richard had already told them. He felt a little guilty for not telling her that—but by any means necessary. "So, I think you should get married."

Simone stopped and turned around. She was confused. "Excuse me?"

Kal plastered a serious look on his face. "My older brother is single and looking for a wife." He lost it at the expression on Simone's face.

What in the hell? She almost fell for his stupid joke. "You jerk." She turned and started for her room.

He quickly retrieved her. "No, no, no. This way. I need help washing."

She struggled as he hoisted her over his shoulder. "I deserve a sponge bath, nurse."

She bit his back as he carried her into his bathroom.

"Oh goodness. Are you still hungry?" He placed her on her feet, closing and locking the door. She knew that look in his eyes. Oh shit. What had she done? He tilted his head and smiled at her. She could see the excitement she'd caused with what she'd done.

"My grandma said Richard wasn't the one."

He frowned at her.

"She never mentioned you, but I don't think she would approve."

His eyebrows rose as that smile of his drove her crazy. He didn't care—this was gonna happen. Oh well, she'd waited long enough. Mister Right was whomever she deemed him to be, so why not Kal? She took a step back and pulled her top over her head. To her surprise, he stopped her.

"I'm gonna hop in the shower. You should take a bath." He moved by her, kicking off his sneakers.

"What the hell? So you don't…"

He turned so abruptly it scared her. "I said I'm going to shower."

She frowned at him. She was sure she'd read the signs correctly. He wanted her; she could see the bulge in his damn pants.

"Look, I don't want to tell our grandkids that the first time I made love to their grandma was in the shower. It won't be a very romantic story."

Simone's mouth flew open. "What the hell…why would you tell your grandkids about you having sex with me?" She was so confused. What the fuck grandkids was he talking about?

He slipped into the shower still half dressed. She just stood there, watching as he threw his wet jeans out of the shower.

"What the hell just happened?" She decided to go shower in her room. The situation hadn't turned out the way she'd thought it would. She wondered what she had done to change his mood. As she entered her bathroom, the words came back to her. Did he say their grandkids? No. That's not what he'd said. She must have misheard him. Simone decided to take her time in the shower then have a drink before bed. Miss Jenna was out at the movies with Felix and Braxton, so there was no one to scold her. Maybe two drinks after the evening she'd had. "I think I deserve two."

She didn't hear Kal enter her bathroom. He took a seat on her sink and waited for her to finish. Simone decided to sing. To hell with Kal—and Richard, for that matter. He had rejected her as well. A sadness came over her, and she found herself envying Kat and Mallory. No one ever turned them down.

"Do you plan on coming out, or should I come in after you?"

Simone was startled. "Oh Jesus! You scared me, you asshole." She hadn't meant to call him that, but it came out. She heard him groan, then the door to her shower flew open.

"Jerk, asshole, what other insults do you wish to hurl at me?" He was standing there, a towel wrapped around his waist. She didn't even bother to cover herself.

"Move! You scared me." She pushed past him and grabbed her towel. "What the hell are you doing in here anyway?" She sounded a lot madder than she was.

"You don't follow directions very well. I distinctly remember saying take a bath." He sighed as if he were disappointed in her. "You should work on listening." He turned and walked back into her room. Simone couldn't believe the nerve. He must not have known who the hell he was talking to. She wasn't one of his damn harem girls. She was going to have to put him in his damn place. She bolted into the room like a torpedo.

"Who the hell do you think you are? Better yet, who the hell do you think you're talking to? I am not one of your concubines. Now get the hell out of my room." She was pissed.

It didn't help her mood when Kal jumped onto her bed with a smile. He nodded for her to get in. It was like he wasn't even listening to her. He patted a spot next to him on the bed.

"Get out of my damn room!"

Kal didn't budge. He laid there staring at her.

"Come here."

Her chest was heaving up and down.

"Please." He didn't look up at her. He didn't want to laugh, but if he looked at the way she was reacting to him, he probably would. "Let's talk, please."

She didn't want to talk. She wanted him out. She was about to unleash hell upon him when a knock sounded at the door. Kal jumped from the bed and ran to the door. A young man was standing on the other side of the door. He'd brought champagne, strawberries, and cheese. Simone threw her hands in the air and headed for her closet.

"I'm getting out of here." She was too tired to deal with Kal but was glad he'd pissed her off. She didn't feel like confronting her rejection by him earlier. She grabbed a sundress and matching jacket and quickly pulled them on.

"Leaving me?"

Simone turned to see Kal standing in the doorway. She rolled her eyes and continued selecting a pair of shoes. She knew which one she'd wanted to put on until he interrupted.

"I think it's best. I would rather spend what's left of my life out of prison."

Kal laughed at her comment. She was feisty, and he loved it. "We need to talk." He didn't want to talk but they needed to.

"Nope, we don't. I have nothing to say to you, sir. Now, if you will excuse me, I am going home." She slipped on some sandals and stalked over to him. "Move."

He tilted his head with a frown. He was serious again, but she just wanted to leave.

"Please." He didn't like this at all. For a moment, she thought she'd seen a flicker of disappointment in his face.

"Just because you've discovered the word please doesn't mean you'll get your way—not with me anyway." She was stubborn like his mother.

"Enough." He reached for her and threw her over his shoulder. A few seconds later, he was throwing her on the bed.

"I swear..." She tried to protest, but he wouldn't let her. He placed a hand over her mouth.

"I will tie you up if I have to." He held both of her hands firmly on her chest. "I would like to talk."

She was fuming.

"Please."

How many times had he said that damn word? He slowly removed his hand from her mouth. The motion of her chest was inviting. Maybe talking could wait. He bent and kissed her, but Simone wasn't having any of that. She bit him the first chance she got.

"Damn it." He pulled back.

"I am not one of your..."

He kissed her again with the same results. "Ouch!" This time it hurt a lot more than before.

She'd bitten him in the same spot. She was really mad. That didn't stop him from trying again, and again she bit him. This time his lip started to bleed. As if he hadn't felt her bite him the last few times, he tried again.

"Stop! Your lip is bleeding." She sounded concerned.

He could feel the stinging in his lower lip. "You did that." He could see regret in her eyes.

"You should have stopped."

He smiled. "You could have turned away."

She scowled at him.

"I just wanted to talk, honestly."

She tried to wiggle from his grip. "Let go of me so I can clean your lip."

He hated he had put her in this position, but now he knew just how to manipulate her. Her heart may have been defective, as she'd put it, but it was full of love and compassion. She couldn't stand to see people she cared about hurt.

He didn't move. "Let's go to Vegas and get married—tonight."

A drop of blood fell onto her chin.

"Oh shit. Sorry." He sat up and wiped the blood from his lip. How freaking bad was it? He sucked his lip into his mouth and applied pressure.

"Shit. I'm sorry. I shouldn't have done that." She felt bad. He was bleeding because she had lost her temper. "Let me see."

He turned away. "Don't act like you didn't hear me."

She had heard him, but he couldn't have meant it. There was no way his family would allow them to elope. "I heard you." She scooted closer to him. "But I enjoy my life." Simone patted him on the back. "You forget who you are?"

He turned to her. "I control my life. My parents either deal with it, or they lose their sweet little boy."

She rolled her eyes at him.

"I'm serious. I want you."

She shook her head at him. "I'm a lost cause."

He didn't care about that. She was tired of explaining this to him. "I know, but I want whatever you've got left—for us."

She felt her stupid heart ache. She wanted that too, but was it worth it? "Okay. What if I say yes and we do this, then what? We hide out on a beach somewhere until I pass?" She felt tears. She didn't feel like crying, but she wanted this. Knowing it couldn't happen, she still wanted it. She deserved it.

"Just say yes and find out." He was smiling again. "We can do it and keep it our little secret until you're ready to tell everyone."

132

She felt a rush as she mulled it over in her head. Kat and Mal would kill her when they found out. She would have a field day with them.

"I know you want to say yes. We can go and be back by morning. No one would even know we were gone."

She giggled. "Okay." She shocked both him and herself. She was terrified and excited.

"Then I can wait until after you're officially mine." He pulled her into his arms and kissed her. Ignoring the stinging in his lip, he claimed what was his. "I'm gonna get dressed and call the pilot. Make sure you don't forget."

She was puzzled. "What?" She waited for him to explain, but he got up and walked to the door.

"After we're married, you never have to wear underwear if you don't want to, but tonight you need to." He left as she started to laugh. He had won this battle. If he never won another, it wouldn't matter—this was all worth it. Simone was his.

*****

Kal and Simone had done it. They had kept their secret from their friends and family for over a week—at least that's what they thought. Richard was throwing one of his parties now that the girls were back from their trip. He'd noticed Kal's increasing protectiveness of Simone and knew something had changed. He hadn't addressed it with Kal, but he was curious.

"I always love your little mix and mingles. So full of…well, them." Kal pointed at the mayor and his wife talking to his older brother. He hated anything that put him in the spotlight as the prince he didn't want to be.

"At least they've left you alone tonight." Richard knew the real reason Kal was irritated. He had been separated from Simone almost all night. She'd been secretly making business meetings with people who'd taken the party as an opportunity to employ her and the girls. Kal did not like any of this. He would have to get her away from all of it soon.

"I can always cause a distraction, and you can kidnap Simone." Kal almost spit his champagne on a passing guest.

"Kidnap?" He gave Richard a puzzling look. He knew his brother wasn't fond of secrets, but this one wasn't his to tell though he'd wanted to. Richard didn't seem as friendly tonight as he had before. Something was bothering him. "I don't think I need to do all that." Kal elbowed Richard and got a chuckle out of him.

"Well, maybe you should get her to kidnap you before the vultures start to circle closer." Richard's tone was sour. He'd been in a mood all night. Kal wondered what had gotten him in such a funk.

"I think you're the one in need of kidnapping. What's gotten into you? This morning you were in a much better disposition." He knew Richard wouldn't tell him right now if it wasn't important.

"Just tired." He was lying but Kal wasn't worried. He would find out soon enough. As they stood talking, the mayor's wife sashayed their way.

"Jesus, here comes one of your vultures now." They both bent their heads and snickered like bad boys at a school dance. The woman was dragging a younger one behind her. Richard knew what was about to happen. He stepped away from Kal as the women came to a stop in front of them.

"Richard, honey, how are you?" Though she spoke to Richard, her eyes were glued to Kal's face. Richard winked at the poor girl she had dragged over with her.

"I'm much better now—and you?"

The woman giggled, causing Kal to give Richard a look that made him laugh.

"Have you met my brother Kal?"

This time Kal slapped him in the back. The sound made the women gasp. Richard knew Kal wanted to kick him.

"Hello, ladies. I was starting to wonder if he'd ever introduce us." He plastered a beautiful fake smile on his face and took both their hands. He placed a kiss on each and bowed. "It is my pleasure." Richard did the best he could to keep from cracking up.

"Oh, you're such a gentleman." The woman was blushing so hard Richard couldn't help snorting. "I'm Loise by the way. We've met before, but you may not have remembered. It was a few months ago."

Richard held his breath. He knew what was coming. "Did we? I would have remembered meeting someone as beautiful as you. I never forget a beautiful woman. Her name maybe, but never her."

Richard had to cough to keep from laughing.

"Are you all right, Richard?" Loise tried to act concerned, but he wasn't buying it. The woman was as phony as they got. He was enjoying Kal toying with her. She was eating out of his hands like the horse she was.

"I'm fine." He wanted to leave Kal to his fate, but he knew he'd pay for it later. He wasn't in the mood to deal with Kal's retaliation tactics tonight—not when Mallory was upset with him. "I think I do need another drink though." He smiled at Loise, causing her to blush.

"I think you've had enough for now." Kal threw an arm around him and whispered in his ear. "If you leave me with these two, I swear I'll have you castrated."

Richard's laugh almost scared the two in front of them.

"You boys are terrible. What are you whispering about?" Loise seemed a bit put off at their lack of attention to her and the woman with her.

"It seems I drink too much." Kal nodded in agreement with Richard's statement. Just as they were about to remove themselves from the situation, another older woman and her companion walked up.

"Oh, this just keeps getting better." He was getting irritated. As soon as he got away from these parasites, he would find a quiet place to drink.

"Oh, Richard, we've been looking all over for you." Joelle walked over and planted a kiss on Richard's cheek. "And this must be that roguish Prince Kalu." She tried to curtsey, but Kal stopped her.

"Oh, you don't have to do that." Kal didn't like that at all. The younger women suddenly became all smiles. Loise didn't seem at all pleased with Joelle's barging in on her territory.

"Oh, I forgot your people are different. How do your subjects greet you?"

Kal's smile fell from his face. Richard folded an arm across his chest and covered his mouth with the other.

"For god's sakes, woman, have some manners." Loise was clearly upset. Not that she was less of a snob, but she didn't want to lose her audience with the prince. His family was oil rich, and that was all that mattered. If she could get close enough to him, she could pawn her niece off on the poor prince. The girl would be set for life. But it seems Joelle had the same idea.

"Which one of my people are you referring to, my African jungle swinging ape mother's people or my brutish sand monkey father's people?" Kal flashed the horrified woman a smile. He had overheard a conversation earlier between Joelle and a few other women. Though he'd plan to ignore their rude ignorant comments, she'd come to him.

"One of the luxuries my barbaric father provided my brothers and I was education—the best of it. From an early age, he insisted that our mother teach us to speak different languages. A rule in our household was that we learn something new and long-lasting every year." Richard had heard this speech several times. "My African jungle swinging ape mother speaks thirty different languages. She has a PhD in language studies and also in education. The woman has traveled to every country in Africa, and yes, there are countries on the continent of Africa." He took a breath and relaxed. "My barbaric father has a PhD in business and horticulture. Now, while he isn't half as educated as his wife, he's still one of the most intelligent men I've ever encountered. My two brothers…" Kal stopped when he heard Richard clearing his throat. "Pardon me, my three brothers and I were sent to the best schools. However, we had to earn our places into those schools. So, I'm more than happy to inform you that we are more than just jungle and sand animals."

Joelle was shaking. She was sure Kal was on the other side of the room when she had engaged in the conversation that was threatening to ruin her now.

"I'm so—"

Kal stopped her. He didn't say anything. Instead, he signed what he wanted to tell her. Richard translated.

"He says no need to apologize for being who you are, and by the way, he reads lips very well, and as you can see, he signs too."

Loise and her companion stood frozen as they watched. Kal waved one of the waiting staff over. He was carrying several glasses of champagne. Kal relieved him of the tray then offered everyone a glass including the waiter. When they all had taken their drinks, he offered a toast.

"To being classy." He took a sip of his champagne. "Something we teach our barbaric ape women from an early age." He never took his eyes off Joelle. She was pale with embarrassment. Richard wondered where all the blood had gone, for there was none in her face. Kal took a step back and bowed. "You ladies must excuse me. I think my wife is in need of my assistance." He winked at the younger women and dragged Richard behind him as he left.

"You're getting soft little brother. You didn't offer to behead any of them."

Kal laughed. He knew Richard, and Richard knew him. The wife comment would be addressed soon enough. They walked past a group of chattering women who stopped talking immediately and plastered their best smile on for them. Richard nodded at them, but Kal kept walking. He didn't feel like mingling anymore tonight.

"How have we managed to survive these things as long as we have?" Kal ignored everyone as he moved across the room. He'd spotted what he wanted and was focused on that. Richard knew exactly where he was headed, so as they got closer, he sidestepped Kal and grabbed Simone.

"May I have this dance, young lady."

Simone smiled and took his hand. She was grateful for the save because she was tired of talking to the man in front of her. Kal wasn't at all pleased especially when Richard smiled and winked at him. He wanted to get the hell out of there before someone else pissed him off. He did not feel like showing Simone the other side of her husband just yet.

"Why are you messing with him?" She smiled when she saw Richard making faces at an angry Kal. She loved that he had someone he could be silly with. Richard was often too serious for her taste. He was different when he was with Kal; they somehow seemed to mellow each other out.

"So is this your thing now? Collecting husbands secretly?"

Simone stopped moving and looked up at him.

"He didn't tell me. You just did." She knew he would find out, but she wasn't ready for this.

"I asked him to keep it a secret."

He leaned forward and whispered in her ear. "Haven't you learned by now that you can't keep secrets from me?"

She felt her knees go weak.

"Believe me, if I know, so does his father." He stepped back and nodded at Kal to take his bride.

Simone felt sick. Kal stepped in and saw Simone was looking a bit pale. The worried look on her face made him look to Richard for answers.

"What did you say to her?" He was no longer amused. He didn't like that Richard had upset Simone. Just as he was about to let his displeasure be known, a woman burst into the ballroom screaming. Richard turned quickly to see one of Simone's new models running toward them. He went to meet her. The woman was out of breath.

"What's wrong?" He was genuinely concerned. Was it Mallory? He glanced around the room quickly and spotted her heading their way.

"Monica!" She could barely speak. She was in tears. Simone pulled the girl into her arms.

"What about Monica?" When she didn't answer, Simone gave her a little shake. "Where's Monica?" She was terrified. Kumiko wasn't easily scared. If she was this hysterical, something terrible had happened.

"She's dead. She's dead." Kumiko's accent was a little thick, but her words were clear. Richard pulled her from Simone.

"Where is she?" He needed to see for himself.

"Cars." Kumiko was shaking. Richard instructed Mallory and Simone to stay inside while he and Kal bolted for the door. God, he hoped Kumiko was wrong. He tried to catch Kal as they darted through rows of cars. Where the hell was she? Was she in one of them? As they searched every vehicle in the area, others joined in the search. There were so many damn cars.

"She's here!" Someone called from across the lot.

Everyone made their way toward the screaming woman that was standing next to the body. Kal was the first to reach her. He quickly pulled Monica's lifeless body from under the car. He checked her pulse and breathing. Richard came to a stop and waited for Kal to perform his task.

"She has a pulse but barely breathing." Kal lifted her as Richard cleared the way for him. He knew there were at least three doctors at his party.

"Get the doc!" he yelled as they made it to the house. Felix was already on it. He was dragging one of the doctors behind him as he headed toward Richard. They all came to a stop inside the doorway. Kal placed Monica on the floor and made way for the doctor. "Call…" He was about to give Felix another order, but the man stopped him.

"They're on their way." He placed a hand on Richard's shoulder. "The helicopter is ready if you just want to take her." Felix was very calm. He was used to emergencies like this. Military life had numbed him to matters like this. "I'll get the girls to the hospital." Richard trusted him to do what he said.

"I think the helicopter will be a much better idea." The doctor stood and waited for Richard's confirmation. He wasted no time.

"Let's go." He stepped aside when Kal retrieved Monica and proceeded him out the door. A young man was waiting in a golf cart to take them to the aircraft.

*****

It was almost five in the morning when the doctors came out to speak with Richard. Everyone was worried. They pulled him aside and spoke to him alone. He didn't look at all pleased. Simone was getting impatient. She needed to know Monica was okay. No one had said anything to them about her condition. When they'd arrived at the hospital, Monica was already in surgery. Simone and Mallory were the only two allowed to stay. Kat and Sylver had been ordered to stay with Felix and the other girls for their safety.

Simone decided it was time to find out what the hell was going on. "Richard, what's going on?" She waited for him to come to her.

"She's still in surgery. Everything is going well."

She knew something was wrong. His facial expression told her enough.

"What?" She was getting more aggressive. "Tell me, goddamn it!"

Kal placed his hands on her shoulder to try to comfort her, but she shrugged it off.

"She's going to be okay, but she has a very bad head injury. They're going to try to drain the blood from her…." Kal put a hand up to stop him. Simone was swaying, and Mallory wasn't doing as well. "You ladies should stay here until she gets out of surgery."

Mallory couldn't believe he was going to leave. "Are you leaving?"

He didn't feel like dealing with Mallory right now. He had tried to keep his anger under control, but things weren't looking any better as he thought they would. Mallory stood before him, and he could see she was pissed. He had to get out of the hospital before they threw him out. He needed to find out who had done this to Monica at his home. Someone was feeling bold enough to hurt one of his girls while he was right there.

"Shouldn't you wait until we know something?" Mallory looked tired and fragile. Had it been her someone had hurt, he would have already found them. Monica deserved the same attention.

He didn't say anything; he simply kissed her on the cheek and walked around her. Kal followed silently. Simone knew where they were going and what they were going to do. She wholeheartedly approved of whatever they unleashed on the bastard that hurt Monica. She went to Mallory.

"We will be okay. They have to go before that idiot detective comes back." Simone hugged her friend. She hoped Mallory would understand one day, but right now she just needed to stand back. Richard needed to work, and she was getting in the way. Mallory pulled away from Simone.

"Where's he going?" She waited for Simone to take a seat then sat with her. "He should be here. What else could he have to do right now?" Simone rolled her head around, trying to relieve some of the tension in her neck. She didn't want to tell Mallory what she knew was going to happen. Maybe she needed to see for herself.

"Maybe you should go. If you want to know Richard, then you need to go."

Mallory gave her a confused look. What in the world was she talking about?

"If you want to spend the rest of your life with this man, then you need to know what and who he is outside of your little love nest." She was serious. "Richard is a complex man. The man you've been spending time with is his relaxed self."

Mallory scoffed. Richard? Relaxed? Was Simone talking about her Richard? The man had a vicious temper that he didn't even try to conceal.

"Go, Mal. Go find out who you're trying to spend the rest of your life with." Simone sighed. She knew Richard and Kal would find whoever had done this to Monica before the police even had a clue. "Go."

Mallory was hesitant, but she stood and ran toward the elevators. Simone said a silent prayer. "Lord, give her the strength she'll need." She watched Mal disappear into an elevator.

Richard was not at all happy to see Mallory. He was even more pissed when she insisted on going with him and Kal on their little trip. He had paid that ass of a detective a hefty sum to back off and let him handle the situation. What he was going to do to the bastard that had hurt Monica wasn't gonna earn him any points with this woman. What if she left him? He couldn't let the disrespect go unpunished, but was it worth losing her? He shook his head to clear his thoughts. Mallory would have to wait. He had something to do.

"We're here sir." Felix pulled the car up to the country club entrance. Richard looked over at Mallory before exiting the car. He stood outside the doors as she and Kal caught up to him.

"Do not open your mouth."

Mallory knew the command was directed to her and her alone. She felt Felix's hand on her back and jumped. She didn't know what the hell was about to happen, but she was scared. What if Richard got hurt? She followed them, not knowing what she was walking into. Felix stayed close to her as he had been instructed.

"Relax, he knows what he's doing." Felix's voice was soft and comforting.

Mal held the hand he had offered her tight. She started praying in her head. They walked to a private dining area marked MEMBERS ONLY. Richard stopped at a beautifully carved door and nodded at Kal before bursting in, Kal in tow. The laughter in the room ceased immediately.

"Gentlemen, don't get up. This is gonna be quick."

Mallory recognized a few faces. She had seen most of them at the party. The mayor was one of those faces.

"Richard. I didn't know you were a member." The mayor was short and chubby. Mallory did not like the look of him. He looked shady sitting here, smoking this damn early. It was barely nine in the morning, and they were drinking.

"I'm not. Not really a golfer."

Richard walked to a showcase and stood admiring the clubs inside. "These look expensive." He opened the case and pulled a club from it.

Mallory had no knowledge of golf, so she had no idea what the damn thing was called. It was the largest one in the bunch. She wondered what the hell he was going to do with it. These men were some powerhouses in their field.

The mayor spoke up again. "Those are going to be auctioned off at our next fundraiser." He looked worried as did several of the other men.

Mallory glanced at Kal, who was standing in front of a young man at the large table. He was staring daggers at the man, who refused to return his gaze. She watched the scene unfold as if it were a movie.

Richard turned to address the group of men. "So all of you were at my house last night."

The men looked at each other as if they needed to confirm with each other.

"But I'm only here for one of you." Richard jumped onto the table. He walked over to the young man who was very much aware he was the reason for the visit. His guilt was ever present on his face. Richard squatted in front of him. "It seems no one taught you the rules."

No one at the table moved, not even the guilty party. He sat still. The shock on the faces of these men scared Mallory just a bit. Why the hell were they so afraid of Richard?

Felix took a step in front of her as if he were shielding her from something dangerous.

"You not only disrespected me, but you hurt one of my girls."

Mallory could see the anger dripping from Richard's face. She reached up and held her necklace in her hand.

"I don't care why you did it. I don't wanna know what you were on, and I damn sure don't want any apologies." The last part was directed at someone who had raised a hand to get Richard's attention. "There are rules to this game that you want to play—rules and consequences." He stood and turned to the older man sitting next to the one he'd just spoken to. "If someone came to your house and raped your daughter then smashed her face and practically beat her into a coma, what would you do?"

The group seemed even more shocked. They were all present last night when Monica was found.

"I would kill him." The man did not hesitate with his response.

Richard nodded. He directed his attention back to the guilty young man.

"I'm not gonna kill you. I'm gonna give you a choice." He leaned on the club as if it were a cane. "You can cut it off, or I can show you what happens when you fuck with me."

For the first time, the young man's head came up, and they made eye contact.

"Cut off what?" He wasn't sure what Richard was asking. Hell, Mallory didn't know what the hell Richard was talking about either. Kal was standing behind the poor man.

"You're not very, smart are you?" Richard's smile was evil.

Mallory held on to Felix, but she couldn't look away. What did Richard want him to do?

"I'm not cutting off shit." The man tried to stand, but Kal stopped him. Mallory wondered why no one else was trying to help him.

"Like I said—not very smart." Richard was serious again. "I think I'll give a little refresher on what happens when you gentlemen forget who I am. Show me the hand you hit her with."

The young man shook his head. He didn't want to participate willingly, so Kal helped him. Whatever he was doing to the man was painful enough to cause a loud noise to echo through the room. His hand slowly stretched toward Richard.

"Now make the same fist you hit her with."

The man did as he was told though Mallory was sure Kal was the reason he was doing it. She watched in horror as Richard lined up and took a strong swing with the club. The sound that filled the room had everyone at the table and her terrified. The young man had pulled the hand back so quickly she couldn't see it. The blood on the table and the finger lying in the mayor's plate told her all she wanted to know.

"Damn that wasn't a bad swing."

The poor man was howling in pain. Mallory unconsciously dug her nails into poor Felix's arm.

"Yeah, it needs work."

Kal was making jokes? What the hell was wrong with them? Kal moved to one side as Richard kicked the man onto the floor. He jumped down and stood over him. He was going to kill him. Mallory had to do something. Before she could move, Richard took another swing at the man, catching him in his ribs. Another blood-curdling scream filled the room. She had to stop him. Without thinking, she moved from behind Felix as Richard positioned himself for another swing. He was slowly torturing everyone.

"Stop!"

The look on Richard's face as he looked up at her was the scariest fucking thing she'd ever seen. She tried to hold it together as she walked to him and his victim. All the other men in the room watched as she knelt at the young fellow's head. "I'm not saving you. I have a friend whose face had to be reconstructed because of you. She's one of the sweetest people I've ever met, and you may have destroyed her." She ignored everyone as her anger rose. She had seen Monica before they'd taken her to the helicopter. "Apparently you weren't aware of the shit you were getting yourself into." She could see the pain taking its toll on the man. He was gonna pass out. "You obviously come from money, and she's gonna need lots of care. Dead men can't pay bills." She stood. "I'll leave it up to you and Richard to work out the details of your payments. Understand this, though, if ever you miss a payment or attempt to hurt her again, I'll turn you into alligator shit." She didn't make eye contact with Richard. "I'll be in the car." She turned and walked to the door. Her heart was trying to break out of her chest. She was sure she was gonna have a heart attack in the car. Mallory heard Kal laugh as she exited the room.

"I hope you plan on marrying her because I think I just fell in love." Kal laughed at the look he was getting from Richard.

"Get this piece of shit to the hospital." He threw the golf club to the nearest man. "Clean that up for me. I'll take the whole set." He wasn't at all shocked at the smile on the man's face at his proposal. He was certain if he had killed the idiot passed out on the floor, they would have buried the body on the course for him as long as they were getting his money. He turned and took one last look around the room. "Are we clear?"

Everyone nodded in agreement. They all knew the woman had tamed the Richard they were used to—not that they were complaining. Had that been the old Richard, the kid would be dead, and they all would have been paying for socializing with him. He had a temper that scared even his grandfather. The old man was happy when Richard chose to distance himself from the family and make his own way through life. They watched as he and Kal left the room, Felix following.

*****

Richard was shocked to find a note on the windshield when he got to the car. Mallory had left. She hadn't waited like she said she would. It was late afternoon, and she was nowhere to be found. He tried calling everyone, but no one had seen her. He knew Simone had known where she was but wasn't saying. If Mallory was truly missing, Simone would have been worried. She wasn't. Richard decided to have a few drinks at the cabin by himself, but Kal had barged in as he always did. They were finishing their second bottle of scotch when Mallory walked in. Both men tried to sit still.

"Ooh, I think you're in trouble. She looks pissed." Kal looked over at Richard. "Fix your face. You look scared."

He and Richard started to laugh. Mallory shook her head in disappointment. She turned and called Felix.

"Can you take Kal back to the house please?"

Kal stumbled to his feet. "Hey, you can't boss me around, little bitty person." He was slurring his speech. Turning to Richard, he said, "She can't tell me what to do. I'll leave when I damn well please." He was smiling at Richard.

"Simone wants you back at the house." Mallory's words slowly penetrated his fog.

"Well, that changes things." He tried to help Richard to his feet. They were both too drunk to be of any help to each other, but somehow Richard was standing.

"I'm going to go get my wife pregnant. Be careful with this one. I don't want you to be crocodile shit."

Felix quickly caught the laughing man when he stumbled.

"Hey, Richard, if it gets bad, jump out the window and run to the woods. She won't follow you."

Mallory tried not to laugh. Felix practically had to drag Kal out of the cabin. She could hear him shouting horrible advice to Richard as he was stuffed into the car.

"Where have you been?" Richard speech was slurred as well. She shook her head as she turned to him. He was serious, but she didn't care about that. He looked hurt.

"I had to think." She tried to walk past him, but he stepped in front of her. "There's something I want to tell you, but not while you're like this."

He squinted at her. Whatever it was, she would tell him now. He wasn't very patient at the moment.

"What?" His voice was low but demanding.

She didn't want to fight with him. "I need to get cleaned up for bed." She looked up at him and regretted it. As angry as he was, she could feel his sadness. "Richard, it can wait until morning."

He didn't move. The man was as stubborn as she was. "Can I please take a shower first?" She pleaded, but he wasn't going to budge.

"What is it?" He would make her tell him. He wasn't so drunk that she couldn't talk to him. "Tell me now." He raised his voice just enough for her to understand he wasn't letting it go.

"Damn you." She stepped back from him. "I haven't decided yet."

He was barely standing up straight. How could he understand what she wanted to talk to him about?

"Decided what?" He was in pain. She could see that. He thought she was leaving him.

"I was afraid of you today. I mean I've been afraid before, but not like this." She went over to the fireplace. The heat felt good on her body. He didn't move. "The man standing on that table today—he was gonna kill someone." She tried not to look at him. "I need to know that's not you. I mean I know you can be sweet and amazing, but that person you were this morning was scary as hell. Your face alone was enough to strike fear in the hearts of those bastards, but you had to terrify them—terrify me." She felt the tears she'd promised to keep at bay flowing.

"I asked you not to come." He was still standing in the same spot.

"I had to." She slid down the wall to the floor. "I needed to see the other side of you." She wiped her face in her sleeve. "I wanted to spend my life with you, Richard, but things have changed." She couldn't look at him. He came to stand above her. "By myself, I'm all yours, but I'm pregnant." She felt like she was on fire. "I can't raise a child like this."

Richard dropped to his knees so hard she reached out for him. He caught her hands in his.

"You're pregnant?" Richard whispered. He seemed to have sobered up a bit at the news.

She didn't want to tell him like this, but it was done. "Yes. I was going to tell you last night, but everything got so crazy."

He pulled her gently into a hug. She held on tight to him.

"It's gonna be okay." He didn't really know how to feel. Mallory was his, but he had to adjust his life for her and the child. Then it happened—the memory he hadn't wanted to share with her resurfaced. He pushed her back from him and sat staring at her. Mallory knew something was wrong.

"Is something wrong?"

He was serious. Something in the look he was giving her scared her a bit.

"It's okay if you're not ready. I will be fine until you are, but I'm keeping this child." She was crying again.

"There was someone else who got pregnant a while ago."

Mallory wiped the tears from her eyes. She tried to tune everything out but his voice.

"She was just a woman I used for pleasure every now and then." He bent his head as if he were ashamed. "I thought I was being careful, but somehow she got pregnant."

Mallory didn't care about all this. She just wanted to know what happened to the kid. Was he already a father? She felt a bit of jealousy.

"She wanted to get married, but I wasn't ready for that. I told her I needed to think about it." He looked up, and Mallory saw the unshed tears in his eyes. His hands were clenched into fists. "I promised her I would give her whatever she needed, but I wasn't ready to get married. I bought her the beach house she wanted and made sure she had everything she wanted." He cleared his throat, but it didn't feel like he'd accomplished the task he'd wanted to. "I went away on business and took a little time to think about what I wanted. I wanted my son to have his father in his life no matter what. I wanted to be a good father, and if that meant marrying her, then that's what it had to be." He tried clearing his throat again.

"I decided I would marry her. I had a ring made and came home, ready to give her what she'd wanted all along." A stream of tears ran down his face.

Mallory couldn't just sit there. She crawled into his arms and held him.

"She told me she'd terminated the pregnancy a week prior. Five months, and she got rid of him."

Mallory couldn't believe it.

"She said she had waited long enough for me to make up my mind, but since I couldn't decide to be a good father, she'd taken matters into her own hands." He was shaking.

Mallory wanted to comfort him. "I could never do that to you or my child." She sat back from him. "I can't explain what she did, but I can promise you I am going to do whatever I have to in order to protect my baby."

He was frowning at her. "Including leaving me."

She knew he wasn't asking, but she responded. "Yes, Richard—if I have to."

He knew she would say that, but he wasn't going to let that happen. "Over my dead body." The calm in his voice scared her more than the words he had spoken. "Or yours."

Mallory couldn't believe what she was hearing. She jumped to her feet.

"Don't you threaten me, Richard Embers!" She felt a rage that quickly overtook her fear. "I am not some gold-digging bitch that you can treat however you please." She was pissed. "I hate you right now!" She couldn't stand the thought of leaving him, but she would have to. He was not the man she wanted to raise her child with. She stormed around him and into the bedroom. She would shower and get the hell out of his cabin. She threw a few clothes into a bag and grabbed an outfit. Stripping down to her panties, she walked into the bathroom and started the shower.

"Leaving?" She turned to see Richard standing in the doorway, smiling. This made her furious. She ignored him and continued what she was doing.

"Are we going to talk or…"

Mallory slammed the shower door closed behind her. She had nothing she wanted to talk to him about. She had already said what needed to be said. She wasn't at all happy when he stepped into her shower.

"I know you don't think I'm about to…" He pushed her against the shower wall. His body pressed against hers. She could smell whatever he'd been drinking seeping through his pores. She didn't struggle, knowing she wouldn't win. She waited.

"So you hate me now?"

She didn't answer.

"I don't believe that for a second." He chuckled when she dodged his kiss. "What do you think is gonna happen, Mallory?"

She didn't feel like engaging.

"You think you'd just tell me you're pregnant and I would what?" He waited for her to answer, but she didn't. "Answer me." His voice was calm, but she knew he was anything but calm.

There was nothing she could say to him. She kept her head low and listened. Neither of them spoke for a bit. Then he placed a hand under her chin and lifted her head. When their eyes met, she didn't like what she saw.

"I'm not willing to lose you or my child, but I can't just walk away. I've built something here."

Mallory closed her eyes, and the tears started streaming down her face. "I know." She knew she had to leave him—just like her mother had her father. He may have loved her in his own weird way, but it wasn't enough. She wouldn't raise her child with a man like him. She would raise her child alone if she had to—but not like this.

"Would you like to talk now?" He hated himself for making her feel the way she had earlier. This wasn't the life she wanted—not for her or their child. He had promised her whatever she'd wanted, and he would give her just that. "Maybe we should save the talking for tomorrow when I'm more fit for it."

She decided one more night with him wouldn't hurt. She did love him, but she needed more than this. Richard knew what he had to do if he wanted to keep her. For her he would sacrifice everything. She turned off the shower, knowing he had no interest in it now. He lifted her into his arms and carried her to their bed.

"I don't like your last name," he said before kissing her.

*****

Richard woke with a headache from hell. He knew Kal was not sharing his pain because he could hear the man's voice louder than ever in the other room. He rolled over and found he was alone in bed.

"Hey, lovebirds, it's damn near afternoon. Are you planning on joining the living?" Kal came bursting into the room. He noticed his friend wasn't looking at all pleased to see him. "Hungover?" He snickered as he watched Richard drag on a pair of sweats.

"Have you seen her?" When he noticed the frown on Kal's face, he knew.

Richard sat on the bed, trying to gather his thoughts. He'd known she was too calm last night. He should have taken her back to the house. "She's gone." He shook his head in frustration. Mallory had slipped away from him.

"What are you talking about?" Kal took a seat at the foot of the bed. "She spoke to Sy this morning. Maybe they went for lunch or something." Kal remembered Simone saying she had a meeting, but she never mentioned Mallory. "What makes you think she's skipped out on you?" Kal knew not to poke fun at Richard right now. He was hungover and worried.

"She told me she didn't want this life." He took a steadying breath. She was gone. He could feel it. "She's pregnant."

Kal's head whipped around so quickly Richard heard his bones pop. "What?" Kal was shocked. "I don't understand. I thought you were going to ask her." He liked Mallory, but he knew what it would do to Richard if she had truly left him. He couldn't have that—not again.

"She said she'd raise our child alone if she had to." He ran his hands over his face. "I told her over my or her dead body." He was regretting every word now that he had time to think about it. He never meant to hurt her. He wasn't thinking straight last night.

"She's not Kim. Mallory is not Kim." Kal hated saying that name. "Why are we sitting here? She couldn't have gotten far." He stood and walked over to Richard. "Let's go. Let's find your woman."

When Richard didn't budge, he squatted before him. He could see hopelessness in the man's face, and that was not like Richard. The man was a fighter, but he looked defeated sitting there on the bed. "Do you believe in karma?"

Richard looked up at Kal with a frown. "Yes." He didn't want to be lectured. He knew what he had done, and he may have deserved his punishment, but Mallory and his child needed him.

"Do you think it's our sins we pay for or our fathers'? Because our fathers haven't been the best of men." Kal was serious. He knew that Richard loved Mallory.

"I don't know." Richard was fighting the urge to call in rein-forcements to find Mallory and return her to him. If she had indeed left him, he would need to prove he was the man she needed, the father she wanted for their child, but he wasn't that man—not yet.

"Not that we've been angelic or anything, but when does it end? Who does it end with?" Kal knew Richard understood what he was saying even if he was only half present. "Someone has to break the chain. I want to be the one who does in my bloodline. My wife is worth it." He stood and started for the door. "I'll find out where she went, then you can decide what you need to do." Kal walked out and left Richard to his thoughts.

He didn't have to think about it—Mallory was worth it. His child was worth it. He decided to be more proactive and get himself together. If anyone was going after his woman, it would be him. Richard stood and walked to the shower. He would find her. Well, he and his brother Kal.

Kal left Richard at the cabin and headed straight for the house. He quickly grabbed his phone and dialed Simone. If he wanted to find Mallory before Richard, he would have to work fast. When the call went unanswered, he became frustrated. "I'm gonna have to have a chat with my sweet little wife about answering my calls." He pulled up to the house just in time to see Felix and Ms. Jenna leaving. "Why hello there, beautiful lady." He pulled Ms. Jenna close and planted a kiss on her cheek. "Have you seen my beautiful princess anywhere?"

Ms. Jenna was too busy giggling to answer. She shook her head and nodded toward Felix.

Kal didn't release her, but turned his attention to Felix. "And you beast! Have you laid eyes on my beauty?"

Felix shook his head and rolled his eyes at Kal. "I have not seen your beauty since she left for the apartment this morning." He stretched a hand toward Kal and Ms. Jenna. "Now, please unhand my beauty before I have to get rough with you."

Kal laughed as he gently shoved Ms. Jenna toward Felix. "Forgive me, for I was unaware she was yours." He made air quotes with his fingers. He winked at a blushing Ms. Jenna before hurrying to the door.

"Hey, is he up?"

Kal turned to answer Felix. "Mallory said he was really hungover when she left this morning. I was supposed to check on him, but I figured he wouldn't want me bursting into his sanctuary." Kal quickly went to Felix. "What time did she leave?" He didn't want to alarm Ms. Jenna, but he needed to get information out of Felix.

"She met Simone here this morning." Felix was getting suspicious. "Why are you looking for them?" He frowned when Kal tried to brush off the question.

"Can a man not look for his woman?" Kal tried to smile, but Felix wasn't fooled. He knew something was wrong. "Richard and I have lunch plans. We wanted to surprise them."

Felix wasn't buying it.

"It's been a frustrating few days, and we wanted to do something special." Ms. Jenna was eating up his deception.

"I think that's a great idea. The girls need a break—they've been doing too much. Maybe you could call Kenneth and have him bring Kathrine as well." She flashed Kal a beautiful smile.

He felt like shit lying to her, but he had to. She didn't need to worry about the women until he knew she needed to.

"Sounds good. I'll talk to Richard when he gets here." He gave Ms. Jenna a polite bow before turning and dashing through the door.

"Is something wrong?"

Felix didn't want to alarm her, but he didn't want to lie either.

"I'm not sure what's going on, but the boys can handle it. Let's get you out and about." He turned her toward the car and started walking.

"Felix, I don't need to go shopping. If the kids need you, then go to them."

Felix stopped and opened the car door. He gently shoved her into the car.

"Young lady, I said I was taking you out today, and that is what we are doing." He closed the door and went around to the driver's side. "You were right there, and I'm quite certain you never heard him ask for my help. If it's one thing I've learned from these boys is to call their fathers when in doubt." He winked at Jenna. "I'm not in doubt." He started the car.

Kal watched the car pull away from the house. He would try Simone again. Now that he had an idea of where to start, he would get to work. Simone had only been gone maybe two hours. He went to the phone and dialed her mobile again. When there was no answer, he became worried.

*****

Simone felt sick to her stomach. She was going to help Mallory even though she knew it would probably kill Richard. He had crossed the line threatening her. She was pregnant, for god's sake. She would take Mallory home. There were so many places to hide her there the baby would be in high school by the time he'd found them. Her phone rang again.

"Shit, that must be Kal." She pulled off the road and sat staring ahead. "I really want to answer, but I can't."

Mallory wished she had just left by herself. She had dragged Kat and Simone into her get away, disrupting their lives. "It's okay. You can drop me at the nearest bus station. I can take it from here." She covered Simone's hand with hers. "I'm so lucky to have found friends like you guys. I know you want to help, but I can't let you do this. I wasn't thinking before, but you can't go with me." She looked in the backseat at Kat. "I love you, guys." She couldn't believe there were still tears she hadn't shed.

"Girl, please. We said we'd help, and we are going to do just that." Kat removed her seat belt and scooted closer to Mal. "Ain't nobody scared of Richard and Kal. You're family, and we take care of our own." She reached for Mallory's hand. "Now stop all that crying before your face shrivels up." Mallory and Simone couldn't help but laugh. They were so preoccupied that they hadn't noticed the van parked behind their car. Just as they were finally gathering their thoughts, a knock on the window startled them. Simone turned to see a suited gentleman standing by her window, holding a badge. He gestured for her to roll her window down. She unconsciously did as he asked. She barely heard Kat screaming something before the car filled with smoke.

"Shit." Simone felt her body relax as the darkness rained over her.

"Are you sure these are the women we're looking for?" One of the men asked as Kat finally succumbed to the gas.

"For the kinda money I'm getting paid, you damn well better believe I'm sure." Another man reached in and unlocked the doors. He gently pulled Simone from the car and carried her to the van.

"What about the other two?" The younger of the men was still standing near the car.

"They come too."

They had been given orders to take Simone and anyone with her. The man quickly pulled his phone out and called the number he was given. "We've got her and two others." He waited for instructions before hanging up and helping with the other women. They left the car unlocked on the side of the road and headed for the airport.

Simone made a groaning noise as she tried to wake herself. She felt groggy.

"Help her."

She could hear a man's voice, but it was not at all familiar. Her eyes flickered open as someone helped her to a seated position.

"Where...where am I?" She could barely get the words out as she tried to gain control of her body.

"You are safe."

Simone tried to steady herself but found it difficult. She was swaying slightly when a large hand rested on her shoulder, keeping her from falling forward. "Maybe you should rest. Those idiots weren't supposed to use the gas unless necessary."

She could barely make out the man shaking his head. Though she was unable to recognize the voice, his blurry features seemed familiar.

"Kal...Rich..." She felt so weak.

"My sons."

She knew it. What the hell? As her eyes adjusted a little more, she could see his smiling face. The king? Why had he taken them? She was instantly frightened. What had she gotten her sisters into?

"Rest. We have plenty of time to talk." He didn't seem upset, but she didn't want to rest. She wanted to know why he had taken her.

"I'm fine. Why did..." She was slowly gaining control of her senses.

"I have no intentions of hurting any of you. Well, not if I don't have to."

Simone didn't like any of this. He'd kidnapped them. "You must understand something, Princess Simone, I will always be the villain so that my children won't have to be."

She gave him a frown. "What do you mean?" She ignored the fact that he'd referred to her as princess.

"My son married you without my permission." His brows knitted together. "He would rather live a humble life with you than be who he was born to be." Her eyes hadn't fully adjusted, but she was focused on his face. "He is a prince! But he chooses to defy me every chance he gets."

She knew they would never have accepted her. She tried to tell him. He raised a hand as if he'd known she would try to defend him.

"There was a beautiful princess waiting for him at home, but without a second thought, he chose to marry you."

Simone didn't like the comment at all. "Forgive me for not being up to standard. I'm sure you can wave your royal hand and dissolve our so-called marriage." She felt a pain in her chest. She didn't want to give him up—not her Kal.

The man before her let out a laugh that startled her. "Oh, I'm afraid that's not possible. You see, the only way you get out of this marriage is through death."

Simone didn't budge. She wouldn't let him see the fear she was feeling—or the anger.

"I see you aren't afraid of death."

She turned to look out the window at the clouds. "I'm already dead." She kept her attention on the passing clouds. There was nothing she could do now.

"Not if I can help it."

Simone's head whipped around as the words registered. What the hell did that mean? He was smiling at her. "I know of your condition. Richard made us aware of your situation." She'd forgotten he was one of them. "I had intended to help him, but then news of your divorce was reported to me a short time later. I had no idea why he'd let you go until I saw you with Kalu."

Simone frowned at him again and got a dashing smile in return.

"I know my sons very well. If Richard thought his little brother was able to give you a better life than he, then he would let you go. It is the only logical explanation."

Simone let the implication sink in. "What?" Her face was hot with anger. "What exactly are you trying to tell me?" Was this some game to them? Had they used her?

He smiled and took a sip of his drink.

"I wouldn't let a woman such as you out of my grasp no matter the circumstances. Once you were married to me, it would be a sealed deal. Is that not the saying, Yusef?" Simone heard a loud laugh from behind her seat.

"I think you mean done deal, Your Majesty." The man's accent was strong, his voice commanding. "Maybe you aren't using the right approach."

Simone sat listening to their exchange.

"You never introduced yourself." He was right.

"Didn't I?" The man frowned at Simone. "I thought I did." He gazed around the woman in front of him, clearly ignoring her. "Well, maybe it is your job to announce me." He smirked at the man behind Simone.

"How can I? Your mouth never shuts long enough for me to announce you."

Simone gasped as the man before her spit the drink he was sipping onto the small table that separated them. She could have sworn she saw a glimpse of humor before he composed himself.

"You insolent bastard. How dare you make me waste my bourbon?"

Yusef didn't seem at all bothered by the rude comment. Instead, he took a sip of his drink and countered. "Well, it's not my fault you can't hold your liquors. I've always been the superior man—you are just too stubborn to accept that."

Both men laughed as if they hadn't just kidnapped her and her sisters.

"I'm sorry, Princess, your father is an ass who can't hold his liquors. Welcome to the family." Again they laughed. This was starting to annoy Simone.

"Why haven't I killed you yet? You are the worst friend anyone could have." Yusef laughed at his friend.

"I'm your only friend, you bastard, and you are always welcome to try."

Simone couldn't believe what was going on around her. This had to be a dream. These two idiots couldn't possibly be real. She had crashed her car, killing everyone, and this was her punishment. She rubbed the back of her neck as she tried to stretch a bit.

"I don't have time for such trivial things." The king waved his hand dismissively at Yusef. This just made the man laugh.

"As you wish, your fearfulness."

Omar frowned at Yusef.

"I meant your fearlessness."

They both laughed again. Omar shook his head and turned his attention back to Simone.

"I am sorry, my little princess. I am your husband's father. King Omar Bashar."

Simone didn't know what to say.

"Now I am your father as well."

Yusef's laugh brought Simone out of her trance.

"This is the most heartwarming thing I've ever witnessed." Yusef laughed again before mocking his friend. "Welcome to the family, princess, why yes, yes, I always kidnap the women in our family." King Omar let out a booming laugh that roused the other two women. Simone undid her seat belt and went to check on her sisters. She ignored the two men as she checked on the girls.

"Where the fuck" Kat was coming to faster than she had. Simone grabbed a bottle of water from the table and opened it for Kat.

"Drink this." She held the bottle to her lips as Kat took a sip. "Take another sip." She handed the bottle to Kat and turned her attention to Mallory. She wasn't even half awake. Simone turned to look at Omar. "You shouldn't have done this to her. She's pregnant." He frowned at her.

"That's what I get for hiring American amateurs." Omar shrugged nonchalantly.

"Who the fuck are you?" Kat felt drowsy. She tried to adjust herself in the chair.

"This one has a filthy mouth. I do not like that." Omar was giving Kat a disapproving look.

She did not like it. "I don't give a fuck what you like. Where are we?" She was so angry that she didn't realize who she was provoking.

Omar sat back in his chair. "Yusef." Omar made a gesture with his hand.

"Your Majesty?" Yusef was on his feet.

159

"Throw that one from the aircraft."

Yusef grabbed Kat by her arm, removing her seat belt as he pulled her from the chair. Before Simone could reach her sister, Yusef had already thrown her over his shoulder.

"*No!*" Simone was screaming, trying to get up, but she was still a bit dizzy. Kat was so shocked that she just froze. Yusef stopped in front of the door.

"You know if I open this door, we all die." Yusef turned to look at his friend, who was smirking. His eyes were filled with tears of amusement. Suddenly the cabin filled with the sound of Omar's laughter. Simone's chest was heaving up and down as she pushed herself onto her knees. What the hell?

"I suppose I could forgive the little one for now. Place her back in her seat and secure her." Omar waved over his shoulder.

"If you really want me to throw her out, I will, but I may have to talk to the pilot first." Yusef was laughing too.

Kat finally got the strength to wiggle violently as she was taken back to her seat. "You fu—" Kat was furious, but Yusef stopped her before she could say anything. He leaned in close with a look that scared the crap out of her.

"Watch your mouth, little one. I may not be able to throw you from this aircraft, but there are other things I can do. You will speak respectfully to His Majesty." His voice echoed throughout the cabin, scaring all three women. Kat nodded nervously.

"Well, now that everyone is comfortable, why don't you return to your seat?" Omar smiled at Simone, who was still sitting on the floor. She slowly stood and slipped into her seat. As she attempted to fasten her seat belt, Omar spoke again. "You don't need that." She looked up at him. "I promise you it's safe. I am not wearing mine." Simone looked over at Kat. She was rubbing her temples.

"I should check on Mal," she said softly.

Omar looked at a seemingly sick Mallory. She was swaying in her seat. He reached over and pressed a button on the table. Simone watched as a woman came dashing into the cabin.

"Your Majesty." She bowed at Omar and waited for instructions.

"Will you see to the young lady. She's with child." He smiled at the woman before turning back to Simone. "She's a doctor. You can trust her." His smile was genuine, but Simone couldn't appreciate it at that moment. She had questions.

She took a deep breath and decided to ask. "What do you want with us?" She tried to hold Omar's stare but found it uncomfortable. The man seemed to be staring into her soul. He was a very handsome man, but she could see he wasn't always kind.

"Not them, you."

Simone's stomach tightened at his response. He stared at her, waiting for her to ask her next question.

"What do you want with me?" She stared at her hands and waited. When no response came, she looked up at him. His face was serious. She didn't like that look.

"My son loves you—both of them."

Simone unconsciously looked over at Mallory. She was performing some tasks for the woman seated on the little table in front of her and Kat.

"Yes, Richard still loves you."

The comment made Simone adjust herself in her seat. She was sure Mallory could hear him. Hell, if he spoke any louder, the pilot behind their closed door might hear him.

"He's in love with Mal. They're having a baby together," she defended.

Omar shook his head. "Yes, but that doesn't mean he cannot love you." He wasn't letting that go. "She must not love him though." He turned his attention to Mallory for a brief moment. His smile was long gone, and a contorted angry scowl held its place.

"Mallory does love Richard. He's just difficult to deal with sometimes." She would defend Mallory until he understood that she was a good woman. Richard didn't deserve her—not when he was still trying to prove he was his father's son. His biological father, that is, not that Omar was much better. Kidnapping helpless women and scaring them half to death.

"Is that why you were helping her run from him? Because he's difficult to be with?" His face had softened, but he was still looking at her with displeasure.

"I don't have to justify her actions. He shouldn't have threatened the woman carrying his child." She felt her temper gearing up for an explosive entrance.

"Hmm. Did you tell my son where you were going?"

Simone glanced up at him to see a smirk on his face. She had kept their destination a secret. Though she was his legal wife, Richard was his best friend, his brother. She couldn't trust him with Mallory's secret.

"What was your reason for running away from my son?"

She wasn't running from Kal. "I wasn't running from him. I was helping my friend, my sister. She needed me." She felt her heart ache. She hadn't answered his calls, and now he would never know what happened to her. "What are you going to do with me?" She needed answers. Would she ever see Kal again?

"I'm going to fix your broken heart. Can't have my son playing with broken toys now, can I?"

The collective gasps of the women in the cabin pleased him. Omar took a strong sip of his drink. There was no readable expression on his face. Simone had no idea what to say or do. She was shocked.

"My son loves you—they both do—and I will not leave this world knowing you could follow me before your time." He turned to look out the window, but she had already seen the pained look on his face.

"What does that mean?" Simone knew there was more to that statement. She ignored the fact that he was threatening to make her get the lifesaving surgery she'd avoided since she'd gotten the news of her condition.

"I may be dying." Omar was known to twist the truth here and there, but he was going to be honest with her about his condition. Simone seemed concerned for him. He could see it in her beautiful eyes. He smiled at her and took another sip of his drink. "I may or may not have cancer." He seemed so nonchalant about the whole thing. Simone wanted to hug him, but she wasn't sure that was appropriate.

"Does Kal know?" She felt her stomach tighten again as she waited for his answer.

"No one but the people in this cabin is aware of my condition, and I intend to keep it that way. If I only have a short time to be with them, I don't want them worrying. I want them to be happy and carry on as they always have." He smiled at Simone, but she could see the sadness in his eyes.

"Isn't that a bit selfish? Shouldn't you tell them so that they can prepare?" Simone sat forward in her seat. She'd almost forgotten they weren't alone.

"I know you're not throwing stones while living in that glass house of yours." Kat was glaring at Simone.

"I haven't decided if surgery is right for me yet. I have to be sure my family wants me around before I go saving myself." Omar tilted his head and winked at Simone.

"Are you crazy?" Simone sat back when she heard a loud grunting noise coming from behind her. Yusef was not at all happy with this conversation. She lowered her voice as if she didn't want Yusef to hear her. "You want to force me to have lifesaving surgery while you die of something that can be surgically altered?" She wanted to be mad, but she just couldn't find it in her now.

"My son would miss you. No one would miss me." He shrugged.

Simone glanced over her shoulder at the monster of a man sitting quietly behind her. Yusef was reading a book.

"I'm sure he would miss you." She heard Yusef make a noise behind her.

"No, I would not. I'm waiting patiently for him to die so that I may marry his wife, give her a daughter, and live quite comfortably in his beautiful palace."

All four women turned abruptly to look at Yusef, who was still reading his book. It was Omar's laugh that disrupted their disbelief.

"And with any luck, I would be reincarnated in your daughter and give you both hell." Both men broke into laughter.

Simone suddenly realized she was in the presence of an older version of Kal and Richard. She shook her head at the thought.

"Well, I'm sure your wife would miss you." Simone was grasping at clouds now. She didn't know much about this man. Neither Kal nor Richard had talked too much about him. They always spoke to each other about Kal's family but never to her.

"I assure you she would not miss her troublesome husband. He is worse than a child in her presence. He screams often when they are alone." Yusef giggled at his own joke.

"Oh, I assure you those aren't screams of—"

Yusef quickly cut Omar off. "I do not wish to know!" Yusef ran a frustrated hand over his face as if he were trying to suppress a memory.

Omar laughed again at Yusef. "Why no one told you to come rushing in." He seemed pleased with Yusef's discomfort.

"I vowed to protect you. I was simply making sure you weren't being killed." Yusef shook his head and grunted.

Omar seemed to be enjoying their private moment. It almost seemed like they hadn't realized others were present. Simone looked at her sisters to see they were sharing her confusion.

"I'm sure your family cares about you." She couldn't understand why these two seemed so at peace with him dying. Her whole family and all her friends had totally freaked out when she'd shared her news with them. "Someone must love you." She felt warm tears in her eyes.

"Maybe you will one day."

She gave him an unsure look. After kidnapping her, threatening to make her have a surgery she didn't want, he thought she would love him. Simone didn't know how she could ever love this crazy man.

"If you live long enough, I'm sure she will come to hate you as we all do." Omar laughed at his friend.

Simone felt sorry for him even if he didn't deserve her pity. "I think your family loves you. Maybe they just don't know how to say it." She turned to look at her little sister. Kat was finishing her water.

"Well, they do, and I love them as well." He sat up straight in his chair. "Did you know Kalu's the only one of my three who carries any resemblances to his mother?" He smiled a genuinely happy smile. "She says he was supposed to be our daughter, but unfortunately I make only male heirs." He was proud of himself, yet she heard sadness in his voice. "He's her baby boy. She loves all our boys, but Kalu is her special boy." He sighed happily. "His happiness means more to her than my life—and yes, she does love me." He held Simone's gaze. "She wants him to be happy, and she wants grandchildren from him."

Simone dropped her gaze at the last of his comments.

"I intend to make sure you are healthy enough to love my son and give my wife the grands she desires." He snapped his fingers, grabbing her attention. "Call it my final act of love—for you, my son, and my family."

Simone tried to wipe the tears from her cheeks. He was doing all this out of love? Crazy misguided love.

"Do not worry so much. All will be well. I've seen it."

Simone tried to force a laugh. He was starting to sound like her grandmother. She would always say she'd seen their futures. Of course, she was right most of the time.

*****

Kal and Richard went over the car, searching for any signs of foul play. Who the hell could have taken the girls? Richard was angry. They weren't taken by amateurs. The two federal agents that had informed them of the situation were being suspiciously helpful and cooperative.

"There's nothing here that suggests they were hurt."

Kal's face was hard with worry. He almost didn't look like himself standing in the dimly lit warehouse. "Who would do this?" He ran his hands through his hair. "It doesn't make sense. This trip wasn't something they had planned. It was spontaneous, so how did they know?"

Richard knew this had to do with him. Kal didn't have people who wanted vengeance in these parts of the world. Then he heard Kal's words in his head: the sins of the father.

"I'm going to see my father." Richard stood and walked out to his car. Felix was waiting patiently for him. "Home—to him."

Felix knew who he was talking about and where to go. He nodded and got into the car. Kal climbed into the car next to Richard. He was deep in thought as they left the parking lot.

"Did you trust them?" he asked.

Richard didn't seem to hear him. He was far away from there. Felix had heard him though.

"No. I didn't like the way those two were moving. Something is off about the whole thing." He drove with a purpose.

"Felix, pull over!" Kal suddenly realized something. Richard looked at him for answers. As soon as the car was pulled to the side of the road, Kal jumped out. He felt a sickness in his stomach. Richard and Felix came to him.

"What?" Richard's anger turned into concern. Kal seemed physically hurt.

"It's not your father." He slid down the side of the car. His body felt heavy and pained. What had he done? Of course, this was his father. He was angry about him marrying Simone without his permission. "Omar did this. This is his work. I know it."

Richard thought for a second before dropping to his knees. "Your brother was at the party. Do you think he told Omar?" He knew Kal was probably right. If he had found out about Kal and Simone's secret marriage, then Omar had known as well. There was nothing the old man and Yusef couldn't find out when they wanted to.

"If he hurts her…" Kal was getting emotional. He would have taken Simone home to them, explained everything, but the old man was pissed at him.

"He won't. You know Nyala would never condone it." Felix was right. His mother would never let his father hurt Simone—not now that she was her daughter.

"Get the jet ready. We're going home." Richard helped Kal to his feet. He knew Felix was right, but Omar was unpredictable. He wasn't at all pleased with Kal not wanting to follow his well-laid-out plans.

Kal had told him he would make his own way in the world, and that did not sit well with Omar. He wanted his sons to be the princes they were groomed to be, but Kal didn't want that life. He wanted to be free like Richard, choose his own life, live the way he wanted.

"I know you two have your differences, but he does love you. He won't hurt her."

Kal knew his father better than Richard thought. They used to be very close when he was a child. He'd wanted to be like his dad, but as he got older, he realized his father wasn't always the wonderful man he'd pretended to be.

"He has a ten-hour head start. I need to get in touch with my mother." Kal opened the door and got back into the car. He needed to call in the big guns. If anyone could talk to his father, his mother could.

"Maybe we shouldn't jump to conclusions." Felix hung up the phone and started the car. He waited for Richard to close his door before pulling off. "If he'd planned on hurting Simone, he wouldn't have taken Mallory and Kat."

Kal wasn't convinced. "Right. The whole kidnapping thing shouldn't be alarming at all." He scoffed. "I'm overreacting. I mean he could have just invited us both home, but he came and stole my wife." Kal shook his head in frustration. What had he gotten Simone into? And why wasn't Richard as furious as he was? He didn't trust anyone right now. He felt betrayed.

*****

Simone sat quietly as the aircraft touched down. She didn't know where the hell they were, but she knew the ocean was close by. She'd seen giant ships floating peacefully a few minutes before they'd reached the desolated airfield. She had moved to the seat closer to her sisters and the doctor. Omar and Yusef engaged in several humorous conversations that had gotten a few laughs from everyone. Had he not kidnapped them, she might have liked him. She tried not to show the terror she was going through. She had to be strong for Kat and Mal. They were also trying to be brave, but she knew they were scared.

"Welcome home, my little princess."

Simone turned to see Omar smiling at her. She looked out the window and saw absolutely nothing. Was he going to leave her in the desert to dehydrate and die? The aircraft was still taxiing toward what looked like a large opened hangar. There were several small planes parked inside.

"Let's have a toast." He snapped his fingers, and Yusef got up, rolling his eyes at him. He disappeared into the cockpit. "So, will you ladies be staying with the princess, or would you prefer something less desolate?" Kat and Mal looked at each other then back at Simone. She didn't look at all worried, but they knew she was. What the hell did he mean?

"We go where she goes." Kat wasn't going to leave Simone.

"I thought you might say that, my feisty little miss." Omar snapped his fingers as Yusef returned with a few drinks. "Ladies, let's toast." He took a glass and held it as he waited.

"I can't have that." Mallory had barely spoken since they were taken. She felt responsible for their current predicament. Had she not tried to run away from Richard, they would have been safe at home.

"I am aware of your condition. This is sparkling grape water." Yusef smiled at Mal. He was clearly being silly, but she didn't care. His smile was comforting, and she was thirsty for some reason.

"Thank you." She took her glass and waited.

"What exactly are we toasting to? The kidnapping or you dropping us off in the middle of nowhere?" Kat didn't really care who she was with. He had taken them without permission. King or no king, he was a damn criminal.

"I would like to toast to family." Omar raised his glass, and everyone did as he did. He watched as the women sipped their drinks. "This is some of the finest wine in the world." He smiled at the women. Simone didn't trust him. She thought he was being too accommodating. Omar sat and waited.

"I feel weird." Kat swayed before slumping down into her seat.

"Shit." Simone knew she shouldn't have trusted Omar. She found it hard to stay awake. That bastard had drugged them—again.

"Oh my god. What'd you do to them?" Mallory was worried for her friends. They both seemed to have just passed out right before her. The doctor checked both ladies before leaving them and going to the cockpit.

"Don't worry, dear. They've been given a mild sedative." Omar nodded at Yusef. "I hope you understand why I'm doing this."

Mallory didn't know, and she surely didn't care. He was forcing her friend to do something she didn't want to even if it was what they all had wanted.

"Why haven't you drugged me?" She was curious as to why she hadn't shared the same fate as her friends.

"Richard wouldn't approve of me hurting you or his child." Omar smiled at her. "He seems very fond of you."

Mallory was starting to regret leaving.

"I wish you to stay with my wife while I take care of your friends."

Mallory was taken back by his suggestion. "I would love to, but I need to be there for Simone and Kat." She was visibly scared. "They would have done the same for me." She didn't make eye contact with the king.

Omar had already made the decision to take her home. He was just asking to make her feel some semblance of control.

"I insist. My wife would love to have you. Besides, these two will have the best care I can provide." He knew she was skeptical. "I will update you as much as I can." Omar crossed his heart with a warm smile.

Mallory was shocked and confused. What happened to the crazy man who kidnapped them and was forcing Simone to have surgery? He was being awfully sweet to her. Mallory knew not to trust him, but he seemed so sincere.

"We are ready, Your Majesty." Yusef returned from the cockpit with the doctor in tow. The aircraft door opened, and a few large men entered. They nodded at Yusef before retrieving Kat and Simone.

Mallory didn't know what to do. She wanted to stop them, but how? She was powerless.

"We need to get airborne immediately, Your Majesty." Yusef seemed a bit uneasy. "Richard and Kalu are heading home." Mallory saw a slow smirk cross Yusef's face as the king realized he had been found out.

"That didn't take them long. I thought we'd at least have a few days." Omar laughed. "Who am I kidding? Those are my boys." He shook his head proudly. "We need to be on our way." Omar seated himself next to Mallory. "A few more hours, and we should be enjoying my beautiful garden."

Mallory sat still, her heart pounding in her chest. She didn't know if she was scared or excited that Richard was coming for her. He did love her. He had obviously dropped everything to find her—or was he looking for Simone? She quickly pushed the thought to the back of her mind. Simone was Kal's now—nothing would change that. Well, at least she hoped nothing could. Simone and Kal belonged together—just like she belonged with Richard. She felt queasy.

"May I have some water or apple juice please?" She was sweating.

Omar noticed and gestured for Yusef. Her breathing was rapid. "I feel…" Mallory's body slumped into her seat.

"I think she has fainted." Yusef adjusted her seat and examined her. "Should we call the doctor back?" He wasn't the worrying type, but he didn't like not having someone to care for Mallory.

"No, she has a surgery to perform. I'm sure we can take care of one tiny little woman, Yusef." Omar waved at the waiting pilot. "Let us leave."

The man bowed and disappeared back into the cockpit.

"I do not wish to be the doctor that let anything happen to either of their women."

Omar laughed at Yusef. "Are you afraid, Yusef?"

Yusef scowled at him. "Come now. She's fainted. We can let her rest until we get home. Thirty minutes will not kill her."

Omar shrugged at a worried Yusef. "If you wish, you may grab the medical bag." Omar shook his head as he watched Yusef hurry off for the bag.

*****

Richard was getting more impatient the closer they got to their destination. He knew Omar wouldn't hurt Mallory, but he wasn't sure what was in store for Simone—or Kat, for that matter. Kal hadn't spoken a word since the conversation with his mother. She was not at all happy with her husband's actions. She'd told them to get there as soon as they could. She would deal with her husband in the meantime. Richard knew she would protect the girls, but she could only do so if she was present. Knowing Omar, he would stay far away from his wife if he was up to no good.

Felix came and sat opposite him. "Is he okay?"

They both looked at Kal, who was trying to relax. He was not at all happy with his family at the moment. His father had taken his wife, and no one seemed as worried for her as he was.

"I can't tell you what he's going through right now, but I know he's terrified. He and Omar had a huge fight before we left." Richard sighed. "Omar wasn't too happy with his decision to leave the family and move in with us."

Felix hadn't known about that. He knew Kal and Richard were close, but he never thought Kal would leave his family like that. Then again, Richard wasn't the reason he had made that decision. He had done it for Simone. Suddenly it all made sense to Felix. He wanted to talk to Kal, but now he knew what was going on; he needed to regroup. Kal was a prince in his father's world; things would change once he was home. No matter what he'd done before, he was still Omar's son.

"I'm going to check in, see how much longer. Shouldn't be more than an hour or so." Felix stood and started for the cockpit. He placed a supportive hand on Kal's shoulder as he passed. "I'm with you."

Kal nodded at him, but his demeanor did not change. Felix left the boys alone in the cabin. Richard knew he had to say something to Kal.

"What's your plan?" He got up and took the seat in front of Kal. "You can't just charge in there pissed. He's still your king."

Kal seemed to become even more furious. "That he is." Kal sounded so defeated, but Richard knew he was calculating what steps to take when he arrived. Kal shifted in his seat. His eyes met Richard's. "Are you still in love with Simone?"

Richard seemed to flinch at the question. He did not expect that. "I love her, but my heart is with Mallory." He was sincere, but that didn't seem to ease Kal's storm any.

"Had our situations been reversed, how would you feel right now?" Kal's gaze made Richard feel like he was sitting under a heat lamp. Kal was upset with him.

"Mallory was taken too." He tried to keep his emotions in check. He didn't want to alienate his brother, but Kal seemed as if he had something on his mind—something that was going to unearth their relationship.

"You know, I was jealous of you." Kal let out a sad snicker. "I wanted to be a father, but I knew when I married Simone, I knew that would never happen." He turned to look out his window. Richard could feel his pain. "I love her, and I would do anything for her." He returned his gaze to Richard. "You once felt that way about her too."

Richard rested his head back to avoid Kal's stare. "Was it ever real for you?" Kal knew the answer to his question.

"She's yours now." Richard didn't change his position. "None of that matters anymore." He closed his eyes and hoped this wasn't going to turn into a fight.

"Why did you give in so easily when I told you I wanted you to give her to me? She wasn't one of your regulars. You loved her." Kal sounded angry. Richard knew he had to defuse this bomb before it exploded.

"Her grandmother. She told her I wasn't the one. She said I would find someone, but I wasn't Simone's mate." He held Kal's stare. "I was supposed to lead her to him."

Kal's brows knitted in confusion. Richard had never mentioned that.

"She pulled me aside and told me not to worry, Simone would be with someone close to me—you."

Kal leaned toward him.

"You were the closest person in my life then. That's why I came bragging to you about our situation."

Kal could see he was being honest.

"I had to see if she was right before I walked away from Simone."

Kal sat back again. "You're not superstitious." He'd known Richard better than anyone. He was not into any of that superstitious fortune telling shit. Why would he have believed the old woman?

"I'm not, but I do believe in fate, destiny, or whatever you wanna call it." Richard shrugged. He did love Simone, but now that he was with Mallory, it was clear to him that he wasn't in love with her—not anymore—but he would never admit that shit to Kal. Not right now.

"Sorry." Kal felt irritated with himself for questioning Richard the way he was. Richard had always been there to support him. Even if Mallory hadn't been taken, he would have been right here with him. "I need you." He exhaled, letting out some of his frustration. "I need you to make sure she's okay no matter what happens with me and Omar." He knew he didn't have to ask. Richard was like a safety net when Omar would push him.

"I will." Richard was worried for Kal. He knew him well enough to know he was going in guns blazing, and Omar would react. He almost wished he could go in without Kal, but it was too late for that. Felix came bursting into the cabin.

"Is all well with you two?" He was serious. Both men nodded at him. "Good. I have news from some friends." He took the seat next to Richard. "They landed a few miles away from the port. Your father had about four oil tankers docked there, but now they're gone."

Kal knew his father was great at distraction.

"I'm gonna have the pilot land there and see what I can find. It may be nothing, but I want to check it out." Felix was good at what he'd done before he worked for Richard. They both trusted his instincts. "Omar is back at the palace with one of the girls. I don't know which one, but he only brought one with him."

Kal ran his hands through his hair. It had to be Simone.

"What happened to the other two?" Richard was worried about Mallory now. Where the hell had Omar taken her and Kat?

"They were taken off at the airfield and taken to the port. They were covered. My guy couldn't see them clearly, but it has to be Kat and Mal." Felix looked at Richard. "I'll get her back." Richard knew he would.

"What about Yusef? Was he with Omar?" Kal knew Yusef hardly ever left his father's side, but he's the only one Omar would trust with his deceptions.

"He's at the palace." Felix didn't want to leave the boys, but he had to find Mallory and Kat. He hoped Richard could handle Kal and Omar without him. He knew Richard wanted to go with him, but Kal needed him. He just prayed he wouldn't have to come back with bad news.

"Thank you." Kal didn't feel much relief at the news. Simone was at the palace with his father. Though he knew his mother would protect her from physical harm, he knew his father could still hurt her.

Felix stood. "We land in ten." He had to change. The situation didn't require Felix; it needed Captain Masters.

*****

The car pulled into the private family entrance that was used when one didn't want to be seen entering or leaving the palace. Richard followed Kal into the palace as they were led to Omar. He had been waiting for them in his famous garden. This was not really a good sign. As they entered, the guards turned and left them. They could see Omar sitting with his roses. This was definitely not good. Richard stepped ahead of Kal as they approached. He knew Kal was not in any shape to address his father.

He quickly took a knee, bowing his head. "Your Majesty." He stayed on his knee as Omar stood to acknowledge him.

"Your Majesty?" Omar seemed shocked at his gesture. "Have I angered you?"

Richard looked up at the man standing over him.

"It was father and a hug last time. What have I done to warrant"—he waved a hand over Richard—"this?"

Richard stood and embraced Omar. The laugh the old man let out echoed across the garden.

"Apologies. I thought you were angry with us."

Omar pushed him back to look at him, clearly ignoring Kal.

"No, my son, you haven't angered me." He patted Richard's shoulders. "You look well."

Richard nodded with a smile. "I hear congratulations may be in order." He smiled a proud smile at Richard. "Though I must warn you, I have become very fond of little Mallory. She is an amazing young woman." Omar turned Richard and threw an arm around him. He was probably an inch taller than Kal and Richard, but he always made them feel short when he did this.

"I know you are eager to be reunited with her, but I must warn you." He stopped again and turned to Richard. "You will have to choose." Richard frowned, causing a smile to overtake Omar's face. "You're either going to be the husband and father they need, or you're going to follow your current path. Either way, it's a choice you'll have to make before you leave here." His smile faded. "I've loved you as a son, but I am aware you have another father. I see you becoming more like him than I'd like." He raised his hand to halt Richard's protest. He knew Richard never wanted to be compared to his father.

"Mallory deserves better than that. She demands it." Richard took in a deep breath.

"She has agreed to stay for a few months. This will give you time to make up your mind. So, if you need to fix things before she returns home, I suggest you do. I know you will make the right decision, my son." His smile was back. "But she will not leave until she is sure you are going to be the man we know you can be."

Richard finally exhaled. He had already made his choice. Mallory and his child would have the man they deserved in their lives.

"I understand." He felt butterflies in his stomach as he prepared to ask the question. "Where is she?"

This brought a loving smile to Omar's face. "Yusef!" He clapped his hands as Yusef appeared, carrying Mallory in his arms.

"We were having such a good time flirting with your roses."

Yusef placed Mallory on her feet. She was smiling at him as if they'd known each other forever and a day. Richard suddenly realized that Simone wasn't the one Omar had brought to the palace. He turned to see a furious Kal charging at his father. Richard grabbed Kal before he could get to his father. He had to practically pick him up to stop him.

"You evil son of a bitch!" Kal was filled with rage.

"You forget your place?" Omar's loud voice almost gave Mallory a heart attack. She stood timidly behind Yusef, whose knife was at the ready. Mallory wondered if Yusef would really hurt Kal. "I am your king, and you will respect me!" Omar was furious as well. He hadn't budged.

"Kal, please." Richard pleaded with his brother. "Don't make this worse." He could feel Kal's rage.

"Let him go, Richard." Omar ordered.

Richard hesitated but did as he was told. He stood in front of Kal. "You know where I'll be when you remember who you are." Kal's hands were clenched into fists. Richard turned and bowed slightly. He watched as Omar walked away with Yusef. Before he could turn around, Kal started to walk away. Mallory ran over to Richard.

"Kal..." She didn't know what she could say, but when he turned, her breath caught in her chest. The look he was giving her caused knots in her stomach.

"You bow when you address me, and it's Your Highness." Kal turned and walked away, leaving her and Richard in the garden.

"Don't worry. He's not himself right now." Richard wrapped her in his arms. He placed a kiss on the top of her head. "We thought it was Simone he had brought here."

Mallory felt a twinge of jealousy and disappointment. He had come for Simone, not her. Richard's arms tightened around her as she started to let go. "No, not yet. I need to hold you for a little while longer."

Mallory could hear his heart pounding in his chest. "I'm sorry," she whispered. Richard could feel her tears soak his shirt.

"I'm the one who should be sorry, Mal." He reluctantly pushed her back from him. "I shouldn't have said the things I said. I love you, and I understand how you feel about the man I am, but I told you I would need time to fix the things you needed me to." His face was pained. "I don't need Omar to tell me what you're worth. I already know. I've always known."

Mallory tried to smile through the tears.

"I didn't come here looking for Simone. I came here for him." He nodded over his shoulder. She blinked back the unshed tears in her eyes. "If I thought for one second that he could do this on his own, I wouldn't have sent Felix to look for you. I would have gone myself."

She understood.

He stood back from her. "When this is under control, I'm going to leave you here."

She stiffened.

"I'm gonna go back and find us a new home—somewhere we can start fresh. I'll sell everything and start over. Cut ties where need be."

Mallory threw herself into his arms. He was giving up everything for her and their child.

*****

Kal burst into his room. He was pissed. His father had betrayed him—his own father—but then again, he knew who the hell his father was. He stalked across the oversized room and hated that the damn thing was so big. He needed to think, regroup. He hoped Felix was having better luck than him. He ripped the clothes from his body, flinging them violently to the ground. A shower would help him clear some of the fog that was clouding his judgment. He was about to jump into the shower, but the hot tub seemed to call to him.

He decided to take a short bath instead. He had almost submerged himself when he heard his door open and his mother's voice.

"My son? Are you in here?" She must have heard of his insolence from his father.

He was tempted not to answer, but he knew she would check everywhere for him. "I'm here." He wasn't at all surprised when she came rushing into his bathroom.

"How dare you come home and not come to me?" She came over to the tub and stood patiently, waiting for his excuse. He had never not found and mauled her with kisses when he came home. She was always his first victim.

"I need to get clean." His head was bent in shame.

She knew he was regretting his encounter with his father. She should have been there, but she'd thought he would come to her first. She took a seat on the side of the tub. "I remembered once you and Richard decided to have a wrestling match in the stables. You did not care that you were covered in dung that day. You ran to me and gave me a great big hug." She laughed softly when she saw the sheepish smile on his face. "Has he told you where your wife is?" She held her breath as she waited.

"No." Kal looked up at his mother with tear-filled eyes. "I don't know…" He was barely able to speak and breathe.

His mother reached for him. He moved closer so that she could embrace him—not just for her, but he needed her comfort.

"I will make sure he returns her to you unharmed." She ran her hand through his hair. "I'm glad you've found someone you love."

Kal held on to his mother. She had always gotten him his way, but this time was different. He'd thought his father had taken Simone to make him return home, but she wasn't here.

"You should hurry. Your father is having tea with Richard and Mallory in a half hour. You need to be there. He will tell you where to find your princess." She wiggled out of his embrace and stood. "I must go speak with him before then."

Kal did not like when his mother was sad, yet his situation was obviously causing her more than enough sadness. She brushed a few tears from her cheeks as she bent and kissed his forehead.

"I love you." She turned and started out the door.

"I love you too, Mother."

She stopped. "Never more than I love you." She didn't turn around as she always did. It was always her response when he'd tell her he loved her.

He watched as she disappeared, then he heard the door close behind her. Nyala stopped outside her son's door. She hated to see him like this. He was strong, a warrior like his father. She took a steading breath as she stormed off toward the solar room. She knew Omar would be waiting for her there. It was the location of all their major disagreements.

"I can hear the storm rolling down the hallway. You should leave before she comes." Omar poured Yusef another drink. They toasted one last toast as her steps became louder.

"I shall be right outside." Yusef stood, but Omar stopped him.

"You will do nothing." The look he received from Yusef almost made him laugh. "You will protect my wife and son at all cost."

Yusef was confused. What the hell did that mean?

"It is my command."

Yusef bowed at his king's command. "As you wish." This was unusual behavior for Omar, but Yusef trusted him. He quickly slipped out the alternate door as Nyala stormed into the room.

"Where is Yusef?" Nyala looked around the room and found they were alone.

"He is elsewhere."

She wasn't happy.

Omar sat with a smile, waiting for the dam to break. When she didn't speak or move from the spot she had chosen, he raised an eyebrow.

"I don't know what you've done with my son's wife, but you have until I leave this room to tell him where he may find her." She was dead serious.

"Then it is in my best interest to keep you in this room for as long as I may need."

Nyala's eyes became slits in her face. This made Omar laugh. The angrier she got, the more amused he became. Even though he knew his actions would only enrage her, he had to poke at her.

"Your son has learned nothing from me. All that prestigious education, and he could not keep his wife safe." He smiled.

"You have gone too far, Omar!" Her chest was heaving up and down as if she had run a marathon.

"What is going on in my palace today? Has everyone forgotten who I am?" Omar stood and walked over to his wife.

"It is you who forget, not us."

Omar reached for her, but she stepped back.

This little gesture infuriated him. "I know who the hell I am. I am your king, and you, your son, and everyone else should do well to remember that." Omar turned his back to Nyala.

"No, my love, you are a father." Her voice was low, but he heard her.

"Am I not both?" He looked over his shoulder.

"You are not acting like the father your son needs."

Omar became angry again. He turned and took a step closer to her. "Have you forgotten that he decided he did not want to be my son!"

Nyala knew Omar was hurt by Kal's decision to leave. She had tried to help him understand Kal's decision, but he did not want to hear any of it.

"If he wants to live like a common man then why should I treat him like my son?"

She realized in order to get through to her husband, she would have to drop the big bomb. "Then why did you take her?"

Omar did not expect that question—not yet anyway.

"Because I could."

Nyala couldn't believe what she was hearing. How could he do that to their son?

"Just like I took you." He stepped closer and soon regretted it.

Nyala reached back and swung. She didn't think about it; she just reacted. She watched as her husband stumbled back into his chair. She hadn't meant to hit him that hard, but she was angry.

180

"You struck me." He didn't know what he had said to warrant such a reaction. He had bragged about kidnapping her many times before, but she'd never hit him for it. Nyala stood firm as she watched her husband try to compose himself. "Do you intend to beat the information from me?" He sat up in his chair, his eye stinging from her punch.

"Tell my son what you've done with his wife." She was tired of fighting. Their fights never lasted long, but none had ever gotten physical. She didn't even know why she had struck him. He had been telling his version of their story for ages. "Kal is my son, and I will do whatever I have to for his happiness." She turned to walk out of the room.

"Do not walk away from me, woman!" Omar did not like the way his wife and son had been acting. Yes, he had stolen his wife, but he was home. She should have been happy he was back with them even if only for a short while. Nyala waited to hear what he had to say. "Do you forget who you are?"

She knew he was angry, but her son's happiness was more important. She turned around to face him. He was still sitting in the chair. "I thought I would always hate you, yet I've spent what seems like a lifetime loving you. I've never once looked at another the way I look at you. I am yours now and forever, but forever may come sooner than you think if my son doesn't have his wife by nightfall." Her eyes were filled with tears.

Omar did not respond well to threats. His ego had turned this situation into a family war.

"Are you threatening to leave me?" He laughed. "I've told you since the day I married you the only way out of this is through death."

The calm look on Nyala's face was very disconcerting. She was a warrior; he expected a fight. Instead, she seemed to be throwing in the towel. This was not like his queen.

"I know." She turned and started for the door. "My son's wife..." She paused at the door. He could see the strain on her shoulders as if she were carrying a heavy load. "For my life."

Before he could respond, she was gone. He was stunned. Where had this all gone wrong? He had threatened her many times, but she had known he would never hurt her. Didn't she? Hell, she had struck him, and he had done nothing. Omar held his face in his hands as he remembered his mother making a similar plea to his father. Her son's life for her own. His father had accepted her offer. Never had he understood how the man could be so cruel. He and Yusef had attempted to poison his father after the king had beaten them for breaking his horse's leg. The poison had only succeeded in giving him the worst stomachache of his life. He had thrown up for days. Had he not run away, his father would not have known of his involvement. His mother had saved him and his best friend by offering her life in place of his. It was the last time he had ever seen her. Now the woman he loved was offering him her life in place of what? He would never hurt their son. He decided it was time to come clean. He would find his wife and explain to her what he had done. She would still be upset, but Simone's surgery had already begun. Omar left the solar room in search of his wife.

*****

Yusef had heard the whole argument and had gone to Nyala's reading chamber. She was curled up in her lounge when he entered the room.

"I will not let you sacrifice your life."

She looked up at a worried Yusef. He pulled her to a seated position and sat with her. Nyala began to cry again.

Yusef quickly undid his saber, placing it at Nyala's feet. "I will talk with him." Yusef pulled Nyala into his arms and placed a kiss on her forehead. It was at that moment that the king had practically burst through her doors. Omar couldn't believe what the hell he was seeing. His best friend, his wife. His queen in another man's arms? He flew into the room.

"In my home?" he yelled.

Yusef quickly shielded Nyala as Omar removed his saber and swung. He felt the cold steel strike his forearm as he blocked the blow. He looked at his saber on the chair but didn't reach for it.

"*No!*" Nyala hadn't had time to react.

Yusef was pinned against the wall with Omar's knife at his throat.

"You dare defend your lover?" He couldn't see past his rage. A sad smile rested on Yusef's face. He didn't try to defend himself. Omar felt someone's arm around his neck. He was being pulled to the ground. He saw Richard attempting to restrain Yusef.

"Stop!" Nyala screamed. Mallory was next to her. "He is my brother, you ass of a man." She pulled away from Mallory.

Everyone stopped moving.

"Yusef is my brother. I am his sister!" she cried.

Omar looked at his wounded friend. Yusef nodded in agreeance.

"What?" Kal had no idea what he had walked in on. He looked from his mother to Yusef. Omar waved Kal off him as the room filled with guards. Richard stepped away from Yusef when Omar stepped in front of them.

"You said your whole family had been wiped out." He looked back at his wife.

She walked over and stood next to Yusef. Omar felt sick. He would have killed his friend.

"How is this…" Kal helped him into a chair.

"We found out a few years ago."

His wife bared a strong resemblance to Yusef now that he was staring at them next to each other. Omar wondered how he'd never noticed that before.

"And you did not tell me?" Omar suddenly realized Yusef was bleeding badly. What had he done? "Get him to the infirmary—now!"

A few guards rushed over to help Yusef. He watched as they escorted him from the room. Kal was at his mother's side when Omar turned around. "Why would you keep this from me?" He stood as Nyala came to stand next to him.

"He did not want me to tell you."

Omar took his wife in his arms.

"You were already his brother."

He was ashamed of how he had acted. Yusef was his best friend. The man would have given his life for him without a second thought. His jealousy had almost destroyed his family.

"I accept your offer."

Nyala stepped back from Omar. He was smiling.

"I will tell your son where his wife is." Omar watched his wife breathe a sigh of relief. "I will accept forever with you."

Kal watched his parents' interaction and it made him miss his wife even more.

"Everyone needs to take a seat."

They all looked at each other as they took their seats silently. Kal and his mother sat close together while Richard and Mallory sat together.

"I would like to apologize to you all."

Those who knew him were shocked. Omar did not apologize for anything.

"First I want to let you know that I love you all."

This was starting to worry Kal; he didn't want to be an ass, but he just wanted to know where his wife was.

"Kalu, I understood why you wanted to make a life for yourself away from this place. I have had some time to think since you and Richard left us." He seemed so tired Mallory was feeling sorry for him. "Your wife is very strong and beautiful. She is on the Iris with her sister."

Kal and Richard shared a look. Why the hell was Simone on an oil tanker?

"You may go now if you wish."

Kal jumped to his feet and ran to the door. Everyone watched as he opened the door and stood there. He needed to get to Simone. He looked over his shoulder.

"Why did you take her?" Kal turned and waited for his father to answer.

"Because I love you." Omar's response seemed to shock everyone. "She is having surgery as we speak."

The simultaneous gasps from Richard and Kal could be heard over the silence in the palace. "She and I spoke, and she agreed to have her surgery as long as I had mine."

Kal walked back into the room. "What surgery do you need?" Kal stopped beside his father.

Omar's attention was elsewhere, but he answered. "I discovered several months ago that I had cancer in my right eye." Omar waved his hand as his wife stood. She was in shock.

"So what happened to your left eye?" Mallory hadn't meant to blurt the question out. She quickly covered her mouth, but Omar started to laugh.

"My wife has a very strong right hook." Everyone's attention was turned to the queen. "She did not approve of my taking your wife."

If his father hadn't just confessed to having cancer, Kal would have laughed his ass off. He could only imagine his little mother socking his giant father. He wanted to be here, but his heart was tugging him in another direction. His father had his mother and the rest of the family. Simone needed her husband. She needed him.

"I need to go." Kal stood waiting for his parents to give him their blessings. He couldn't deal with this right now. Richard would have to. His mind was on his wife.

His mother was the first to embrace him.

"I love you." He held his mother tight.

"Never more than I love you." Nyala stepped aside as her husband embraced their son.

"I love you more than I could ever express to you, my son, and I hope you understand I always will. You are my son, no matter where you decide to live or who you decide to become."

Kal kissed his father's cheek before releasing him. He planted a kiss on his mother's forehead, nodded at Mallory and Richard.

"Go."

Kal turned and ran from the room. He couldn't believe Simone had decided to do the surgery. He raced down the hall and out to the waiting vehicle. But why the hell did he put her on a ship in the middle of the ocean to have this surgery. What if something went wrong? He shook those thoughts away. He had to get to her.

*****

Omar was sitting at Yusef's bedside when Nyala found him.

185

"How is he?" She walked over and took Yusef's hand.

Omar was tired. He had been worrying all afternoon. "How long have you known he was your brother?" Omar was staring at Yusef. Nyala knew how much they meant to each other.

"Two years." She knew it was going to be harder for him to forgive her than it would be for him to forgive Yusef. She was fine with that.

"I am your husband, your king! You should not keep secrets from me." Omar was furious again. He looked at his wife and saw she was feeling the same.

"Well, I do, and apparently so do you." She suddenly remembered how hard she had hit him.

Omar knew she was going to cry when her hand covered her mouth. His wife didn't make it a habit to cry no matter what she was going through. He knew why she was brought to tears. She loved him. A smile slowly lit his face. He stood and gestured for her to come to him. She did.

"I am sorry, my love. I didn't want you to worry." He placed a kiss on the top of her head. "I suppose I now have to rethink my plans to leave this world."

Nyala stiffened in his arms.

"Yusef had threatened to marry you and make you happier than I ever could." He chuckled when she made a disgusted noise.

"There is no proof she is really my sister. I still may just make her happier than you." His voice was faint, but Yusef was awake.

Omar gently pushed his wife aside and went to Yusef. His eyes were barely open.

"You fool. I could have killed you." Omar placed a hand on Yusef's shoulder. "I am sorry." He felt his chest tighten. "I'm sorry for how I…"

Yusef raised his uninjured hand, and Omar took it. "If you wanted me dead, I would be." Yusef's eyes finally opened. He tried to sit up, but Omar stopped him.

"Rest. Your doctor has ordered it." Omar smiled. "In fact, she had ordered that I give you time off for a vacation to somewhere tropical."

Yusef knew that smile. He frowned at his friend.

"I think this one loves you. She almost cursed me." He wiggled his eyebrows at Yusef before wincing in pain.

"No, thank you." Yusef shook his head. "She is too much for me."

Omar chuckled at his friend.

"Well, since you two idiots do not require my company, I shall enlist the children to help me destroy your precious roses." Nyala walked to the door.

"She is jealous." Omar was smiling when she turned around.

With a scowl she pointed at both men. "I am not, but if you were a woman, I would kill you—sister or not." She frowned at them before continuing out the door. "Have someone call on me if you need me." She closed the door behind her.

Omar shook his head. "You know, we should wait until she is back in her chambers." He looked to the door as if he expected someone to enter. "Then we have a guard rush to her and bring her back here. When she arrives, I'm lying in bed with you, pretending to be asleep." Omar looked down at his friend and saw not amusement but concern. He was obviously joking.

"Have you seen your face?" Omar tried to laugh at Yusef's observation.

"I don't have to see it—I can feel it."

They both laughed as Omar tried to touch his half-swollen black eye. "This is your doing. A woman should not train the way you train her." Omar returned to his chair next to the bed. "Thirty-six years of marriage, and she has never struck me in anger."

Yusef scoffed. "I find that very hard to believe."

They both chuckled.

"Why didn't you want her to tell me she was your sister? Are you ashamed of me?" Omar was trying to joke, but Yusef knew him too well. He was hurt. They had never had secrets. Things he would never tell his wife he had told Yusef.

"What would you have done if she had told you?" He knew the answer to his question. That was the only reason he had kept it a secret. Omar thought for a second.

"Yusef, I have many men trained by you who are more than capable of keeping me safe." Omar sighed. "I trust no one as I've trusted you, but you can't spend the rest of your life alone. You need children."

Yusef made a grunting sound that made Omar laugh.

"I've seen what children do to men. I have no need for them." He tried to laugh, but Omar didn't believe him. He had helped them raise their boys. He was an excellent role model for the children.

"I will not hear it. You will marry the doctor and be happy." Omar waved his hand as he always did to end a conversation in his favor.

"I shall do no such thing. She is eleven years my junior." Yusef thought for a brief moment but decided it was not possible.

"How do you know all this?" Omar clapped his hands in triumph. Yusef was interested in the doctor. "Ha! You do love her." He giggled. "I'm going to tell my"—he stopped for a moment—"your sister that you wish to wed the doctor."

Yusef turned to look at Omar. "That is not true." He knew Omar didn't care. He would tell his wife, and she would push until there was a wedding. "She is too young. She will want children and her own home. I am comfortable here. I do not wish to leave." And that was the reason he hadn't told Omar the news before.

"You have always been my brother, my protector. We have been through life together, but I have been selfish. You deserve happiness." Omar looked at Yusef. He stared intently at the man.

"What?" Yusef was concerned.

"How have I never noticed how much you look alike?"

Yusef rolled his eyes at him. "Hmm. Well, you did say all you Africans look the same."

Yusef pushed himself to a half-seated position. The mischievous smile on Omar's face amused him.

"I said all you sand crickets looked the same. I said nothing of us Africans." Omar slapped his knee as he laughed. They were only boys when Yusef had told him that. It had made him angry then, but now he laughed at the reference. "I do not wish to leave this behind." He was talking about their strange relationship.

"You do not have to. We can always make an addition to the palace for you and your bride." Omar had already seen it.

"I did not agree to anything." Yusef knew he wouldn't let it go.

"That's because I have not yet told Nya." He laughed when Yusef sighed in defeat. "You'd better take tonight to come to terms with this." Omar was enjoying tormenting Yusef. They both quieted down when the door opened, and Doctor Verose walked in. Yusef slowly turned to see an excited Omar getting to his feet.

"Good evening, doctor."

She bowed at him before turning to Yusef. "How is my favorite patient?" Her smile made his stomach ache. Before he could answer, Omar did.

"Oh, I am well. However, Yusef seems to be having some issues with his testicles. He's somehow lost them." Omar patted Yusef's thigh while pushing the blushing doctor closer to him. He turned and strolled briskly to the door. "Just in case you don't find them, he was hoping to speak to you about marriage." Omar didn't turn around to see the death glare he was getting from Yusef. He exited the room and strolled triumphantly down the hall toward his garden.

*****

Richard was ready to get back to Mallory and the rest of the family. He hadn't been able to talk to her since he'd left nearly two weeks ago. He had one last meeting before his flight, and this was getting on his nerves. He wasn't too excited, but he had to see this one personally. As usual, Vinny was late. Richard was ready to call the whole damn thing off. He had no patience left. No one else had made him wait. Just then his office door flew open, and in walked Vinny and his bodyguard. He never traveled without the man and for good reason. He wasn't a well-liked man.

"Richie Boy."

Richard hated that he called him that. He wanted to hit the stupid little man. "Don't call me that." His face was bland. He didn't want to have the man in his house any longer than needed.

"Good to see you."

Richard smiled his business smile.

Vinny laughed, knowing the smile wasn't genuine. He and Richard's family never really saw eye to eye on anything. He hadn't been shocked when Richard had called him to squash whatever beef was between them—not the families', theirs. He had heard Richard was getting out of the game, and as much as he would miss the competition, he was happy to see him go.

"So, I heard from a little snitch, that you were getting out the game—permanently." Vinny took a seat in the couch. He rubbed the material, admiring the softness of it. "What's this, velvet? Feels good. You should get me one." He laid back in the soft couch, enjoying the feel of it. "I can only imagine what you've done in this thing." He laughed as his bodyguard shook his head in amusement. Richard, however, was not amused. This was a business meeting.

"Look, I have a flight to catch." Richard grabbed the file from his desk and walked it to Vinny. He handed it to him and went back to sit on his desk.

"Listen to this guy, huh." Vinny shook his head. "This man has two private jets, but he still keeps a tight schedule. As if they would leave without him." Both Vinny and his bodyguard laughed. "I wonder what's more important than this, huh?" He didn't open the file. Something on the table in front of him had caught his attention. Richard followed his gaze. It was Mallory. She and Simone were sprawled across the cover of the magazine that Vinny was staring at. "Are those two a part of the deal?" He never took his eyes from the magazine.

"No." Richard knew why he was asking. He almost wondered what Vinny would say if he had told him yes.

"They quitting with you?" Vinny seemed a bit disappointed.

"No." He didn't mind telling Vinny that Simone had started a new company, one where she didn't have to answer to anyone, but he wouldn't. He would let that surprise him later. A slow smile crept across his face.

"I don't know if this magazine is worth shit without Simone and…" He hesitated. He couldn't say her name without getting emotional. "Anyway, the boys were wondering if you could get them to sign some of the mags for them." Vinny tried to force a smile. He wanted to see Mallory but wasn't sure he could face her.

"They aren't in the country." Richard was growing wary. He just wanted the damn meeting to be over.

"Oh." Vinny finally opened the file. "So, I hear it's a woman that has you trying to get on the right side of the law. Is that true?" Richard knew the rumors had started once he decided to go straight. Everyone had their own thoughts on why he was doing it.

"I have good reasons." He didn't trust Vinny, but he had been serious about cutting ties with this life.

"You know women leave and take half your shit if you're not careful." He nodded at his bodyguard and laughed. "You could've been big—well, bigger than your father. Hell, maybe even your grandfather." He shook his head in disappointment. Truth was he admired Richard. The kid had taken his family's failures and turned them into profit. "I hope she's worth it." Vinny took out a pen and signed the papers. He knew Richard was a man of his word. If he said he was getting out of this life, then he was done.

"She is." Richard watched as Vinny stood and brought him the file.

"Good luck, man. I can't say I understand." Vinny shrugged and shook Richard's hand.

Richard held it tighter than expected. "Not that it means anything to you, but Mallory and I are getting married."

Vinny stiffened. His eyes were as wide as they could get. Not Mallory—anyone but Mallory. The shock that crossed Vinny's face pleased Richard. Vinny quickly took control of himself and snatched his hand from Richard's. He took a few steps back from the man. Richard knew.

"After everything I did to keep her out of this life, she ends up with you." The anger was clearly displayed on his face. "I gave up a life with my kid so that she could have a normal life, and she ends up with you." He looked over his shoulder at the man he had come with. With fist balled at his side, he turned back to Richard.

"Like I said, I'm done with this life. She's too important to me." Richard stood toe to toe with Vinny. Though Vinny was significantly shorter than Richard, he was not intimidated at all. Most men didn't stand this close to him especially when they were aware of his past. Vinny looked up at Richard.

"I guess you're a better man than me then, Embers. I sent my family away to keep them safe." He unclenched his fists. "I never thought for one second to go with them." He stepped away from Richard and turned for the door. "I pray for your sake you can keep away from this life. Many men have tried, but the moment you dip so much a fucking finger back in this shit, you'll get that stink on you again."

Richard didn't need him to tell him that. He was well aware of the ramifications of coming back to this life. Any unfinished business would stay that way. "I leave nothing behind that I'll ever need again in my life." He had realized as he sold off his businesses and paid old family debts that none of it ever mattered to him. He was trying to outdo his predecessors, but this life was meaningless. Well, since he'd met Simone, he would have given it up for her if she'd ever asked him to. Had she not rejected him, he would have given her the life she'd wanted, but she had given him more than he could have ever asked for. She had given him a chance to find Mallory—his happiness.

"I'm sure I won't see an invitation, so congratulations." Vinny continued to the door that was being held open for him.

Richard didn't plan on telling the man anything, but he knew it would have been better coming from him.

"She's pregnant."

Vinny stopped.

"Looks like you're gonna be a grandfather." Richard didn't know what to expect, but he wasn't expecting Vinny to be happy about him knocking up his daughter.

Vinny turned slowly. "You love her?"

Richard was shocked by the question.

"Or is this about the kid?" Vinny seemed concerned. If Richard didn't know better, he would have thought the man was holding his breath.

"Yes, I love her." This time the smile on his face was genuine. "Since the first time I met her, I knew I was going to marry her."

This pleased Vinny. Though he hadn't been in Mallory's life, he still wanted the best for her. "Good." He walked back to Richard. "Congratulations. I hope it all goes well." He took Richard's hand. "As much as I would love to meet my grandchild, I know it's not possible—not if you want to leave this life behind. I can't be a part of your lives."

Richard almost felt sorry for him. "I know. If it's any comfort to you, my family won't be able to meet our children either."

The comment drew a smile from both men. It pleased Vinny to know he wouldn't be the only one suffering. He knew Richard didn't have a good relationship with his biological family, but he had found everything he couldn't have with them elsewhere—in powerful arms. It was what had made him a bit untouchable.

"I wish I had known she was with you." Vinny knew Richard could and would take care of his daughter. He wasn't at all worried now.

"If you had known, would you have been okay with it?" Richard was quite sure Vinny would have intervened and made things worse. Knowing now what he did, Vinny wouldn't have condoned their relationship. Their families hadn't been on friendly terms for decades.

"Hell, no. I might have killed you." Vinny chuckled. He was glad he hadn't known. He wished he had the courage Richard had shown. If he did, he would have been with his family. "I guess I better get the hell out of here." He wanted to ask about Mallory, but it would only make losing her again worse.

"One last drink?" Richard gestured toward the small bar in the room. He knew Vinny wouldn't pass up a drink—especially when he'd known Richard always had the good stuff.

A smile lit his face and he walked over to the bar. "I can make you an offer on this place." He reached for an unopened bottle of scotch. "Boy, you sure know how to treat yourself." He returned the bottle and poured himself a drink from the monogramed decanter displayed before him. "You should think about it. I'll offer full price." He liked the place, but more importantly, he liked that Mallory had spent her time here. He may not have given her the things she had deserved, but she had done well enough for herself.

"If you want it, you have to talk to Felix. It's his now."

Vinny almost choked on his drink. "Masters?" He seemed shocked at what Richard had revealed. How could Felix afford a place like this?

"Yes. I've decided to leave it with him." Richard smiled at the thought of Felix and Ms. Jenna living in such a huge house.

"Well shit. The servant becomes the master." Vinny chuckled as he finished his drink and poured another. He downed that one in one gulp. "You're a good kid—dumb but good." He smiled at Richard, stretching his hand to him. "I know you'll make sure I get the paperwork in a timely manner."

Richard nodded.

"I guess you better walk us out. Wouldn't want to run into you know who now that he owns the place." Vinny and his bodyguard shared a laugh. He decided he'd have another drink for the road before he left.

"I hate to rush you, but I have a flight to catch."

Vinny didn't seem at all bothered by Richard's statement. He poured another drink and swallowed it down.

"Yeah, you said that." Vinny finally started toward the door. He wasn't sure why he felt a sense of loss. He had hoped to see Mallory while he was visiting, but fate had intervened. "I better let you on your way before you miss your flight."

They walked side by side to the front door before Vinny stopped. Richard continued, opening the door, and stepping out.

"Shit." As he stepped outside Ms. Jenna was coming up the stairs, Felix directly behind her. Richard hadn't meant for her to be around when Vinny showed up. He'd told Felix to keep her out until he'd left, but here they were.

"Hey, honey, I thought you'd be gone by now. You must not miss Mal as…" Jenna froze. She took two hasty steps back and into Felix's arms. Her breathing was rapid. Felix realized immediately what had caused her reaction. He quickly stepped in front of Jenna as Vinny stepped from the house.

"Masters." Vinny walked out and stood next to Richard. "You're looking"—he gave Felix the once-over—"fed."

Felix didn't budge. He was in no mood for this. He had been so caught up with Jenna he hadn't noticed Vinny's vehicle. He was starting to hate limos. Had he checked the license plate; he would have known not to bring Jenna into this situation.

"Our business is done." Richard turned to Vinny. "You should go."

Vinny didn't move.

"Now would be a good time." It was his last warning.

Vinny recognized the tone. He knew not to test these two without his army. He gave Richard a nod.

"Do better than me." Vinny took a deep breath and started around Felix. He stopped at the bottom of the stairs. "I'm happy you two found"—he didn't turn around—"what you deserve."

Jenna watched as he got into the waiting limo. She hadn't expected to ever see him again.

"Wait!" she yelled from the top of the stairs. Felix tried to stop her, but she was determined to confront Vinny. She pulled away from him and ran down the stairs. Vinny stepped from the limo and waited for her to approach him. "I didn't know what I would say to you if I ever saw you again." She stopped a few steps away from him. "I want you to know that letting us go was the best thing you could have ever done for Mallory." Her voice started to shake. "After I left you, I lost my daughter." She tried to hold the tears at bay. "I couldn't tell her the truth about her father. She loved him too much." She closed her eyes and took another step closer to him. "I had to protect us, but I couldn't take the man she loved from her. So for all those years I had to be the bad guy."

Vinny bent his head. He was ashamed of what he had done to her. "I've tried so hard to protect her from men like you that I almost lost her to someone worse."

Vinny's head came up so quickly she unconsciously took a step back. His eyes went to the top of the stairs where Richard stood.

"Since she's been with Richard, I've had my little girl back." She took a steadying breath. "She's happy." When a tear streamed down her face, Vinny had to fight the urge to touch her. He wanted to comfort her, but the men at the top of the stairs wouldn't have understood his actions. He was in the business of self-preservation.

"My daughter is finally happy, and I intend to make sure she stays that way."

Vinny smirked at her when he finally realized what she was trying to tell him.

"It's too late to apologize for what I've put you through, but I hope you understand that I did what I had to—and I will always do what I have to." He turned, got back into the car, and slammed the door. Rolling down the window, he took one last look at the woman he once loved. "He doesn't deserve you"—Vinny glanced at Felix—"but he is a good man." He smiled at Jenna.

"You didn't deserve me, Vincenzo, but I know that I belong with Felix." She turned and ran back to the stairs, back to Felix. Vinny could do nothing but watch as Felix pulled her into his arms. It was like losing her all over again. He recalled the night she had taken Mallory and left him. He'd watched from the window as they got into the taxi. It was almost the hardest thing he'd ever had to do. He took one last look before instructing his driver to leave.

"Well, if he didn't hate me before, I'm sure he does now." Felix held Jenna close. He heard Richard scoff and turned to him.

"Do you give a damn?" Richard knew Felix very well.

"Hell, no."

They laughed as Jenna wrestled herself from Felix's embrace.

"Cut it out, both of you." She playfully smacked Felix's chest. "And don't you have to get back to Mallory, or shall we set a plate for you?" Richard made a face before reaching for her. He placed a kiss on her cheek.

"I'll see you two in a few days." He hugged Felix then turned and ran to his car. He would never see this place again, and that was fine with him. As long as he had Mallory and their child, he would be all right.

*****

Mallory was excited to see her new house. Richard had kept everything so secret she thought she would burst from curiosity. After he had returned to her, they'd spent most of their time getting to know each other better. Nyala insisted they spent time together before she'd let them get married. The queen was too excited about all the weddings she'd seen in their future. She was especially excited about Richard and Mallory's. Though it was a small intimate wedding, Nyala had made it perfect. Everything was perfectly planned. Had she not been a queen, she would have made an amazing wedding planner.

"Why can't I see a picture of the property?" Mallory couldn't wait to see where they would be raising their family. She'd tried almost everything to get some information out of Richard or one of the guys, but they were tight-lipped. Not even Simone knew where they were moving to. The women had banded together to gather information from their men, but they hadn't budged.

"I'm your wife. You shouldn't keep secrets from me. Remember what happened to Omar when he tried to keep secrets from Mom?" She gave him a mischievous side glance. Richard could do nothing but laugh. He slid to the floor in front of her.

"Do you intend to assault your husband?" He kissed her swollen fingers. "I don't think my little one would like his mommy beating his daddy—especially while he's trying to relax in there." He rubbed her swollen stomach and got the reward he sorted. "Our little soccer player is awake." Richard bent and kissed her tummy. "Two more months, and you can play all the soccer you want with Daddy."

Mallory loved how excited he got when he spoke to her tummy. "What if your little man is a girl?" she asked.

His head came up slowly. She could see he was thinking about it. "Does she have all her fingers and toes?" He looked at her, and Mallory laughed.

"I should hope so. Why?" She was smiling at him.

He couldn't get enough of that smile of hers. "If it doesn't have all the parts, we have to send it back."

His response shocked her even though she knew he was joking. "Our baby is not an '*it*', sir." She playfully smacked his shoulder. "We would know everything we need to know if you and Omar would let me have that scan." She tilted her head and gave him a pleading look, but she knew it was futile. He was not taking any chances with Nyala's grandchild. She had threatened to castrate him if anything happened to her daughter and grandchild.

"Can you not wait a few more months?" He kissed her tummy. "Is everything all right with you in there? Are you well fed? Do you have the expected amount of limbs, fingers, and toes?"

Mallory laughed when he put his ear to her belly and nodded as if he was getting responses to his questions. "He says not to worry. He's as normal as he could possibly be—given the circumstances." He smiled mischievously at her.

Mallory rolled her eyes at him. "What circumstances?" she asked, knowing she was about to smack him.

"Well, for one, you're his mother. He has no chance at anything but normalcy with you." He laughed at the look he received from her. "However, we've reached an agreement." He didn't look up this time.

"What agreement?" When he didn't answer, she thought he hadn't heard her. "What agreement have you and our child made?" He still didn't answer. She wiggled under his head.

"Careful, woman." He turned his head to look at her. Still resting on her tummy, he winked at her. "He understands that breast-feeding will be limited to only four weeks."

She scowled at him. "And why?" She shook her head when the baby moved as if he were really communicating with his father.

"Well, we have decided that you will be pregnant for as long as it takes to make us a small basketball team." The look on her face made him burst into laughter.

"Should I not have been consulted since I'm the factory that has to produce this team you wish to have?" She watched as Richard whispered to her belly and got a gentle kick in response. He nodded before answering her. She loved this Richard. He had been so different since he returned to her from his business trip several months ago. He had promised her the man she could raise a family with, and she was more than satisfied with him.

"We just did. This was your official update." Her belly moved again, and he acted as if he had forgotten. "Oh, yeah, the little one would like to be fed. It seems you haven't eaten since we took off six hours ago."

She rewarded him with a smile. She was a bit hungry.

"What am I gonna do with the two of you?"

She giggled when he lifted her dress and kissed her tummy then blew a raspberry on her nonexistent bellybutton.

Neither of them saw Kal with the camera. "This poor kid is gonna be so traumatized when he sees this."

Mallory looked up to see Kal recording Richard assaulting her tummy with raspberries as the baby fought back. "This is awesome. He's actually kicking your ass."

Simone slapped her husband upside his head as she took the seat next to Mallory. "Language, sir. I don't want my nephew learning that type of language." She reached over and popped Richard in the forehead. "And stop tormenting him. He needs his rest."

Mallory rested her head on Simone's shoulder, trying to catch her breath from all the laughing she was doing.

"Thank you," she whispered. "Thanks for rescuing us." She giggled as Richard rolled his eyes at them. "I think all that playing made me hungrier." She rubbed her tummy when she felt a soft kick from its tenant.

"What would you like, princess? Omar has everything you could possibly want on this aircraft." Kal laughed when Mallory and Simone's faces lit up.

"Almost everything."

He shook his head at the women. "I'm the one who's hungry. Why are you asking Miss Picky what she wants?"

Mallory had misunderstood. Kal wasn't talking to Simone.

"I didn't ask her anything. I asked you what you wanted." He tilted his head and smiled. "Has your awful husband not told you?"

Mallory was confused. What was he talking about?

"Told me what?" She sat up, fixing her disheveled garments.

"Haven't you asked him about the brand on his right hip?" Kal seemed shocked that she had no idea what he was talking about.

Richard, however, sat quietly next to him. He hadn't told Mallory because he was afraid the story would bleed into their past. He only hoped Kal would keep his grandfather out of the story he was sure would come to light.

"Don't you have one as well?" Simone asked.

Kal's eyes grew as he turned to look at his wife. "Shush, woman. That is none of her business." He laughed when Simone rolled her eyes at him.

"I'm gonna get my wife something to eat while you lie to her." Richard stood and walked to the front of the aircraft.

"Does he not want you to tell me?" Mallory watched as he left. He didn't seem to want to tell her much about his past.

"He prefers I tell you since I'm a master storyteller." Kal scowled at Simone when she laughed at his comment. "Well, it all started with a birthday disagreement—something we haven't solved even now."

Mallory and Simone shared a look.

"Richard and I were born on the exact same day at almost the exact same time. Shocking, isn't it?" Kal raised his eyebrows at the women.

"I knew you shared a birthday, but I didn't know that." Mallory was intrigued. She was invested in whatever this was.

"Yes. So we have debated for what seems like forever over who is actually older." He smiled when Richard returned with a milkshake and a tray of fruits. "I say I am, but he doesn't agree." Richard placed the tray before Mallory and Simone then handed the milkshake to his wife. "Technically, we were born seven hours apart but at the same time."

Simone and Mallory stopped eating and looked at each other.

"What?" Both women asked.

This made Richard and Kal laugh. It was the response they were used to.

"I was born at 10:36 a.m. He was born at 5:36 p.m. on the same day." Richard quickly grabbed Kal, covering his mouth as he continued. "Now, if I was born in the morning, doesn't that make me the older one?"

Kal wasn't even struggling. He just relaxed and waited for the women to process what they had been told.

"Wait a minute." Simone was the first to respond. "So, seven-hour difference but same day. Then it doesn't really matter if it was a.m. or p.m. The kid that popped out first is the oldest." This made Richard let go of Kal.

"No, no, no, no, no…" Kal was not a fan of this answer. "That's not fair. My day was coming to a close, and his was just beginning. I'm older." Kal waved his finger at his wife.

"What does it matter?" Simone didn't see why it mattered so much to them.

"Because that's how the fight started."

Again both women gave each other a confused look before asking.

"What fight?"

Kal and Richard laughed at their wives.

"We were both at the same boarding school. It was almost our birthday, and we both had plans to throw a party. Well, neither of us knew the other was planning anything. Hell, we didn't even know we shared a birthday." Kal waved the stewardess over. This story was going to take a while and he needed a drink.

After requesting some wine for him and Richard, he continued. "When I found out that he was trying to ruin my day, I went to see him in the library—the library that my father had donated to the school several years prior." The girls wondered why he threw that bit of information in. "When I confronted him, the little bastard was not at all receptive to any of my suggestions. He didn't think he should share shit with me since he was older."

Kal shook his head at Richard who seemed to be ignoring him. "As irritating as his rudeness was, I tried to be diplomatic as my father would have wanted. I offered to throw us a party to rival any the school had ever seen, but this jerk wouldn't hear of it. So after he'd insulted my kindness yet again, I removed my jacket and offered him a beating. His response, and I am quoting him here, was 'Bring it then, your royal dick juice.'"

Both Mal and Sy burst into laughter, spitting milkshake and mango pieces on their men. This didn't seem to bother either of them though.

Kal continued as if nothing had happened. "I'm glad you find that amusing because I didn't. No one had ever spoken to me like that. I was a fucking prince, and he didn't seem to realize that." Kal shook his head. "Well, we fought and fought hard, knocking over columns of books and breaking chairs. Now, the windows in this library were floor to ceiling, so it was inevitable that we were gonna go flying through one if someone didn't stop us."

Richard couldn't hold the snicker that escaped him. "Since my royal detail was asked to keep out of the fight, that is exactly what happened. He and I went flying out of the second-floor window and, thankfully, into the flowerbed below." Mallory was more shocked than Simone at this point.

"Needless to say, the headmaster was pissed. However, he was more lenient with me because of said library. He called my father and asked what he should do with me. He had expelled Richard and was waiting for his family to respond."

Mallory noted the discomfort on Richard's face at the mention of his family.

"My father told them he would be there in two days to retrieve me. That old bastard told them to expel me as well—his son."

Richard covered his face with one hand and chuckled.

"When he showed up, Richard's parents hadn't responded to the notices the school had sent. So Omar, being Omar, pulled some strings and had him released into his care. I didn't like that shit one bit. I knew what he was doing, but poor Richard had no idea what he was about to endure."

Mallory wondered why Richard's parents hadn't come for him and how they could let a complete stranger take their child.

"We were taken back to the palace where I was put in charge of his safety—me, the same guy he had thrown out of a second-floor window."

Richard did not agree with Kal's claims. "What? I recall us both going through that window." He shook his head in disbelief. "I think I better tell this part. I don't trust you to be honest right now."

Kal laughed. "I spent a total of three months at the palace with his family before we were enrolled in another boarding school." He took a sip of his wine and avoided eye contact with the women. "Two weeks into my stay, I finally met his mother."

Richard rubbed his face in frustration as Kal doubled over laughing. "I had gone looking for the lion I'd heard roaring one morning—no idea that the thing was loose in the garden. No one told me that it just walked freely. I thought it was probably in a cage or something. Well, it wasn't. I came around a corner, and there he was, mouth covered in blood. I saw him, he saw me, and then I turned into Jesse Owens. Don't ask me how I made it back into the palace, but I was muddy when I got there." He paused and took another drink while his audience laughed. "Anyway, I was coming out of the shower and didn't have a towel. By the time I realized there was a woman in the bathroom, the towel rack was a good distance away. I don't know why the hell this man's bathroom was so big. I tried to run back to the rack and slipped, knocking over everything as I did, hitting my friggin' head on the floor—I still have that scar—but she never moved. I grabbed the closest thing to a towel I could get, and by the time I made it to my knees, the bathroom was a theater. Omar, Yusef, Kal, and his brothers were all standing there." Richard let out a sad sigh.

"It was quite possibly my most embarrassing moment, but here I was trying to cover myself in a tiny hand towel in front of the royal family. I was so dazed from my fall I couldn't understand a word they were saying. I just knew all these men were pissed at me. The boys started to charge at me, but she raised one finger, and everyone stopped." He smiled at the memory. "I once saw my grandfather slap the chief of police, and I thought that was power, but this little woman raised one finger, and the king, the princes, and Yusef stopped." The admiration in his voice was ever clear. "She told Yusef to collect the doctor to look after her son. Then she scolded everyone else. It was the first time I'd met her. Well, I hadn't met her yet, but that was our first encounter."

Kal interjected, "And he was naked."

Richard laughed at the comment. He had known from the way she'd handled the situation that she would always be his ally. "She said he was now one of her children since she'd seen him naked." Another round of laughter flowed through the cabin.

"My parents eventually adopted him."

The revelation shocked Mallory. "Wait, what?" She had no idea Richard was adopted by Kal's parents.

"That's why he has that brand on his hip. He is my brother— legally." Kal was more than proud to share this with the ladies. They both sat shocked, staring at the men.

"I was the youngest of the family. My brothers were months apart and me almost four years younger, so we really didn't have the kind of connection my parents saw between Richard and I." He patted Richard's thigh. "This jerk has gotten me into and out of trouble many times." Richard made a face. "I love him."

Mallory's heart felt like it would explode. She was happy Richard was part of Kal's family. Though she didn't know much about his biological family, she didn't much like them. They had left him all alone at that boarding school. She would ask him about that one day, but right now she was enjoying this moment.

"So what does the brand actually mean?" Simone was curious.

"Property of Omar." Richard and Kal laughed, but the women didn't. "It's an out-of-date practice, but we chose to have it done. Way back in the day, it was used to identify a bloodline. If a royal was killed in battle and his body couldn't be brought back to his family, the brand would be cut from the body and returned to their father." The shock on Simone's face made Kal continue. "Our children won't need one. Since I have no intentions of ruling, they won't be branded." The relief on Simone's face made him smile.

"What if someone copied it?" Mallory was now curious.

"Then death was either instantaneous or the king could order something more horrific. My father told us the last person to fake one was beaten then buried alive. His family was weighted and thrown into the ocean, but you can only believe half of what Omar tells you sometimes." Even though the conversation had gotten a bit dark, Mallory was still enjoying the information she'd gathered from it.

*****

Mallory was more than impressed with her new home. The three-story mansion stood proudly above most of the other homes in the area. Though adequately spaced, Mallory's home seemed to dominate the neighborhood.

"Does my queen approve of her new dwellings?" Richard was hugging her from behind. He was proud of his work. Mallory didn't care where they lived as long as they were together.

"I was not expecting this." She turned and kiss her husband. "This house is beyond anything I could have imagined." She held him tight as close as she could.

"Wait until you see the inside. I had an elevator built in for you to get around."

Had she heard him correctly? She stood back from him in amazement.

"What?" He was concerned about the look she was giving him.

"Why do we need an elevator?"

He laughed knowing his response would get him into trouble. "I thought it would be easier for you to get the baby up and downstairs."

She smiled at him as he turned and led her into their home. Mallory was even more impressed with the inside of their home. She was not consulted on anything having to do with the building or furnishing of their home, yet everything seemed perfect. She suddenly realized that someone else had decorated their baby's room, and she got emotional. Richard noticed right away that something was wrong.

"You don't like it?"

She didn't want to be sappy, but her hormones made it hard for her to keep tears in her eyes. "I wanted to decorate the baby's room, but I'm sure that's already done." The sadness in her face made him reach for her. Nyala had already warned him that the baby's room was off limits. It was Mallory's to decorate.

"Would you like to see the third floor? That's where our bedrooms are."

She wiped her tears and nodded.

Richard tried not to smile as he led her to the elevator. He wrapped her in his arms as they ascended to the third floor. "Would you like to see your room or the baby's room first?" He escorted her from the elevator. Even though she was a bit sad, curiosity forced excitement to her surface.

"The baby's room." She wanted to see what color he had painted it, what furnishings he had chosen. She waddled behind him as they made their way to the nursery.

"Are you ready to see our son's room?" Richard stood before the double doors and waited for her to catch up. When she was finally with him, he opened the doors. Mallory was shocked to see the empty bland room. There was nothing in the room at all—no carpet, no paint on the walls, no curtains, no furniture. The room was completely bare.

"Richard?" She stepped in, wondering why their child's room had been left bare.

"This is the room I've chosen for our child. Now you, my beautiful wife, must complete it." He pulled her into a hug. "I thought you'd like to be the one to prepare our baby's quarters."

Mallory was excited about the task. She was happy he had considered her feelings about decorating the room. She had so many ideas on how to proceed.

"Thank you, Richard." She was emotional again. They stood entwined as she took in the massive room their child would be staying in. "Can we keep him in our room for a few weeks?" She was starting to get anxious thinking about their child alone in the massive room.

"Whatever you want, but I must tell you that our room is significantly smaller than this." He took her by the hand and led her out of the room. He closed the door behind them and walked her across the hall. "This is our humble chamber."

Mallory entered the room and was awestruck. The room reminded her of her chambers in the palace. It was identical to the one she had spent the last several months in. She loved every inch of that room. "I thought since you loved your previous chambers so much, I'd duplicate it for you." She was happy. Everything was perfect.

"I love it!" she cried. "This is absolutely amazing." She tried to attack her husband with hugs and kisses. Richard simply lifted and carried her to their bed. It was enormous.

"This is where we will create our basketball team." He wiggled his eyebrows at her, causing laughter to spill from her. "Are you happy?" He knew she was, but he wanted to hear her say it.

"I've never been happier." That was the truth.